Adolescent
escalation

By David Nash

Adolescent Escalation
By David Nash

Published by Amnesia Castle Publishing
Copyright © 2008 David Nash
David Nash photo by Lisa McCracken
Layout and design by Firman Design Studio, Kansas City, MO
ISBN: 978-0-6152-0489-5

www.amnesiacastle.com
davidnash@amnesiacastle.com

Adolescent *escalation*

By David Nash

CHAPTER ONE

It was the winter of 1963 when it was announced by my mother we were to leave New Orleans the city of my birth for California where my mother and grandmother who lived with us were originally from. I was surprised at the news but somewhat excited at the prospect of going west. I had always dreamed of moving out to the West Coast because all I loved seemed to be there. I loved hot rod cars and greatly admired surfing, which I couldn't wait to try. I knew of cars from the hot rodding magazines I read regularly and the monthly drag races that took place a few miles from my home. Surfing had attracted me through films I had seen and a few television shows had portrayed surfing in their plots.

It seemed the timing was right for such a move because my sister would be going off to college at some fancy east coast school, and I would be entering high school in September of that year. My parents had long been divorced and I knew I would get to see my father in the summers between the school years. I became excited about leaving and began to tell my friends after the month of June, I would no longer call the city of New Orleans my home. I settled in and resigned myself to finishing the eighth grade at the private school I had attended since kindergarten. I wasn't exactly a good student and I soon found out I would be attending public school in California. I worried about this but was told public school out west was of good quality and I hoped I would like the school I would wind up attending.

Those last few months in New Orleans went quicker than some had in my life and my excitement level increased as our departure date grew nearer. I was fourteen when I left the south, and the thought I would have to wait an extra year to get my drivers license was troubling but I was told we would move close enough to the beach where access to the water would be within my reach by my bicycle. I was also promised a surfboard when I got to California and I began to save the money from my paper route for the purpose of being able to outfit myself properly when I arrived.

The day finally arrived and after all of our belongings was carefully packed and placed into a moving van my life in the south was over. My grandmother was flown to the west and my sister went to the summer camp where she had worked for years to spend the summer as she usually did. I would not see her until the following Christmas. My mother and I drove the 2000 miles to Southern California and it took us a week of easy driving to get there. There was little of interest on the way, but we stopped at some of the tourist stops such as the Alamo and Carlsbad Caverns for some sight seeing. We crossed the border into Juarez, Mexico from El Paso and I got to be in another country for the first time in my life. I bought a few presents for a couple of close friends in New Orleans and I mailed the purchases to them when we were back across the border. I got to do a lot of the driving on our way west as my mother grew tired of sitting behind the wheel and I had been a proficient driver since I was twelve. My father had taught me at a young age and I enjoyed handling cars as much as anything during those years.

We finally made it to the border of the "golden state," where we were checked for fruits and vegetables which were not grown in California. I was told California was very serious about their produce industry and the border stops were their way of keeping unwanted insects and vermin from getting in to the state and possibly decimating their crops. I remember the border stop in Parker, Arizona was hot as hell being in the middle of the desert and it was my first experience with desert heat. It was as hot as a furnace and twice as dry. I had a lot of experience with tropical heat being from the south, but the lack of humidity made my skin crawl. We drove the rest of the way through Southern California that summer morning and a few hours later, finally pulled up in front of a house belonging to some of my relatives in the western part of the city of Santa Ana, California. My grandmother was there with my mother's cousin and I brought all of our belongings inside while my mother reacquainted herself with the cousin she had been missing for a number of years. We finished when the sun was going down and after dinner the first night I went out to give my mother's Volkswagen Bug its first California bath and get the 2000 miles of dirt off of our only transportation. When I was finished I went inside where I took a shower and went to my cousin's room where I was to sleep my first night in the west.

My mother's cousin lived with her daughter and family and I had been told they were on vacation and would not be home for two more weeks. I would have to wait until their return to meet my cousins who were close to my age. I hoped they would be cool and interested in some of the same things I was. I liked California right off, from the cars I saw on the street to the temperature drop that took place at night. In New Orleans we had air-conditioning but it wasn't necessary in the arid climate of Southern California and I was pleased that first night when the temperature dropped considerably. The wind from the Pacific ocean turned onshore after dark and I could smell the salt from the ocean and the decaying algae from the jetty's that were at the beach which were only a couple of miles away from where I was staying. I woke up early the next morning and fixed myself some coffee in the kitchen making enough for the family as I did so. I was soon chastised for this by my mother's cousin who was up earlier than my mother and grandmother.

She said, "What are you doing?'

"Having my morning coffee thanks, would you like some?" I replied.

She said, "Children don't drink coffee, not in this house."

"Why not, I've been having coffee before breakfast since I was a lot younger than this. Do you take cream and sugar?"

She said, "Children in this house don't talk back either."

I said, "Well I was merely offering you some coffee and I wasn't talking back. I was explaining my morning habits to you. How would you like your coffee?"

"You're talking back again," she said and moved to take my cup from me and after pouring it down the sink she said, "Don't let me catch you using the kitchen again."

I asked, "Well how am I going to eat if I can't cook?"

With a look of surprise she said, "And where did you learn to cook?"

I said, "In New Orleans, I usually fend for myself around the house as my schedule is pretty different from the rest of the family's."

Just then my mother came into the kitchen and said, "What's going on?"

I said, "Cousin Claire and I have just quarreled in an almost polite manner about me drinking coffee. Would you please tell her I do this on a regular basis and there's nothing for her to be worried about."

My mother said, "Claire he's not making this up. He's been drinking coffee for years at home and he loves it."

Claire replied, "The next thing you're going to tell me is that he drinks beer."

"Well as a matter of fact he does drink beer. There is no drinking age in New Orleans and he's been drinking in bars and at home since he was twelve or thirteen."

Claire said, "Well this will never do at all. I can't have him setting a terrible example for his cousins when they come home. This will have to stop immediately."

I said, "Why."

Claire said, "Because I said so. Now I don't want you doing any more of this in this house. Especially when your cousins get home from their vacation. This is a nice family."

I said, "Nice and provincial. Mom I'm going to the beach. Is that okay?"

Claire said, "Grace does he always talk back like this?"

"He's not talking back," she said, "he's expressing an opinion and his father and I have always encouraged him to say what he thinks."

Just then my grandmother came into the room and after fetching herself a cold soda from the refrigerator, she sat at the table and lit her morning cigarette saying, "What's the row about?"

I said, "Apparently I'm not allowed to drink coffee or beer in California Maw."

"Ridiculous," she declared, "Claire let the boy be, he's not hurting anyone. We'll be in our own home in a few weeks and out of your way. David come here and kiss Maw good morning."

I walked across the kitchen and kissed Maw on the cheek and my mother in turn. I said, "Is it okay for me to go to the beach now I'm dying to see the waves and check out the scene."

Claire said, "How will he get there? I'm certainly not going to drive him there."

My mother said, "Can he borrow one of his cousin's bicycles. David will be very careful with it I'm sure."

"To ride all of the way to the beach?" Claire asked, "Certainly not, the beach is several miles and he doesn't know where it is."

I said, "Several miles? As far as that? I think I can find it. If I can smell it I can find it."

Claire said, "Grace you have the most insolent son. The bicycles are out and if you wish to let him go I'm not going to take any responsibility for what might happen."

I got up from the table and said I'd be back later and that Claire shouldn't worry. She inquired as to how I would get to the beach while I was getting a towel and as I was walking out of the door I said I would probably hitch hike there. I shut the front door behind me and walked to the street smiling at the look on Claire's face when she heard me say I'd be hitch hiking there. I walked out to the road nearby and standing on the corner in my T-shirt, shorts and sandals I stuck out my thumb and waited. A few cars passed and in ten more minutes I had a ride with a bunch of kids who were older than I was and they said they were headed to the Huntington Beach pier for a day in the sun. I told them that that would be fine and settled in for the ride there. Another fifteen minutes passed and they pulled into a parking space about a hundred yards from the pier and we all got out. I thanked the bunch for the ride to the beach and headed for the sand and the waves. I walked to the water's edge where I stripped to my shorts and walked into the water for my first swim in the Pacific Ocean. The water was much colder than I was used to in the Gulf of Mexico and I loved seeing the surfers on their boards riding the waves and seemingly having a ball. I thought I would need to get a board very soon and take part in the fun. I looked around the short downtown area of the town and the big building that was at the end of the pier and saw a small surfboard shop on one of the corners. I went about my swim and was ready to get out when I saw a group of kids who were about my age standing by the spot where I'd left my things on the beach. I caught a small wave and body surfed in to where my things were. When I got out they walked towards me and the biggest of them said, "You're not a local. What do you think you're doing here?"

I said, "Swimming," and reached for my towel. It was kicked out of my reach and a second time when I reached for it again.

I said, "What's the deal? May I have my towel?"

Another of the group said, "This is our beach and its locals only. We don't like it when strangers come here and make things crowded for us."

I said, "I was only swimming, what's the big deal?"

I was answered by a swing from the second boy who spoke. I dodged it and came back hard and put the boy on his ass. He looked at me with great surprise and I reached for my towel. I was no stranger to fighting as New Orleans was a tough town and I had learned from confrontations in the bars I went to and the rougher kids in the neighborhood I had lived in. As I grabbed my towel I felt the back of my head sting and knew I'd been hit hard. I stood up and got another on my upper lip and paid that back with a couple of good ones to the biggest who had first complained about me being on their beach. That did it. As he reached for his face the rest of them jumped on me and I pretty much got the shit beaten out of me then and there. The next thing I knew a yellow Jeep with two lifeguards in it pulled up and one of them grabbed me as I was busy making knuckle marks on one of the kids who had jumped me. I turned around and calmed down some and the lifeguard who grabbed me said, "Hey, hey simmer down now!"

I looked around and the kids that were giving me trouble were running into the water and down the beach. The guard said, "You mind telling me what that was about?"

"You tell me." I said. "I came out from my swim and that bunch told me I wasn't local and had no business here. I was under the assumption this was a public beach. Am I in trouble?"

He said, "No, those were just some of our local surf punks welcoming you to Huntington Beach. Are you hurt?"

I said, "No I'm all right. I think I've got a split lip though."

The guard said, "Do you want some first aid? It's all right here in the Jeep."

I said, "No thanks, the salt water will fix it up. I'll be okay in a few minutes."

He said, "You're going back in the water? They'll jump you again first chance they get and I might not be around to break up the next one."

I said, "Not a problem. I can handle myself. Is this normal behavior for West Coast beaches?"

He said, "I'm afraid so. You must be new here what's your name?"

"I'm David Parish," I said, "I just moved here yesterday. This is my first day at the beach."

He said, "My name is Larry and I have to say you've got balls to stay. My station is tower 47 so come on by if you have more trouble with those punks."

I told him I would and went back into the water to get some salt water on my lip and it did sting but I knew it'd be fine in another few minutes when I got out of the water to go and get some lunch at one of the stands closer to the pier. I got out and went to the sand where my things were and after shaking the sand out of my towel I put on my shirt and sandals and walked towards the pier for something to eat. Even with a sore lip I couldn't help noticing the girls were the best I'd ever seen on the beach. It seemed like they were all beautiful and thin with blond hair wearing bikinis which would have been considered much too small for New Orleans. I liked the view and took it in as I walked along the sand to the pier.

When I got to the pier I found a hamburger stand and bought myself lunch. I paid for my food and went to sit in the shade to eat. While I was eating I looked up and saw some of the group who had jumped me on the sand. I was still eating when one of them I'd tagged with a hard right came up and said, "You're toast new guy. If you step off this pier we'll be waiting for you."

I looked up casually at him and said, "If you want more of what you have on your upper lip then come ahead. I'm not afraid of a bunch of punks. Especially a bunch of chicken shits who have to fight in groups. If you want a piece of me why don't you try me alone and see what you get?"

The young punk grunted and walked away leaving me to finish the lunch I was halfway through. I thought about what was going on and decided I would forget about what had happened and would head to the surf shop and see what new surfboards cost. I walked off of the pier and found my way through the sidewalk crowd to the entrance to the shop. I went inside and began to peruse the shiny new boards that were on display. They cost more I thought they would and I checked them out carefully. Pretty soon a guy about five or six years older than I was came up and said, "Just looking or are you interested in buying?"

I said, "Both, I'm new to all of this and I'm planning on buying something as soon as I learn enough to know what I want or will need."

He said, "Well from your size I'd suggest that you get a board about nine feet long but not too wide so you can get your arm around it when you carry the thing."

He pulled a board out and handed it to me saying, "This one would just about be right for you or for a few dollars more I could make something custom for you."

I was told the price of a custom board would raise the price by about thirty percent and thanked him for the offer. I stood and talked to my salesman who I found out owned the shop and discussed prices and the materials modern boards were made of. I told him about my experience with fiberglass and boats and before I knew it I was taken to the back of the store where he made his boards which were displayed in the showroom. We talked for awhile longer and finally he said, "That's a pretty big lip you've got there. Do you want some ice for it?"

I said, "Sure, some ice would feel good. This is a souvenir from what I was told was a surf punk welcoming committee."

"Sorry about that," he said. "Those punks are giving real surfers a bad name around all of the beaches these days."

I said, "Not a problem, I'm not scared of them and I don't plan on it in the future."

He said, "That's a good attitude to take. They'll leave you alone a lot sooner if you stand up to them and don't take any of their shit."

I said, "That's what I figured. They're no different than the punks where I came from. Punks are punks and that's about all there is to it."

The owner and I stood in the shop and talked for another hour or so about boards and all of the things relating to surfing. Finally as I was starting to talk about going for a swim before hitchhiking home he said, "How did you like a job here? It's not much of a job but I need someone to do the itch work for me. It pays minimum wage but if you're a good worker I'll cut you a deal on a board and you can go surfing with me on the weekends sometimes if you want?"

I said his offer sounded good and asked what I'd actually be doing. He told me I'd be finish sanding nasty fiberglass all of the time but there would be surfing breaks periodically during the day especially when the surf was up and breaking good. I thought about his offer and told him I'd take the job.

He said, "What's your name?"

I said, "I'm David Parish, what's yours?"

"Terry Boyer," he said, I open at nine in the morning and I'm pretty much open seven days a week. If you do good work at the sanding I'll teach you how to shape boards. That's more fun and it doesn't itch so much."

I thanked him for the work and told him I'd see him in the morning. I also told him my thumb was my transportation and said I might be late for work if the rides to the beach were slow. He said that would be okay and we shook hands as I left the shop. I felt pretty great about finding a job as my paper route was left in the south and I would need to have something going to make my life more comfortable. I walked across The Pacific Coast Highway or El Camino Real as the sign was posted in Spanish and headed for the water. I went in for a long swim and when I body surfed in there were the surf punks waiting for me. I walked straight up to them and asked if the wanted to start right away or did they need some more of their friends to come and help. This was taken as I dished it out and I was punched immediately. I answered back and caught another in my sore lip. I was doing okay and getting my licks in when I heard a bullhorn blare and heard Larry the lifeguard's voice over it. The punks scattered and Larry walked up to where I was standing feeling for any extra damage to my face.

Larry said, "You again? You okay?"

I said, "Yeah, I'm okay. I'm getting tired of this though. Thanks for running them off. I'm glad you did."

He said, "Two fights in one day? You don't frighten easily do you?"

I said, "Not very. I've had to deal with worse back home."

Larry laughed and said, "Well you do seem to dish it out as well as you take it. Most people would have left after the first problem."

I said, "Well this is going to be my home beach if I can get my family to move here and I'm not about to roll over where I'm going to live and work."

Larry said, "Where are you going to work?"

I said, "Terry just gave me a job in the itch room of his surfboard shop. I took it and have to be at work in the morning."

Larry said, "Terry gave you a job? That's amazing. Do you have any idea how many guys want to work there for him?"

I said, "No but I can imagine it would be a lot. I feel pretty lucky to have some work."

Larry said, "I'll say, jobs like that don't come up easily. I guess I'll be seeing more of you from now on. Terry is a good friend of mine and he and I surf on the weekends sometimes when his sister takes the shop over for him so he can get some time on the swells. Look, I have to get back to the tower. Take care of yourself on your way home and tell Terry I was looking after you tomorrow."

I said I would and after thanking Larry for bailing me out a second time I picked up my things and headed for the highway and extended my thumb to get home.

It was dark when I walked in the front door and after kissing my grandmother I headed for the refrigerator for a cold beer to drink with Maw and tell her about my day. We sat and talked with me holding the ice-cold bottle to my sore lip and she was delighted I had found some work. We sat and talked together until I got up to get us each another beer and my mother and Claire came through the door. I said hello and went back to the living room where Maw and I were drinking when Claire came into the room and said, "What are you doing drinking that beer?'

I said, "Having a cold one after a long day in the sun. Can I get you one? It's hot outside."

She said, "Certainly not. I told you I don't want you drinking in this house. You're going to be a bad influence on your cousins. I just know you are."

My mom came into the room with her drink and said, "Oh Claire, leave the boy alone and sit down. He's fine and has been out all day. Hello dear how was your day?"

"Good," I said, "I had some trouble but it was nothing I couldn't handle. By the way we have to move to Huntington Beach as soon as possible."

Claire said, "What kind of trouble and how did you get your lip split like that? Why do you have to move to Huntington Beach?"

Maw laughed and took a drink from her beer and lit another cigarette as my mother sat on the opposite side of the room. I said, "Not much trouble and I got this lip from fighting with a bunch of surf punks at the beach."

Maw smiled and took another drink from her beer puffing on one of her strong French cigarettes she loved so much. I went on, "We have to move to Huntington because I got a job there today at the surf shop on the corner. I have to go to work in the morning. When's our stuff being delivered? I need my bicycle and I have to take my savings to work with me tomorrow."

Claire said, "I don't believe you. You've only been here twenty-four hours and you claim to have a job already."

I said, "Yep, I need my savings because I'm buying a surfboard tomorrow. The shop I'll be working in had good boards and I'm getting a discount on a new board tomorrow."

"Your cousin can't get a job, how did you do this and what are you going to be doing?" She quipped.

"I'm going to be sanding surfboards for Terry Boyer who owns the surfboard shop in Huntington. He's really nice and please remember I did come here from the south with a few skills that can get me work."

Maw walked into the room and without a word handed me another beer and lit another cigarette. I took the beer from her and holding it against my sore lip I said, "Mombo who's cooking tonight? I'll chef if y'all are tired."

Mombo said, "That would be nice, we just got back from the store and the makings of a meatloaf are in the fridge."

I said, "No problem, did you bring more beer?"

Mombo said, "No, but I'll tell you what though. While you make the groceries I'll go out and get another sack of beer."

I said, "Great, another beer and I won't mind this lip tonight. It'll be okay in the morning anyway. I'll have to get up early and head for the shop. I don't want to be late for my first day at work. Tomorrow you need to find a Realtor who can deal with Huntington Beach."

Mombo got up and getting her purse walked out of the door to her car. I headed for the kitchen and began to make the meatloaf while Maw made the salad. Cousin Claire sat with a scowl on her face while we waited for Mombo to get back with the beer.

When she got back I drank another while I waited for the meatloaf to be done. We had quite a nice meal and I went to bed as the nightly news began on television anxiously waiting for the next day to begin.

I woke with the sun coming up and dressed for work and the beach. I took a few things with me to sand the fiberglass in and walked out of the door to the road. It was early with the sun just barely coming up and there wasn't much traffic at that time of morning. I got a lift eventually and made it to work on time. Terry was pleased to see me waiting for him and we entered the shop together. The smell of fiberglass wafted through the shop as Terry opened the doors to get some ventilation going. I dressed for the itch room tying the long sleeves down on my shirt to keep the 'glass particles out and began sanding with one of the electric sanders that were on the bench. Terry seemed pleased to see I knew what was up with the task and after a couple of pointers he left me alone to sand and I didn't see him again for a couple of hours until he came in and inspected what I was doing. He told me "Good job," and said to take a break from what I was doing. I blew myself off with the air hose and peeled for the water. I went across the street and hit the waves staying just long enough to relax and let the salt water get the 'glass off of my body. I felt better when I came back and Terry was smiling at me when I walked in the door. I said, "Got a minute?"

Terry said, "Sure, what's up?"

"Transaction," I said, and reached into my bag for the cash I'd brought with me. I counted out the price of the board he'd said would be good for me the day before and holding the board said, "I'll take this one."

Terry laughed and said, "okay but you have some money coming back. I told you I'd give you a discount and here's your change."

He handed me back a pile of bills and I put them back into my bag after saying thanks. I dressed for the itch room again and after putting my new board in the back of the shop I went back to work sanding. Three hours later Terry came up saying break time and when I'd taken off my sanding clothes, I was handed my new board freshly waxed with Terry saying, "Better go and try this out."

I smiled and nodded to him and putting my new board under my arm I headed across the highway and crossed the hot sand to the water. I put the board in and climbed on it to paddle out where the two to three foot waves were breaking. Once I got past the soup of breaking waves I turned my board around and waited for something to catch. A small wave came soon enough and I paddled hard and took off on it. As my board was picked up by the wave I stood up and was surfing. I fell moments later and retrieved my board and paddled out again. I repeated this process until I had my balance better and could ride for a bit before falling off. That would be enough for today I thought and surfed in to the beach. I was met by the surf punks from the day before and they immediately started in kicking at my new board and me. I dropped my board and began to fight back when I heard a familiar voice say, "You punks don't mind if I even the odds up some do you?"

The punks looked around and there was Terry standing there behind me with his board and offering to fight all of them. We stood together and the punks decided the odds weren't good enough for them and backed off immediately. When the incident was over I thanked Terry and headed back across the highway where I started to put my board away and dress for the itch room again. As I was getting ready to work a very beautiful girl who looked only a couple of years older than me came from the back of the shop and said, "You must be David. Terry said you'd be back pretty soon. I'm his sister Jolene and nobody calls me Jo. It's nice to meet you. Terry says you're doing a great job already."

I said, "Pleased to meet you. I'm David and nobody calls me Dave. I heard Terry had a sister but I didn't think I'd meet you until the weekend."

Jolene laughed and said, "I just came down today to give him a break and ride some waves when the evening glass-off gets here. Do you want something cold to drink before you go back to work?"

I said I would and took a soda from her as I dressed for the itch room again. I nodded my thanks to her for the soda as I went back to work with my long sleeve shirt on and began to change the sandpaper in the sander I was using as I drank from the bottle Jolene had given me. I thought to myself she was incredibly beautiful and wondered how old she was. She looked much older than I was and I put any romantic notions about her out of my head as I started the sander and buried myself in the whine of its electric motor. I worked until there was a tap on my shoulder and Terry was standing there with a cold beer in his hand offering the cold brown bottle to me. I nodded at him and took the bottle as the noise of the sander died. He said, "Closing time, let's go across the street and get some waves."

I immediately took off my shirt and put the tools I was using away and picked up my board. There was no sign of Jolene and I wondered where she was as the two of us crossed the highway heading for the water and the waves that were becoming glassy and smooth from the offshore wind which was blowing in the now late afternoon. We walked to the water and Terry went in and began to paddle out not saying a word to me. I followed him dealing with the shore break from the waves that had grown in size from a few hours ago. I finally was making my way out through the soup when I looked up and saw Jolene slicing towards me on her board showing perfect form and looking dazzling in a very tiny bikini. I rolled over on my board to get out of her way as I'd seen other surfers do and looked up as she passed me with one of her hands petting the top of the wave as it curled up to meet her. I got back on my board and paddled to the lineup where it was best for taking off on the now five foot waves. Terry was just taking off on one as I got there and I watched as he scratched water and dropped into a perfect piece of translucent green. There were few of us in the water and I tried for the first wave in the next set that was moving towards me. I paddled hard and caught what was getting taller and taller behind me. I stood up on my board as I slid down the face of the wave and leaned towards the shoulder of the green. I felt like I was going to hit the water when suddenly my board turned under me. Before I knew it my board was back underneath my feet and I was slicing across the face of a good sized wave. I caught my balance as I speeded up and crouched as my board began to stall on me. I moved forward on my new board and it sped up and matched the wave's speed. I kept my balance and as the wave began to break up in the shallows I leaned in and went over the top of the shoulder making my first nearly perfect ride on a good sized wave. I paddled back out to the line up and ran into Terry who said, "Hey that was pretty good. Are you sure this is the first time you've surfed?"

I said, "This is it. My first day ever and I'm pretty sure that was just beginners luck. Thanks for the compliment though, that ride felt pretty great."

Looking beyond me Terry said, "Hey! Here comes a good set. Take the second or third wave and do the same as you did before. Be sure to bend your knees and keep your weight forward."

I said I would and after the first wave I paddled hard for the second wave of the set. I felt the back end of my board start to lift and stood up and got my balance. The result was the same as before and I got a good ride this time using my balance and practicing turning my board up and down the face of the wave as I rode with it. When I had all I could get from the swell I rose up over the top of it and dove off of my board into the green water feeling exhilarated. I was paddling back to the line up when I saw Jolene again slicing down a really big wave and working it back and forth as she screamed along. I paddled so I would be in no danger of conflicting with her ride and she waved to me as she went by. She was standing almost erect and her blond straight hair was trailing behind her shining in the afternoon sunlight. I thought then and there she was a beautiful sight on the water. Terry passed me next and waved as he went by. His physical motions on his board were effortless as he moved back and forth on his board to adjust his angle and speed. I paddled out to the line up and rested while Terry and Jolene worked their way back out. I was getting tired because of not being physically used to all of the paddling. I knew my shoulders would be sore the next day but I didn't care. I was surfing and having a great time. I sat on my board out beyond the break when Terry and Jolene glided up to where I was sitting on my board looking out to sea for the next sets that would be rolling in. Terry said, "Jolene would you look at this guy. He's been on the water for one day and he's already watching the horizon like he's been doing this for years."

Jolene said, "David I can't believe how well you're doing. I've never seen anyone learn as fast as you are. Are you having a good time and don't you just love it?"

I said, "Thanks, I sure do. This is everything I dreamed it would be. I can't believe how much fun I'm having."

Terry said, "Well we might just have to take you south this weekend. You're doing well enough to handle some of the surf further south."

"Thanks," I said, "I'd like that. It would be great to see more of the coast."

By this time I was rested and ready for another wave. I waited and watched as Jolene and Terry both took off together on a big wave and they quickly disappeared out of my sight. I skipped the next wave and took the one after it. I took off and stood up feeling my board under my feet and getting used to the response the board made as I adjusted my feet on its surface. The three of us surfed until almost dark and then we walked back across the highway to put our boards inside of the shop and get our things we needed to take home with us. I collected my pack and thanked Terry and Jolene for helping me to have a great afternoon. It was as good an afternoon as I could remember and I felt like I was glowing as I stood on the corner with my thumb out waiting for someone to give me the ride I needed. It came soon enough and I was home in good time. I walked in the front door and went to the refrigerator to get a beer and relax before dinner.

CHAPTER TWO

I sat in the living room to relax and my mother came into the room in a few minutes. I said, "Hi, Mombo did you find a Realtor today?"

She said, "As a matter of fact I did. I called one today and he said he had some nice rental houses that were close to the beach he wants to show me tomorrow. Do you want to come along?"

I said, "No I have to work so I'm just going to have to trust you on this one. I really don't care what it looks like, I just want to be close to the beach."

Mombo said, "Close to the beach it is. How about close to school?"

I said, "That would help but I'm more interested in being near the water. School won't be starting for two more months so I'm not worried about it."

"Well the beach here seems to really agree with you. You're positively glowing from the sun tonight. Did you buy the board you wanted and did you get to use it today?"

I said, "I sure did. I surfed with Terry and his sister until almost dark and had the best time I've had in years. Surfing is great and I seem to be able to stand up and make things happen."

"That's wonderful David, I'm really happy you're having a good time. How was work?"

"It was okay. Its nasty work but the perks of being at the beach are definitely worth the effort. How about you, are you looking for a job yet?"

My mom said, "I looked at the classifieds today. There seems to be quite a market for Registered Nurses here and I don't think it will be hard to find what I want."

I said, "Where's Maw?"

Mombo said, "She went with your cousin Claire to the store. She wanted to find out where she can get those awful cigarettes she likes to smoke. She said she'd be happy when she can get you away from Claire though. She really thinks you're the greatest and doesn't much like Claire telling you what to do."

I said, "No big deal, I don't mind Claire. She's nice enough to let us stay in her house. I just think she's not used to having someone like me around."

"You mean someone young and independent?"

"That's it exactly." I said, "Did you see the look on her face when I volunteered to cook last night? I gather her daughter's children don't do much or at least aren't allowed too."

Mombo said, "That's what it sounds like to me. We left you alone for years so you could have a chance to learn something. I have to say I'm pretty proud of you for getting a good interesting job so quickly."

I said, "Thanks, I just got lucky. I have met some nice people though. Terry's sister is a complete knock out."

Mombo said, "Do tell."

I said, "She's just about perfect but I'm pretty sure she's a couple of years older than I am. Too bad 'cause I think she's great. You should see her surf. She's fantastic. In fact I've seen more beautiful women here in 24 hours than I've ever seen in New Orleans. The beach here is great for girl watching."

Mombo said, "How about the men? I'm ready for someone other than those conservative bastards in the south."

I said, "I guess you'll have to buy a bikini and come to the beach then."

Mombo said, "I most certainly will not. Not until I can join a gym and get some of this fat off of me. Then maybe I'll buy a bikini and head for the beach. Are you ready for another beer?"

I said, "Sure I'd love another. What's for dinner? Should I start to make something?"

Mombo said, "Don't worry about it. Maw said she would try and bring home some Chinese food tonight so we won't have to cook."

Just then the front door flew open and Maw and Claire came in toting bags of groceries and plenty of Chinese food. I went to help and when I took the biggest bag from Maw I could see she had the cigarettes she wanted. She kissed me on the cheek as I took the bag from her and I set it down on the kitchen table as I was handed another beer by my mother. Claire grunted her dislike as I took a drink from the cold bottle. Maw was opening the take out and my mother went to the cabinet for the plates. I sat back and enjoyed the warm feeling I had inside of me from the sun and the surf that afternoon. The Chinese food was gone in minutes after it was served and we settled in for some television. I was falling asleep during the movie that was on the network and soon gave up the film and went to bed. I wanted to get up early and get to the beach and hopefully ride some waves before work.

Morning was in my face before I knew it and I was quick to get out of bed and start the coffee. It was still dark outside and I drank my Joe from a styrofoam cup while I walked to the corner with my pack to start the process of hitching to the pier and all I was beginning to love. I got a ride very quickly that morning and I was dropped off right in front of the surf shop as the sun was just beginning to light up the water and the pier. I looked around and as I did Jolene came riding up on a bicycle which was built for racing and had a number of gears. She rode up to where I was standing and said, "Hi, you're up early. Want to go surfing?"

I said, "That's what I'm here for. I was hoping one of you would be here. I don't have a key."

Jolene said, "No key and with your board here? I'll get you one today at the hardware store. We can't go around with you not being able to get to your board. The way you were riding yesterday you're going to be dangerous in another couple of weeks."

I blushed and said, "Do you really think so?"

Jolene said, "Definitely. You should have heard Terry bragging on you last night to his friends. You have all of what it takes to be one of the best. I've really never seen anyone learn so fast."

I said, "Well thanks for the compliment. I thought you were pretty great out there yourself. You seem to really know what you're doing."

Jolene said, "That's just experience. I've been surfing since I could first swim and I can't remember not surfing. I just wish more girls would surf. I'm usually the only girl out there and the others just sit on the beach and try to look pretty. Come on David let's get our boards and go grab some waves before the crowds get here."

Jolene took her keys and opened the store and we walked to the back and got our surfboards. We changed our outer clothing to what was underneath in front of each other and left our clothes on the floor in the shop. We went out to the street and locked the door to the shop and, disobeying the traffic light, ran across the street to the sand. We were in the water in minutes and were riding perfect waves which were about four to five feet high. I was having the same good luck as the day before and I was having a wonderful time surfing with Jolene. She was great about helping me and made several great suggestions that made things a lot easier for me. I felt I was really learning and by the time the sun was fully up and the water was getting crowded, we were both tired and getting hungry. We surfed into the beach and took our boards across the street and put them away in the shop. Jolene said, "David are you hungry?"

"Yes I am."

Jolene said, "Come on then."

We walked three doors down the strand to a small coffee shop where there were coffee and doughnuts for sale. We ordered what we wanted and I paid for mine and hers with the wet money which had been in the pocket of my shorts the whole time I was surfing that morning. Jolene laughed as I handed the wet bills to the counter person and we went to sit on a bench to drink our coffee and watch the surfers across the street.

She asked, "David, where are you from?"

I said, "I've just moved here from New Orleans. This is my third day here."

She said, "Really? I can hardly believe that. You've really made quite an adjustment very quickly."

I said, "Thanks, I've always been pretty self reliant. I was really lucky to have your brother give me a job at his shop. I'm really doing what I used to just dream about."

Jolene said, "What year are you in school?"

I said, "I'm going to be a freshman this coming year at whatever school I go to."

"Me too!" she said. "I'm going to go to the new high school they call Marina. I'm excited to be going to high school."

I said, "You're going to be in the same year as I am? I thought you were a lot older than I am."

Jolene said, "That's really funny David, I thought you were a lot older than me."

We both laughed and looked at each other. I said, "Well it's nice to know we both look older. Maybe we'll have some classes together."

She said, "Maybe we will. I'll be taking college prep courses. If you're going to take the same thing we could register together and make sure we get what we want. It would be good for homework too. We can each do half of the home work and then switch."

I said, "Great idea, we'll have quite awhile to work out the details. I have to get my mother to rent a house here before I can think of enrolling in school."

Jolene said, "What kind of house are you looking for?"

I said, "Anything that will hold my mother, grandmother and myself that's close to the beach. It's just the three of us. My dad is on the gulf coast of Mississippi and there's no surfing there."

Jolene said, "I have an idea. My oldest brother rebuilds houses here and I think I heard him say he is about to rent one he's just finished out. Let's go and call him to see if it's available."

We got up from the bench we were sitting on and headed back to the shop. We went inside and while Jolene got on the phone to her brother I began to open the windows and get the shop ready for business. Jolene was off of the phone in a minute and said, "You're in business, he was just going to call the realtor he does business with and list the place for rent tomorrow. All we have to do is get your mother and him together."

Jolene extended the phone in my direction and I took the receiver from her. I had to look up the number in the phone book and when Claire answered I asked to speak with my mother. When Mombo got on the phone I said, "Mombo, I've found us a house to rent."

"Great! How did this happen?" she asked.

I said, "The Boyer family who own the surf shop have a house for rent. Jolene said it's what we're looking for. Will you call her brother and go look at it."

Mombo said, "Sure I'll call after we get off of the phone. What's the number?"

I gave her the number and hung up the phone. Jolene smiled at me from where she was wiping off the new boards with Windex making them shine like mirrors. I said, "Good deal, she's calling as we speak and if he's got time she'll go and see the place this afternoon."

Jolene said, "That's great. Can I ask you something?"

"Sure, ask away."

Jolene said, "Why do you call your mother Mombo?"

I laughed and said, "It's kind of a beatnik thing from New Orleans. There are lots of subculture people there and she's kind of an intellectual beatnik. You'll understand when you meet her, she's pretty cool."

Jolene said, "Well she must be if she lets you call her Mombo. She sounds pretty neat."

I said, "I'd better get to work. I don't want Terry to think I'm slacking off around here. I want to be hard at work when he comes in this morning."

Jolene laughed and said, "Good idea. I'll dig you out of the itch room in a couple of hours for a break. We can go for a swim."

I said a swim would be fine and headed for the itch room and the work which was waiting for me there.

I worked past ten and Terry dropped in once to see how I was doing. I suppose all was well with what I was accomplishing as he just patted me on the back to let me know he was there and left for the front of the store as I was turning around. Jolene came and got me a couple of hours later and we walked across the street to go for a swim. We were having a nice time in the shore break when the surf punks came up and started to mess with me and her as well. I was busy with two of them and I noticed Jolene was being harassed by two more while the others hung back and watched. I moved closer to where she was and was about to help her with her battle when she hauled off and kicked one of the guys between his legs and he went down hard. I was busy beating the crap out of one of the two who were after me when the one she kicked went down onto the sand. The rest of then jumped back in horror as their friend lay writhing on the beach. Jolene and I looked at each other and ran for the highway while the others were distracted by their friend's misery. We were laughing by the time we got to the highway and were laughing harder as we ran into the surf shop. Terry looked up from the books he was dealing with as we came in and said, "What are you two running from?"

Jolene blurted out, "Surf punks!" breathing hard and then said, "They got after us when we got out of the water and while David was fighting them off I kicked one of them in the balls and put him down hard."

Terry laughed and said, "No shit! I wish I were there to see that. Those guys have been asking for it for a long time. I'm happy they're getting their share. David thanks for looking out for Jolene but as you can see she doesn't need much help."

I laughed and said, "I learned that. I'm glad it wasn't me who was kicked. That guy won't walk for a week!"

Jolene laughed again and went to hug Terry laughing as she did so. I went back to the itch room, started the sander and didn't take a break until Terry came to me in the afternoon and handed me a cold beer signifying that the day was over and it was time to go and ride some waves. We all had a beer before walking across the highway and as we walked along the sand with our boards we could see the punks point-ing at us and I watched as Terry looked at them almost daring them to come and bother us. We made it to the water without incident and the three of us paddled out together. We all got to the take off spot together and I let Jolene get the first wave. I took the second one and was having a good time on it when I noticed Terry was riding the same wave right next to me. We surfed the wave together and kicked out at the same time. We had a great ride and we paddled back out together. While we were paddling out we heard a yell and when I looked up Jolene was bearing down on the two of us intent on passing close enough to scare us and spray water in my face. When she passed us I could hear her laugh and thought she was wonderful. She was right about what she had said to me earlier. She was the only girl on the water and she was also as good a surfer as any of the men who were out with us. The three of us wore out that day as we had the day before, and we all left the shop as night was falling but this time with Jolene giving me a key to the front door and asking if I was coming early in the morning again the next day. I answered I was planning on it and she said she'd meet me at the shop at sunrise and then walked with Terry to his car. I stepped to the curb and walked across the street and put out my thumb. I got a ride right away that night and I was home earlier than the previous night. I walked into the house and found Mombo and Maw sitting together in the kitchen while Claire was making something that looked like it might turn into a casserole at some point in time. I got myself a beer and said, "So Mombo, how did things go today?"

Mombo said, "David you are an angel. I don't know how you did it but you found us a house. It's perfect. It has three bedrooms and it is two blocks from the beach and two blocks from where the Boyers live. It's affordable and you're going to love it. I halfway expect you to find me a job next."

I said, "Well thanks mombo. I'm glad it worked out. It's one less thing to worry about. By the way I had a great day today and I found out my boss' sister, who I thought was older, is the same age as me and it looks like we'll be going to school together in the fall."

"David that's wonderful." she said. "I'm glad you are making friends. You really seem to like this girl. Are we going to get to meet her soon?"

I said, "You can meet her tomorrow if you want to get up at dawn and drive me to work. Jolene and I are going surfing when I get there."

Mombo said, "No thanks, I'll wait until sometime when the sun is up a little higher."

I laughed and said. "No doubt it can wait. I have a feeling you'll get more than one chance to meet her and her brother."

Maw was laughing as she drank from her beer and lit one of her cigarettes. When she had her light she said she would finish cooking dinner and I got to relax after another wonderful day at work and the beach. I went to bed that night seeing the green translucent waves in my mind and thinking about how great Jolene looked on her surfboard.

I woke up before dawn the next morning and headed to the corner drinking my coffee and hoping for good waves that day. I caught a ride with some other surfers and they took me with them to the pier. I got out of their car just as Jolene rode up on her bicycle. I got out my key and opened the door so she could put her bike inside. She looked at me and said, "Are you ready?"

"More than ready. I went to sleep last night thinking about riding waves," I said.

Jolene smiled and said, "You've got surf stoke. I would too if I was doing as well as you are out there."

I said, "I guess that's good?"

Jolene said, "Yes, that's good. Surf stoke just means you get really excited about what you're doing on the water. You've got it good. I can see it all over you."

I smiled and we went to the back and got our boards. We headed across the street and went into the water at the same time. We paddled out next to each other and spent the early morning riding small but perfect waves. When the sun got higher we surfed in and started to walk back to the shop on the highway. At one point I said, "What's that big building at the beginning of the pier?"

Jolene glanced in the direction I was pointing and said, "That's the Pavilon. It's a place where bands play on the weekends and it's really fun. It's been here since the old days when the big bands played ballroom music. Almost every city has one. Newport has the Rendezvous at their pier. They're used mostly for young people and surf music now. The Crossfires from Redondo Beach will be there this Saturday night. Do you want to go?"

I said, "Sure I'd love to but I have to tell you I don't know much about surf music. Remember, I'm from New Orleans and all we had there was the radio and heavy Rhythm and Blues."

Jolene said, "That sounds great. We don't get much of that here I always like to hear different things."

I said, "Is that tomorrow night?"

Jolene smiled and said, "That's right. You can meet me there or bring your clothes to the shop and we can go from there. Whatever you'd like to do."

"Jolene, I have absolutely no idea what to wear. All of my clothes are from the south and I have nothing but shorts and T-shirts that look like anything out here. Can you give me some help with this?"

Jolene said, "Sure, tell you what. I'll raid my brother's closet for you and find something for you to wear. The biggest thing is men have to wear a tie to get in. They're really intent on keeping the place nice and us respectable looking."

I said, "I have no problem with a tie but what will you have to wear?"

Jolene said, "I'll have to wear something girlie. At least some nice shoes, pants and a blouse. Do you think you can take it?"

I laughed and said, "If you can deal with me in a neck tie then I can handle it."

She laughed too and said, "Tomorrow make sure you remember to bring some shoes to wear. I'll take care of the rest for you."

We walked the rest of the way back to the shop and got to the front door just as Terry was getting out his keys to open up. He said, "Hey, how were the waves?"

Jolene said, "Fantastic. You should have been with us. We had a great morning and I'm taking David to the Pavilon tomorrow night to hear the Crossfires."

Terry said, "Well I'll be there too with Marcy. I think just about everybody will be there. They haven't played here for months. It should be really bitchin'."

I headed for the itch room and the work I knew would be there while Jolene went about polishing the boards and cleaning the shop. Terry headed for the shaping room to build the boards I'd be sanding in a few days. I liked the thought of going out with Jolene and was pleased she'd invited me. That Friday was another great day and the three of us said goodbye at the front of the store after putting our boards away. It was the same as the day before except Jolene turned before she got into Terry's '49 Ford Woody Wagon and gave me a soft wink as she was getting inside. I headed across the street and began to make my way home, warm from the sun and the thought of Jolene smiling at me.

I got back to the house and Mombo and Maw were sitting with Claire having a cocktail and talking. Mombo said, "Hi David would you like a cocktail?"

I said, "No thanks I'll have a beer. I've wanted one since I got off of work."

Mombo said, "Did you have a good day?"

I said, "I really did. The waves were good and I have a date tomorrow night."

"With the girl at the surf shop?"

I said, "Yep. She asked me to the dance at the Pavilon tomorrow night. It's a big dance hall at the end of the pier. From what she said it sounds like great fun."

Claire spoke up and said, "Grace I wouldn't let him go there. I've heard terrible things about that place and the trouble that can happen there."

Mombo said, "Oh nonsense. If David can handle himself on the wicked streets of New Orleans I'm very sure he can handle Huntington Beach."

I was laughing along with Maw and said, "I think I might be able to. I don't think the crowd will be too rough as all of the men have to wear a tie to get in and the girls have to wear nice clothes and shoes."

Mombo said, "David a tie? I haven't seen you in a tie since your cousin's wedding. What are you going to wear?"

I said, "I don't know. Jolene said she'd raid her brother's closet for me. I'll change at the shop and go from there. I guess I'll be home late."

Mombo said, "She's bringing you clothes for the dance? David this girl likes you."

I said, "Apparently so. I like her as well and I'm flattered to go out with her."

Mombo said, "David you're flattered to go out with her? I have to meet this girl. You've never talked like this about any of the girls you've been out with before. Is she that nice?"

I said, "And then some. By the way, when are we moving to the beach? I'm getting tired of thumbing my way there every day."

Mombo said, "Next weekend if that's not too far off. It's the earliest I could get the moving company to bring our things. Will that be soon enough?"

"That will be fine with me," I said. "Make sure I know what day so I can tell Terry what day I'll need to be off so I can help."

Mombo said, "I think it will be next Saturday but I'll check and make sure for you. What would you like for dinner tonight?"

I said, "How about some of that leftover casserole we had last night. I'm tired and I want to eat and go to bed early. Tomorrow will be a long day."

Mombo got up and went to the refrigerator to get out the leftovers and I helped myself to another beer to continue relaxing. Maw smiled at me and got up to make some salad holding her beer with her cigarette dangling from her lips. I did the dishes and cleaned the kitchen with Maw after dinner and then headed for the shower and my bed. I went to sleep thinking of my good fortune and what tomorrow night would be like.

I woke up late the next morning and after chastising myself for it I made it to the road and stuck out my thumb. I got to the shop after Jolene had been there and there was a note saying she would be across the street where the waves were cracking at five feet plus. These would be the biggest fastest waves I'd yet surfed and I watched for awhile before I went in to paddle out. I was halfway to the line up when I saw Jolene take off on a fantastic wave. She dropped into the wave and made a beautiful bottom turn rising up to let the wave break in a perfect tube over her head. I was really impressed and watched as she disappeared inside of the tube for almost a full minute. Just when I thought she had wiped out she came flying out of the end of the tube with all of the spray and the air the breaking wave had compressed steaming behind her. I could hear her scream as she kicked out over the shoulder of the wave and began to paddle back to the line up. I caught up to her on the outside and said, "Nice ride there!"

She said, "Did you see it? I thought I was toast when I was inside! It was just fantastic! I'm glad you saw me because my brother will never believe it if I tell him. I need a good witness. Come on let's paddle over and get you into one of them."

We paddled over and got to the right takeoff spot. I went for a big one and wiped out on my first try. On my way back out I saw Jolene take another wave and the result was almost as good as the wave she was on previously. I caught up to her again on the outside and after a few pointers I took off on the wave she suggested and dropped into it. I made the drop and guided my board up the wave as the peak started to curl over my head. I crouched a bit and let my board speed up. The next thing I knew the wave had completely engulfed me and I learned the meaning of being inside of a green cathedral. It was the most exciting thing I could imagine and the sun through the translucent green water brought chicken skin to my back and arms. Before I could get used to the feeling I was blown out of the end of the tube where I could hear the crowd on the beach yelling at something. I kicked out over the shoulder of the wave and lay back down on my board to paddle out to the lineup. When I got back out Jolene was laughing and saying I'd had a perfect ride. She leaned over and squeezed my arm smiling as she did. I was very pleased she thought I'd done well and when I asked what all of the people on the beach were yelling about. She said, "David, they were screaming at you. You were in the tube for almost a full minute. You were fantastic and they were yelling because you gave them something to yell about. Wait until I tell Terry. He won't believe either of us. I can't believe how proud I am of you. You were fantastic. Let's paddle out and catch a few more before we have to go to work."

We both went back out and spent the morning riding pipes before Jolene said, "Oh shit I'm sure that we're late for work. Terry will be so jealous."

I said, "He won't be mad at me for being late will he?"

Jolene said, "Not at all. When I tell him what you were doing he'll be amazed.

Besides he's opened late on many mornings when it's been breaking good. Come on, let's go in and get some coffee and doughnuts to have before we start work."

Jolene and I surfed in and carried our boards through the crowd that had gathered to watch the tube riding that was going on. When we got to the shop she grabbed Terry and said, "Terry, you should have seen David. He had the wave of the morning and got the whole beach on their feet by the end of his ride. It was fantastic."

Terry smiled and said, "Well that's a good excuse for being late to work. What's yours?"

I said, "Her is the same as mine. Jolene had as ride as good as she says mine was when I was paddling out. You should have seen her. She was completely out of sight for most of her ride and I almost couldn't believe what I was seeing."

Terry was smiling and said, "Well you two are either conspiring to be late for work or you've been having all of the fun. I think I'd better go across the street and get in a few waves before people start telling me my sister surfs better than I do. You two get to work and I'll be back in a few hours."

I dressed for the itch room and Jolene started her daily routine of cleaning and setting the store right for the day. I didn't see either of them until Terry alerted me it was time for lunch. The beach was too crowded to go and fight for waves and Terry sent Jolene down the street for some sandwiches and soda. We ate together and watched the action across the street from the bench in front of the store while we ate. The waves were getting bigger and bigger throughout the day and by the evening there was no way we could surf at the pier as the waves had gotten too big and I was told it was closed out. When it came time to leave Jolene said, "Terry, David and I are going out tonight to see the Crossfires. Is it okay if we take him home with us and let him clean up there?"

Terry said, "Sure, we can feed him dinner too if you want."

Jolene said, "Great, David let's go, you can meet my parents. Terry has been telling them all about you and after we eat you can shower and get ready for the Pavilon."

I said it would be great and after we locked the door to the shop we got into Terry's car and drove the short distance to their home. My new home was pointed out to me on the way there and it looked as nice as I'd hoped it would be. We pulled into their driveway and while Jolene and I went inside Terry began to wash his woody. It wasn't dirty but I understood the California esthetic of never having your car dirty especially when you would be going out that night and would be seen by the whole town. Terry definitely had an image to keep up. Jolene took me inside and taking me by the arm, introduced me to her parents who were in the living room having cocktails. I met Stan and Laura Boyer for the first time and they seemed to be very nice. Jolene went and got the two of us each a beer when the introductions were done and we went out to their backyard to sit by the pool and watch what was left of the sun going down. We were called to dinner soon after dark and the conversation at the table was very nice and polite and I enjoyed my meal. When it was done Jolene and I took over the kitchen and cleaned up the mess that was left. When we were done she left the room and came back a minute later saying she'd put out some things for me to wear on her brothers bed and told me where the shower and the clean towels were. I was told she had a few things to do for herself and she'd meet me in the living room when she was finished dressing. I took my shower and got into the clothes she'd picked out for me and they fit fine. I finished dressing except for my shoes and socks and looked at myself in the mirror in the hallway. The white Levis with a nice shirt and tie looked good and I waited until we were ready to leave to put on my shoes and socks. I sat talking with her parents until she was ready and came into the living room. Jolene looked fantastic with her blond hair brushed and she was wearing makeup that made her look not only gorgeous but a couple of years older. I was amazed she could look so good and told her how nice she looked as she came into the living room. She asked if I was ready and laughed when I said I had to put on my shoes and socks. She said she hated wearing the things too and when I was done with my footwear I stood up. Her mother offered us a ride to the Pavilon but Jolene put her off saying it was a great night and that we'd walk there. She promised her parents she'd come home with Terry and we set out for the pier at the beach. It took us about fifteen minutes to walk there and the night air was wonderful. I knew then I was going to love living in her neighborhood. We could smell the salt in the air from the ocean and hear the big waves breaking as we walked and Jolene held my arm as we walked along talking about other surf spots she wanted to take me to.

When we got to the pier I went up to the box office with her and we each bought a ticket to the event. Inside the place was deceptively large. We went and got two cold drinks and waited for the band to start playing. When the Crossfires began to play the building buzzed loudly with the energy of the surf guitar. The music was thrilling and was very reminiscent to the feeling I had when I'd had been locked inside of the tube that morning. Jolene seemed to know a lot of the other kids who were there and I did get some strange looks as I stood beside her. I watched as the kids began to dance and realized I didn't know how to dance to this kind of music. I said, "Jolene I'm afraid you're going to have to show me how to dance to this music. It's like nothing I've ever heard."

She laughed and said, "Okay, let's go over here."

We walked away from where the majority was standing and she showed me how to dance to the music. When I was confidant enough we went to the dance floor and danced until the band took a break. When the music stopped Terry came up and we stood there talking until the band came back and the music started again. Jolene and I went back to dancing and having fun watching each other. When the music stopped again Jolene gave me a big hug and as I felt her beautiful body against mine she said into my ear, "Want to get drunk?"

I said, "Sure, what are we drinking?"

"Scotch," she whispered, "I brought some with me but we'll have to go outside."

I nodded and she turned around and I followed her to the door of the massive building. We exited and she took my arm and we walked towards the end of the pier which was shaking from the waves breaking against it. The end was quite a way and when we got to the railing she reached into her purse and took out a small bottle of what I recognized as pretty good scotch whiskey. She opened it and drank from the bottle handing it to me. She said, "Here's to you. Welcome to California."

I lifted the bottle towards her and said, "Here's to you. Thanks for having me."

Jolene laughed and took the bottle back and took another drink saying, "I'm very glad you're here."

When she took the bottle from her lips she leaned against me and putting one hand behind my head she kissed me on my lips. Hers were as soft as I could have imagined and I was just getting lost in their softness when she opened her mouth and kissed me with her tongue. I was amazed at this girl. She could kiss like no other girl I'd ever kissed and was completely sensual in my arms. We stood on the end of the pier kissing and trading drinks from her bottle until the contents were half gone. She screwed the top back on the bottle and said, "Okay, I'm nearly drunk. Let's go back inside and dance until we're sober."

I said, "That's fine with me," and we walked back to the Pavilon where our hand stamps got us back inside and we pushed our way through the crowd until we were in front of the band and the sound was close to deafening.

We spent the next hour dancing and when the band stopped again we went outside and finished the rest of the scotch. We drank and kissed until the bottle was empty and we went back to the dance floor. The end of the dancing came all-too soon and we were disappointed when the band stopped and we yelled for more with the others in the building. We got two more songs out of the band for an encore and then the lights were turned on and we walked outside where Terry and his date Marcy were leaning against the pier railing. We walked up to them and Terry said, "Have you two been boozing?"

I said nothing and Jolene said, "Yep, got anything left?"

Terry smiled and said, "Sure, in the car. Come on let's go."

I followed Terry and Marcy with Jolene walking next to me holding my arm. We found Terry's Ford Wagon and we all climbed inside. Terry smiled and pulled a bottle out of his glove compartment and handed it back to Jolene who drank from it and handed it to me. I handed it to Marcy and said, "After you."

Marcy took a drink and handed the bottle back to me saying thank you. I took my turn and handed the bottle to Terry who drank and passed the bottle to his sister. We passed the bottle this way until the contents were gone and it was beginning to get late. Jolene said, "Terry can we take David home? It's getting late and I don't want him to hitch this late at night."

Terry said, "Sure, David where do you live?"

I ran down the directions to him and he started out of the parking lot and down the Coast Highway. Jolene turned and kissed me while we were driving and out of the corner of my eye I could see Terry and Marcy taking small glimpses of us kissing as Terry drove the two of them smiling at each other and seemingly pleased about the romance that was going on in the back seat. I was dropped of at my front door and after kissing Jolene good night she said, "Surf stoke at sunrise?"

I said, "Definitely," and kissed her again. I got out and walked to my door as they pulled away feeling drunken and very pleased about what was happening to me.

CHAPTER THREE

I woke up the next morning feeling tired from the night before. After getting out of bed slowly I went to the kitchen and made some coffee to take to the street with me. It was Sunday morning and I had to wait for awhile before I got a ride. I had left the house early on purpose so I could meet Jolene on time at the shop and I got a ride just when I was getting worried about being late and wound up beating Jolene to the shop. She rode up on her bicycle a minute later and I smiled when I saw her. She got off of her bike and kissed me as soon as she was near enough. I kissed back and when we stopped she said, "David, I just love kissing you."

I looked her in the eyes and said, "I love kissing you too."

We kissed again and without another word went to the back to get our boards and head for the waves that had calmed down from the day before. It was the same walk as we had taken before except Jolene held my hand as we walked down the beach. We surfed for a couple of hours until Jolene pointed out Terry's Woody in front of the shop. Jolene said, "Want to go and surf Newport?"

I said, "Sure I would. Let's go."

We surfed in and caught up to Terry as he was loading boards into the back of his wagon. We put ours in as well and when we'd finished loading Terry turned the car around and we headed south on the highway. We drove through Costa Mesa and turned onto the Newport Peninsula continuing to 59th Street where Terry hoped the waves were good. Jolene nodded her approval and we parked the wagon on a side street and got out our gear. We settled in on the sand and I started to watch the break. The waves broke off of a jetty and they looked great. The break was to the left, which would be different for me from the rights at the pier and I was ready for anything by this time. Terry and Jolene were well known by the locals here and there was a good commotion of welcome when we got outside of the break. Terry got upright on his board and said loudly, "This is David, he works for me and I don't want to see any of you kooks dropping in on him and spoiling his ride. You do and you'll have to answer to Jolene and you know you don't want that."

Most of the group laughed and Jolene blushed enough for me to notice. I was treated with great respect that morning and had some very good rides that some of Terry's friends complimented me on. I felt really great about how I was doing at the sport. We got out of the water at about noon and went for the towels we had left at the beach. We stayed until we dried off and Terry said, "I have to go and meet Marcy at her house. What do you two want to do?"

Jolene said, "I want to go to David's house and hang out there with him if it's all right."

I said, "Sure. That would be fine. I'm sure I can get you a ride home later. Would that be all right?"

Terry smiled and said, "Perfect. If you have trouble with a ride for Jolene call home and someone will come and get you. David if I don't see you later I'll see you tomorrow at the shop. By the way, you rode really well today. I'm impressed with how you're doing."

Terry drove us to where I was staying and I walked inside with Jolene. We walked into the living room and found my cousins had returned from their vacation. Claire's daughter Jo Ann and her husband Ralph were there along with their kids. I was introduced to my cousins Connie who was one year younger than me and her brother Gary who was the same age as I was. I introduced Jolene to them and we sat in the living room with Maw who was sitting there listening to cool jazz on the radio. She smiled when she saw Jolene and I said, "Maw this is Jolene. Where's Mombo?"

Maw said, "I'm very pleased to meet you. Can I get you something to drink? We have beer and soda which would you like?"

Jolene said, "I'd like a beer please."

Maw got up and headed for the kitchen to get us some refreshments as we sat on the couch. Mombo came into the room and said, "Hi you must be Jolene. I'm David's mother Grace. It's a pleasure to meet you."

Jolene said, "It's a pleasure to meet you as well."

I got up and went to the kitchen while Jolene and Mombo sat on the couch and began to talk. I was back with Maw in a few minutes and after handing out more refreshments I sat with the group and listened as stories were told about their vacation. My cousins were dressed like they were from southern California but were nothing like Jolene. The two kids were pretty quiet and they seemed extremely conservative. We all sat in the living room to talk and after awhile my cousin Gary said, "David what are you two doing drinking beer?"

I said, "Having a cold one after a morning at the beach and great surfing."

Gary said, "You went surfing? Where?"

I said, "Huntington Pier at dawn and then at the 59th Street jetty in Newport Beach after that. It was really great."

He said, "How did you get there?"

I said, "Jolene and I went with her brother this morning after we surfed Huntington Pier."

Gary said, "David where did you get a surf board and how did you get to Huntington Pier?"

I said, "I hitchhiked there like I do every morning. Jolene and I go surfing every morning before we go to work. I bought my surfboard from Jolene's brother who owns the surf shop on the corner in Huntington Beach. How about you? Do you and your sister surf?"

Gary said, "No we don't surf. It's too expensive to buy a board and I wouldn't be able to take it anywhere because they're too big. How do you get yours to the beach everyday?"

Jolene said, "David leaves his at the beach at the shop where I leave mine."

Gary said, "Ha! The next thing you'll tell me is you have a job at the surf shop there!"

Jolene laughed and said, "David does have a job there at the shop. My brother gave him a job on his first day here and that's where we met."

Gary said, "Does your brother own the shop?"

"Yes he does. I work there as well."

"I don't believe you two," Gary said. "You're just making this up. I've asked for a job there and I couldn't get one. I think its unlikely David got a job there on his first day in California. How did you learn how to surf anyway?"

Jolene said, "David learned at the pier last week. He's really learning fast. You should see him."

I said, "Gary you should see Jolene surf. She's one of the best on the water. She continually impresses me on the waves."

Gary said, "Girls don't surf. You two are making this all up."

Jolene was more than amused by now and said, "Gary why don't you come to the shop tomorrow. David and I will take you surfing if you want."

Gary said, "How would I get there?"

I said, "Well you could ride your bicycle or hitchhike."

"I'm not allowed to hitchhike and I'm not supposed to ride my bike that far."

I said, "That's too bad. Huntington Beach is really fun. We had a great time last night at the Pavilon."

Jolene said, "Yes we did. The Crossfires were there and we danced all night."

Gary said, "Your mother let you go to the Pavilon? I hear people get beaten up by surf punks there."

Jolene said, "David's got the punks afraid of him already. We've both had run-ins with them."

Gary said, "Well maybe my mom would drive me there sometime during the week if she has time."

Jolene said, "Well if she does we'd be happy to take you surfing across the street."

We talked for awhile longer and then Jolene said, "David, can we take a nap? I'm really tired from last night."

Mombo said, "Of course you can darling. David get another pillow for Jolene and you two go and crash for awhile. Jolene you're welcome to stay for dinner if you wish or it would be my pleasure to drive you home when you wake up."

Jolene said, "Thank you very much," and the two of us went to my room where we lay on my bed with pillows under our heads and kissed with our arms around each other as we fell asleep.

We slept for a couple of hours and woke up in each other's arms. Jolene stretched and said, "What time is it David?"

"I think it's about four o'clock."

Jolene said, "I can't believe your cousin. He's nothing like you. It doesn't seem like he's done anything except stay in the house all of his life. He didn't even have a tan."

I said, "I'm sorry. I had hoped he would be someone who's fun. Do you really think we should take him surfing? I'm not sure he can swim."

Jolene laughed and said. "That's right, we didn't ask him if he could swim. I hope if he comes we don't drown him. Will your mom drive me home?"

I said, "I'm sure she will. What time do you have to be home?"

Jolene said, "At six for dinner so it's still early. I'm enjoying being here with you and I want it to last for awhile."

I said, "I like this too. I've never slept like this with a girl before."

Jolene said, "Well I've never slept like this with a boy before. I really like lying here and having my arms around you."

I said, "Do you want to have dinner here?"

Jolene said, "No, I have to be home to eat with my family. We have a big dinner every Sunday night and I have to be there. Are you sure it's not a problem for her to take me home?"

I said, "No, it's not a problem. I wish I was older and could drive you home myself."

She smiled and said, "That would be nice but I'm really enjoying being with someone that's just my own age. Ever since I started to look this way I've been chased by men much older than I am. Terry's been doing double duty for the last year to try and keep me safe. That's why he likes you and I together. He likes you and thinks you're a gentleman. He told me he doesn't worry about me when we're together."

I said, "That's great. I really like being with you and you kiss better than anyone I've ever kissed."

Jolene's face turned harder and she looked at me and said, "Have you kissed a lot of girls?"

I said, "Not really, I've had a couple of girlfriends down south but no I haven't kissed a lot of girls."

Jolene looked at me harder and said, "David have you ever made love?"

I looked back at her and said, "No I haven't. Have you?"

Jolene looked at me and said, "No, I haven't made love yet. I think I'm too young for that now. Making love was what most of the guys I went out with last year wanted to do. In fact it was all they wanted to do."

I kissed her beautiful cheek and said, "Well I'm content to hold you for now but don't get me wrong. I do think about those things."

Jolene said, "I know. I think about them too. I just want it to be right when I do make love to someone."

Just then there was a knock on the door and Mombo was there and I said, "Come in."

Mombo came into my room and smiled when she saw us holding each other. She said, "Jolene do you want to stay for dinner here or would you like me to drive you home?"

Jolene said, "I'd love to stay but I was just telling David my family does a big Sunday dinner together and I have to be there."

Mombo said, "Well dear there will be plenty of time for dinner sometime later. I'm ready to drive you home anytime you wish. You two take your time and get up. It's just after four now."

Gary's mother Jo Ann stuck her head into the doorway and said, "What's going on here?"

Mombo said, "I was just waking David and Jolene from their nap. Jolene will have to go home soon to have dinner with her family tonight."

Jo Ann said, "What are you two doing sleeping together. This is a nice family and I won't stand for any of this dirty behavior. You two get up immediately and get into the living room."

Mombo said, "Oh come on Jo Ann. Dirty behavior? You've got to be kidding.

David and Jolene just took a nap together and they still have their clothes on. What could be wrong with that?"

Jo Ann said, "I don't want him giving Gary or his sister any ideas. I'm trying to raise a nice family here."

Jolene looked at me and gave me a hug before she got up and followed Mombo into the living room. We sat in the living room with Maw while my mother got her keys. We left the house and drove to Jolene's. When we got there Jolene kissed me again and she said, "Good night David, "Surf stoke tomorrow?"

"Yes, most definitely. I'll see you at sunrise."

Jolene winked at me and after thanking my mother for driving her home turned to walk up to her door and enter. We waited until she was inside before we drove back to where we were staying and without much talk. When we got there Mombo and I went inside and began to make dinner for the family.

I woke the next day with thoughts of the beach in my head and as I was getting up Gary said, "What are you doing getting up at this hour? It's still dark outside."

I said, "I'm heading for work at the surf shop in Huntington Beach but first I have to get Jolene at the shop and we'll surf until it's time to open the store."

Gary said, "Well you'd better ask permission or you'll get into trouble going that far."

I said, "Ask permission? For what? To go to work? I don't think so. I've been going every day since I got here and Mombo knows and doesn't care. I'm going to make some coffee. Do you want some?"

Gary said, "Coffee? I'm not allowed to drink coffee. You're really weird. Why do you drink coffee and beer is just nasty."

I shook my head and left Gary in bed and went to the kitchen and started the coffee. It was done in a few minutes and I poured some into a Styrofoam cup and walked to the corner and began to hitch to work. I made my way to the pier in two short rides and I was just getting out my key when Jolene rode up smiling. She got off of her bike and hugged me hello in front of the store. I hugged her back and she said, "Good morning David. I want you to know I thought about you all night. Every time I woke up you were on my mind. Did you sleep well?"

I said, "I did and you were the first thing on my mind when I woke up this morning."

Jolene said, "Excellent, let's go surfing."

We went in and got our boards together and crossed the highway to go to the beach. The waves were perfect but small and we had a wonderful time nose riding on the small but fast waves. We played until nine that morning as it wasn't very crowded being a Monday. We left the surf when we saw Terry park his woody in front of the shop and we went to meet him and start our day. Terry smiled at us when we came in the door and said, "Great, Huntington Beach's newest couple. How were the waves?"

Jolene threw her towel at Terry saying, "Stop that Terry! David might not want to be a couple with me. The waves were great, now quit teasing or I'll let you do your own cleanup this morning."

Terry dodged the towel and said, "okay I'll stop. Everybody to work."

I said, "Thank you very much," and headed to the itch room and began to sand a newly glassed board. I was hard at work when Jolene came and got me at lunchtime. I dropped the clothes I sanded in and went into the front of the shop. Jolene had bought sandwiches for us both and we sat together behind the counter eating and drinking soda. Terry was not in sight and Jolene told me he was running errands and we were alone. She said, "David, you didn't mind what Terry said this morning about you and I being a couple did you?"

I said, "Not at all. I thought it sounded nice. We seem to really like each other and we're spending all of our time together as well. I guess it fits."

Jolene leaned over and kissed my cheek saying, "I think so too. My parents started calling you my boyfriend last night at dinner after Terry told them I had spent the day with you. Before I met you I mostly kept to myself except for going out sometimes. I like thinking of you as my boyfriend. I can't imagine I wasn't with you before."

I said, "I like that too. Meeting you was certainly a surprise. I never expected to find you the first week I was in California."

Jolene smiled and said, "When are you moving by my house. You live entirely too far away."

I said, "Saturday coming. Will you remind me to tell Terry I'll need the day off to help my family move?"

Jolene said, "Consider it done. Is it all right if I come and help?"

I said, "Sure but moving is a lot of effort. Are you sure you want to work that hard?"

Jolene said, "I do. I love your family and your mother is just too cool. It will be fun to be around them for the day and your grandmother is priceless. Those French cigarettes she smokes are too funny. They smell horrible and she chain-smokes them. She's really a character. I can tell by the way she looks at you she loves you very much."

I said, "My whole family are characters and you're right. She does love me tremendously. She has always been great to me."

Just then Terry came into the shop saying, "Hey, where's my sandwich?"

Jolene said, "Still at the store on the other corner. I just got food for the two of us."

Terry said, "That's great you bought David lunch."

Jolene said, "I didn't buy David lunch, you did and mine too."

Terry laughed and said, "Okay I guess I had it coming. Did anyone come in while I was gone?"

Jolene said, "One person and I sold them the blue and white nine five."

Terry said, "Great, I'm glad I could afford to buy you two lunches."

Jolene said, "We are too. We've decided we like being a couple and it was nice of you to help us celebrate."

Terry looked at me and said, "David is Jolene forcing you into this?"

I said, "Not in the least. We decided we might as well be. We're together almost all of the time anyway."

Terry smiled and said, "Couple or not, am I going to get any work out of you two this afternoon?"

I laughed with Jolene and got up to head back to my sander as Jolene cleaned our mess from the counter.

The afternoon went quickly and before I knew it Terry was tapping me on the shoulder saying it was time to go surfing. I put down my sander and striped my sanding clothes off. I was down to my shorts in a second and met up with the two of them when I got to the front door of the shop. The three of us walked across the street and we went straight for the water. The waves were still small but they were very glassy from the afternoon offshore breeze that was blowing. This helped hold the peaks of the waves up and gave us more time before they broke on us. We surfed until almost dark and then went back to the shop. While we were walking up to the highway Jolene said, "Terry, David needs Saturday off to help his family move and I volunteered to help. Will that be all right?"

Terry said, "Do I have a choice in the matter?"

Jolene said, "Nope."

Terry laughed and said "Okay, I guess I can stay and run the shop by myself for a day. Sure, you two can take the day off."

I smiled at Jolene as we crossed the highway and dodged the cars on the way to the shop. We put our boards away and as Jolene and Terry drove off I went to the opposite curb and stuck out my thumb. I was home an hour later and as I walked in the front door I was greeted by my mother. She said, "Hello David. How was your day?"

I said "Mombo it was great. I have the day off to move on Saturday and Jolene has volunteered to help us."

Mombo said, "David that girl is just the best. She's so beautiful and she has the best figure. You're a very lucky young man."

I said, "Don't I know it. She's more than I ever dreamed of. What's for dinner?"

She said, "Maw is in the kitchen making up something. Let's go and give her a hand."

We went into the kitchen and got beer from the refrigerator. Maw smiled and sipped her own beer as we came into the room. We started to help and by the time dinner was ready Claire came into the dining room. The bunch of us that were home sat down to eat and after we were all served Claire said, "David, I hear you have found a girlfriend."

I said, "I sure have. She's the sister of the guy who owns the surf shop in Huntington Beach. She's fabulous. If you had been here yesterday afternoon you would have met her. We spent the afternoon here and Mombo drove her home."

Jo Ann said, "Well she's hardly a lady. Young ladies don't sleep with boys in the afternoon."

I said, "Jo Ann, we just took a nap together. What could be wrong with that?"

Jo Ann said, "Nice girls don't behave like that."

Mombo said, "Jo Ann you apologize to David. Jolene is every bit a lady and she's wonderful to David. Just because other people think differently than you do is no reason to condemn them. Jolene is a wonderful girl and I won't have you run her down to David."

I said, "Thanks Mombo but it's not necessary to defend Jolene. She's perfect and if she were here she might have a few words for Jo Ann herself."

Jo Ann looked at me and scowled, I said, "Don't worry Jo Ann, we'll be out of your hair in no time. Will you bring Gary to the beach so Jolene and I can take him surfing?"

Jo Ann said, "I suppose so if you insist."

I said, "If you brought him tomorrow you could see where I work and Gary could come home with me after work."

Jo Ann said, "Gary isn't allowed to hitchhike. I'll come and get him when you're done."

I said, "That's great. I know he'll have fun."

I woke up the next morning and being careful not to wake Gary I slipped to the kitchen and made coffee for the morning. I took my cup with me to the corner and finished it as I rode to the beach with a couple of guys I had seen before out riding the waves at the pier. Jolene was waiting for me when I got there and we took our boards across the street and started to have some fun. When we were done and walking towards the shop I said, "Gary is coming to surf today if his mother brings him."

Jolene said, "Good, then he can see what a wonderful surfer you're becoming."

I said, "What board can we give him. Do you have something that won't matter if it gets bruised?"

Jolene said, "Sure we've got a couple of old boards Terry keeps around for friends who drop in unexpectedly. He can use one of those."

It was at about one thirty when Gary and his mother came into the shop. Jolene brought them into the itch room and tapped me on the shoulder. I immediately shut the sander off and put it down on the bench. I was taking off the clothes I sanded in while the whine of the sander died and my cousins watched as I got down to my shorts. We went to the front of the shop and while Jolene took off her outer clothes and got down to her tiny bikini. Gary more than noticed Jolene in her bikini when she took off her shorts and his mother simply looked the other way pretending not to notice. Terry came out of the back and Jolene asked him to watch the shop for us while we took my cousin surfing. Gary was not particularly talented at the waves and the water and Jolene did her best to teach him enough so he could at least have some fun. He spent the majority of his time on the water staring at her breasts and making her feel just a bit uncomfortable. He was amazed at how well I surfed and couldn't believe how great Jolene was on the water. We played for a couple of hours and when we got out of the surf the surf punks came up to us when we were getting our things off of the sand. Gary was visibly frightened and Jolene said to the group, "Well which one of you punks wants to eat sand first today?"

I said, "Yes, where's your friend who Jolene punted halfway to the highway?"

The punks came closer and I said, "One more step and whoever takes it gets me to deal with."

The biggest of the punks said, "We don't want you, we want the new guy."

Jolene said, "He's our cousin and if you want him you'll have to go through us."

I said, "Now which of you chicken shits wants to go first."

I had no takers and Jolene said, "What's the matter? None of you guys wants his balls in his throat for the next few days?"

I said, "I guess not. Come on and let's go back to the shop. These guys will never take us on again. We're too tough for them."

We picked up our things and with them watching we walked to the highway and the safety of the shop. When we got there Gary said, "You two have a lot of nerve. Those guys could have beaten us up."

Jolene said, "No way Gary, we've already fought them and beaten them. That's why they're afraid of us. David has been kicking their asses since day one here and I've had a piece of them myself."

Gary shook his head in amazement and went and called his mother who came and got him as we were drinking a soda before we went back to work. He left without thanking Jolene or I and I said, "Jolene I'm sorry about my cousin. He just isn't the person I hoped he would be."

Jolene said, "David don't worry about it. Not everyone could be like you, you're one in a million and that makes you very special. I'm sorry your cousin isn't more fun. I have some relatives who aren't fun either. Remember you don't have to spend any time with him and after you move to Huntington Beach you'll probably never see him. I can't imagine he'd come looking for you at the shop."

"You're probably right. He doesn't seem to be able to get out on his own and we'll only have to see him at family get togethers."

I went to the itch room and put my clothes back on and with the noise of the electric sander in my ears, contemplated my future in Huntington Beach. Jolene tapped me again when it was time to close and we walked across the street to catch some waves before we parted company that evening.

I hitched home and when I got there Claire was asking my mother what Jolene was like as she had been out when Jolene was over on Sunday.

Claire said, "What does she look like?"

Mombo said, "Blond and really beautiful and she has a wonderful personality. David says she's a great surfer. I'm sure you'll like her."

Jo Ann said, "She dresses for the beach in those awful tiny bikinis."

My mom said, "And I can't blame her. If I had her figure I wouldn't wear anything else. She's a beautiful young girl."

Claire said, "When will I get to meet her?"

Mombo said, "Saturday. David and Jolene are both taking the day off to help us move in at the beach. She's going to help so if you're around then you'll get to meet her."

Claire said, "It's very nice of her to help you move in. I hope she knows what she's in for."

I said, "I think she does. She just want's to be around us mostly. She thought Mombo and Maw were great."

Mombo said, "Well that's fantastic. She's a wonderful girl and I'm personally happy to have the help."

Claire asked, "Where does she live and how old is she?"

I said, "She's my age and we're both starting high school together. She lives about four blocks from the house we're going to rent."

Jo Ann said, "That girl is the same age as you are. I don't believe it. I was sure she was much older."

I said, "That's funny, she said the same thing about me."

The dinner conversation changed to the weather and Mombo's prospects of getting a job. I did the dishes after dinner while my two cousins' quarreled in the living room over something completely stupid. I kept on with the dishes and rolled my eyes at the ceiling to make Maw laugh while she dried what I'd washed. Maw and I joined the rest of the family in the TV room and relaxed for awhile before I went to bed thinking of the next day, Jolene and the waves we'd be riding in the morning.

Jolene and I spent the days leading up to Saturday meeting each morning and surfing twice a day. I was getting better and Jolene continually impressed me with her abilities on the waves. There seemed to be nothing she couldn't ride and the size of the waves meant little to her. She was great on everything and the big waves that made me nervous didn't seem to bother her in the least. The Friday before we were to move into our new home Jolene came into the itch room to stop my work for lunch. We sat to eat as we usually did together and as we sat she leaned over and gave me a very sexy kiss. I said, "That was nice, what brought that on?"

Jolene said, "You my wonderful boyfriend."

I said, "Well my wonderful girlfriend, will you tell me what I've done so this kind of treatment will continue?"

Jolene smiled and said, "You're turning into somebody very special. This morning while you were sanding boards a customer came in and asked about you. The customer wanted to know what kind of board you rode because they've been seeing you ride and they wanted a board just like the one you bought."

I said, "You're kidding. Did they buy the board?"

Jolene said, "Yes they did. They paid cash for it and took it with them. Terry will just flip when I tell him. You're getting noticed because you're getting so good out there. I'm very proud of you."

I said, "You surf much better than I do why didn't they want one like you ride?"

Jolene smiled and said, "Because I'm a girl. When they look at me they just see a bikini and that's about it."

I said, "That doesn't hardly seem fair to me. You're a much better surfer."

Jolene said, "Fair or not that's the way things are. I don't mind but I need to talk to Terry. We should build a custom board for you. A David Parish signature model and sell them."

I said, "I think it's a little premature for that but if it happens again maybe you should."

Jolene said, "I'm sure it will. I think you're good advertising for the store and I love that you're doing so fantastic and already getting attention out on the waves."

We changed the subject and planed on Jolene meeting us at our new house in the morning and what would take place all day. After we finished eating I went back to work and wasn't bothered until it was time to close and go surfing.

I went to bed that night thinking about how nice it would be to be able to get up in the morning and ride my bike to work with Jolene. It would certainly make things a lot easier and I liked that she and I would be able to spent time together in the evenings.

CHAPTER FOUR

The next morning I helped load the belongings we had with us into the car for the drive to our new home. Jolene was waiting for us when we got there and helped us put the things from the car into the new house. Just as we were finishing the truck from the moving company rolled up and I was pleased our things were finally here and I could once again live with the personal items I enjoyed. The movers went into action and in a few hours all of our things were in the house and the big truck was gone. I was helping with the kitchen things getting them out of boxes and dealing with the unwrapping of everything when Jolene said, "David what do you want to do with the furniture in your room?"

I turned and said, "I don't know. Why don't you surprise me, I'm not particular about what you do."

Jolene smiled and said, "Okay, one bedroom coming up. Do you want your TV where you can see it from your bed or your couch?"

"Whatever you think is best. I trust you completely."

Jolene smiled and left the kitchen. I put my attention back to what I was doing with Maw while my mother was dealing with her room and Maw's room. The kitchen was done in a couple of hours and I set my sights on the washer and dryer that needed to be hooked up and made operational. I was done in another hour just as Claire was pulling up in front of the house with her daughter Jo Ann and my cousins. I kept on with the house and was setting up the living room, as I knew we liked it, when I heard Claire's voice speaking with Jolene and Maw in the back of the house. I thought nothing of it and kept doing my job. Claire was finally being introduced to Jolene and was saying the house was very nice and it was nice to meet Jolene. Jo Ann walked around the house and seemed to approve of what we'd rented. She said, "This is nice. How far is it to the beach?"

"Two blocks," I said. "It'll be nice not to have to hitch to work every day. Jolene and I can walk there or ride our bikes."

Jo Ann said, "What time do you get there in the morning?"

I said, "We get there right at first light. We surf as soon as we can see the waves."

Jo Ann said, "Gary said some surf punks bothered you three the other day when you got out of the water."

"They did at that. They're afraid of Jolene and me though. They wanted a piece of Gary but we told them they'd have to get through us to get to him."

Jo Ann said, "How are they afraid of you and Jolene?"

Jolene said, "Because if they mess with us we'll beat the crap out of them. We have already."

Jo Ann said, "You're not afraid of them?"

Jolene said, "Never. The last time they fooled with us David was busy with two of them and I dealt with the other two. It'll be a long time before they fool with us again."

Jo Ann looked strangely at Jolene and said, "Well fighting isn't nice."

I said, "No it's not, but we're not going to take any crap from a bunch of punks either."

I finished with the living room while the conversation was still running and everyone came into the room for a break. Mombo was hugging Jolene and telling her thank you for all of her help. Jolene, I was told, helped her set up all of the beds and move the dressers into place. Even helping to get clothes out and putting sheets on the beds. Claire and Jo Ann volunteered to go and get Chinese food for all of us as it was getting later in the afternoon and, because we had skipped lunch, we were all starving. I hugged Jolene in front of my cousins and she said. "David come see."

I walked into the room that was previously designated to be mine and took a look. It was wonderful. Jolene had set it up beautifully and put sheets on my bed, clothes on hangers in my closet and everything in my drawers. My personal items I liked to keep out and on display were on my dresser. The pictures and posters I liked were hung on my walls. I immediately hugged my wonderful girl and said, "Thank you, it's perfect."

Jolene said, "Is it really?"

"Yes, just perfect. Thank you so much."

Gary said, "You put this room together for David?"

Jolene said, "Of course. He's been working hard with the kitchen and the living room. I came here to help with things."

Claire and Jo Ann were back soon with the take out and we all went into the kitchen to fill our plates and eat to fill the voids in our stomachs. It had been a long day and other than me putting the garage together and making the television antenna functional, I was done. We would get our telephones on Monday and I was beginning to feel like I was home.

The sun was going down when Jolene said, "David if you're not too tired would you like to walk down to the pier and see what's up?"

Jo Ann said, "Grace, the pier is a pretty wild place at night. Are you really going to let him go there?"

Mombo said, "Jo Ann of course I am. David's perfectly capable of taking care of himself and Jolene. It's only two blocks."

I said to Jolene ignoring my cousin Jo Ann, "That would be great. It will really make me feel like I live here."

She said, "Well go and change and you can walk me to my house and I'll do the same."

I got up and went to my room and in my closet found Jolene had separated my things into groups which would be appropriate to Southern California. I dressed quickly and went back to collect Jolene and walk to her house with her. We walked the four blocks holding hands and enjoying the evening. We got to Jolene's house and I was re-introduced to her parents by Terry while she went to change. Her parents, Stan and Laura seemed pleased to see me and I sat on the couch while Terry told the story about my admirer who had come in and purchased a board which was the same as the one I had been riding. Terry was thinking the same as Jolene, I needed a custom board with my signature which could be sold at the shop along with the boards that carried his signature. I was just starting to explain my protest about this as I had to Jolene when she walked into the room looking very Californian and stunning. She explained to her parents we were walking to the pier and they bid us goodbye after telling us to be careful and not to be out too late

We left the house and started our walk to the pier. We were half way there when Jolene reached into the bag she was carrying and produced a bottle of scotch. She opened it and drank as we were walking and then handed the bottle to me. I took a drink and we walked hand in hand sipping whisky and talking about what we might find to do that night. When we got downtown there were kids of all ages hanging around and great hot rod cars were cruising up and down the highway. I was having a wonderful time taking the scene in and Jolene seemed pleased I was enjoying myself. We walked out onto the pier and down to the end where we first kissed and kissed again. We stood there holding each other and kissing passionately when Jolene said, "David, I want you to know It's all right to touch me. I want you to touch me wherever you want."

We kissed again and she took my hand and put it on her breast and put her other hand on my ass and squeezed gently. Our passion level went up accordingly and we stood there kissing and petting each other for a long time. We drank more and when we started to get chilled from the wind we turned and went back to the highway and the action that was there. We went to the bench that was in front of the shop and sat to enjoy the scene passing in front of us. I began to comment on the fantastic cars I was looking at when Jolene said, "David you know a lot about cars. How do you know so much?"

I told her they had been and were one of my passions when I was in the south and she smiled and said, "Is there anything you're not good at?"

I said, "Yes there is. I'm afraid I'm not much good at school. All I've been able to get are C's at best. How are you at school?"

Jolene said, "I get straight A's without much effort usually and I'm ready and willing to help you get better grades if you want me too."

I said, "Thank you. I can use all of the help I can get. Fortunately my parents don't put too much stock in school and they don't worry about me like that."

Jolene said, "I should hope not. You're like a grown up around the house. You're fantastic at the shop and everything else. If I were them I wouldn't worry either."

We changed the subject and Jolene said, "David, I'm tired and I want to go home and watch TV for awhile and then go to sleep so we can get up and go surfing in the morning. Is that all right?"

I said it was fine and we got up to walk home. As we were getting up the surf punks walked nearby and other than a few nasty comments in our direction they left us alone. We finished our bottle on the way home and went to my room when we got there where we lay on my bed holding each other and watching a movie on TV. Jolene was almost asleep when I reminded her that although I'd love to have her spend the night, I was pretty sure her parents wouldn't approve. We both got up and I walked her home. We kissed good night at her door and I walked back to my new house loving where I was.

A tapping noise at my window woke me before dawn and I heard the screen being taken off of the window. Before I could get up I saw Jolene climbing through the window and without a word she got into my bed and hugged me long and hard. I said, "What are you doing here? Is it time to go already?"

She said, "I couldn't sleep thinking of you so I left the house early and came here to be with you. You don't mind do you?"

I said, "No, of course I don't mind."

We kissed for a few minutes and the next thing I knew it was breaking dawn and Jolene was sleeping beautifully next to me. I kissed her awake and watched her stretch as she opened her eyes. She kissed me good morning and said, "Good morning, are you ready to go?"

I got up out of bed and put on my shorts while Jolene watched and rubbed the sleep out of her eyes. We went to the kitchen where I put the coffee on as we sat at the table looking at each other. When the coffee was done I poured us each a cup and we drank our wake up Java as we walked to the shop to get our boards and head for the waves that were breaking nicely across the street.

The surf was up and fast that morning and we each got several great rides before the crowds began to come. As the Week Enders came there were people lined along the rail of the pier and we could hear them yelling when someone got off a spectacular ride. They all screamed at Jolene on one particular ride as she wove her way in and out of the huge concrete pilings that held up the pier. They were covered with nasty sharp barnacles and wiping out under the pier could cause serious injury to body and board should one lose control while underneath. Jolene made her ride perfectly and the crowd went crazy when she came out from under the pier at the end of her ride. She paddled back out to the line up and when she got to me I said, "That was really something. Is it scary?"

Jolene said, "A little. I've been doing it for years but it can get hairy under there because of the differences in the currents caused by the pilings."

I said, "It looks fun."

Jolene said, "I don't want you to try going under the pier until you've been riding the waves for a long, long time. I don't want to take any wild chances with you so would you please do me the favor of waiting?"

"This is important to you, am I right?"

Jolene said, "Smart boy. Right again."

I said, "I'll stay out here if you say so. Will you tell me why it's so important to you?"

She said, "Because I'm in love with you and I don't think I could stand it if you were hurt or worse."

I said, "Well that's a good enough reason. I think you should know I'm pretty sure I'm in love with you too."

"David, you have no idea how good that makes me feel. I was pretty sure you felt the same way. This has happened so fast. I can't believe it but my mother always told me this is the way love is."

I said, "I suppose it is. I've never loved anyone before. I really like it."

Jolene said, "I like it too. I want the way I feel to go on forever."

I said, "Do you have any feelings about our age? We're pretty young to be feeling the way we are."

Jolene said, "I know we're young but I don't care. I can't stand to be away from you. That's why I came to you this morning."

I said, "What do you think your parents would say if they found out."

Jolene said, "I don't think they would like it very much but I don't care. I'm going to have to find a way to get them to understand us. What would your mother say?"

I said, "I think Mombo would first worry about what your parents would say and then she might worry about us getting into trouble."

Jolene said, "Trouble like me getting pregnant?"

I said, "Something like that."

"Well we'd have to make love first and we will some day when I'm not afraid anymore. Remember I'm smart and you're smart. I know we can have this love and make love without getting into trouble."

I said, "I think so too. I'll leave it up to you. When you're not afraid anymore we'll make love. I'm sure of it."

Jolene said, "Thank you David. Look it's getting too crowded do you want to go and get something to eat at home?"

I said, "Yes, We have today off and I want to spend it with you. Do you want to go to my house and raid the fridge?"

Jolene said, "Yes I would. I'm starving and I'm in love. Can we sleep together in your room after lunch?"

I said, "Yes, sleeping with you is wonderful. Let's go."

We surfed in and got out of the water to the crowd of people and to my surprise we were both asked several times what our names were and what kind of boards we were riding. Jolene pointed out the shop on the corner and told the ones who asked the shop was where we could be found during the week. I was even more surprised when a man came up and introduced himself to us as one of the invitation committee from the Invitational Surfing Contest which was held each year at the pier. We were both invited to be in the contest and Jolene was surprised to find for the first year there was to be a women's division. She smiled when she heard this and the man told us he would be around at the shop to have us sign the proper forms and put up posters for the contest. Jolene was smiling ear to ear as we crossed the highway to the shop. We put our boards away and locked the shop and walked along the beach for two blocks until we walked inland the few blocks to my new house.

When we went inside, Maw was in the kitchen beginning to make some brunch.

She smiled when she saw us and said, "Are you two hungry?"

Jolene said, "Yes ma'am we are."

Maw said, "That's enough of that. I appreciate your manners Jolene but you can just call me Maw like everyone else does. Now what would you two like to eat?"

I went to help fix the brunch and Jolene pitched in as well. It was done in a few minutes and we all ate together in the kitchen. After we ate we went to my room and stretched out on my bed holding each other. Before we went to sleep Jolene said, "David I'm very happy to be in love with you."

I smiled and said, "I'm very happy to be in love with you too."

We woke up two hours later feeling very refreshed and very close to each other. Mombo and Maw were in the living room watching a program on television that afternoon. Jolene and I walked into the room and sat together on the sofa and began to watch what was on TV. When it rolled around to commercial time Mombo said, "Jolene would you like to have dinner with us tonight?"

Jolene said, "Thanks but I have my family get together tonight and I'm afraid I'll have to get home for it." Then she asked, "David, would you like to eat with my family tonight? I'm sure it will be all right. Marcy eats with us Sunday evenings all of the time."

I said, "Sure if it's okay with your family. I want to get to know them better anyway and we need to tell them about you being invited to be in the big contest today."

Jolene said, "And we need to tell them about you being invited as well."

Mombo said, "What contest were you invited to?"

Jolene said, "Mrs. Parish, David was invited to participate in the annual Invitational Surfing contest they have here that will be held at the end of next month. I'm very proud of him aren't you?"

Mombo smiled and said, "That's wonderful. Jolene did you teach him all of this?"

Jolene said, "Some of it, but David has learned most of it on his own. He's very talented."

Mombo said, "That's very flattering of you to say so dear and please call me either Grace or Mombo. I'm only called Mrs. Parish at work and I'm much more informal than that."

Jolene said, "Thank you Mombo. I was just trying to be polite."

Mombo said, "I know dear. It's sweet of you to try but you don't have too. I think it's wonderful that you and David are together. That's enough for me."

Jolene said, "David should we go to my house and tell my mother you're coming for dinner? We can swim in the pool before we eat."

I said, "Sure let's go. Should I change clothes?"

Jolene said, "No, we just eat together. Nobody dresses up and you look fine."

With that I helped Jolene up off of the couch and we walked the short distance to her house. When we got there her parents and Terry and Marcy were outside by the pool and we went out to see them. As we passed through the big sliding glass windows from the living room to the patio Jolene said, "Hey there, what's going on?"

Her family extended their welcome to her and me as Terry got up to get us each a beer from the cooler. We sat down and there were many questions about our morning surfing and Jolene told the story of how we were invited to be in the contest. Terry was very impressed and very happy about Jolene being invited to participate in the new women's division. He said, "It's a good thing they don't let you surf with the men. You'd blow most of those guys away," then adding, "And David you're getting a custom board starting tomorrow. I'm going to have you help make the shape so it can really be yours. It's getting time for you to start shaping anyway and I'm definitely not going to miss any opportunity to use you for advertising."

I said it would be okay and Jolene smiled at me as she took off her shirt and went to dive into the pool. Marcy was right behind her and I was next. We played in the water for awhile and I was surprised at how different the pool was from the ocean, which I had gotten used to in the short time I'd been in California. When I was getting out of the pool I was invited to dinner with the family and I accepted. It was quite a meal and I enjoyed the company and the conversation. Jolene's parents were certainly liberal and I liked them very much. They seemed to like me as well and I felt good there might be hope for the relationship which was growing between Jolene and me. I watched TV with her family until nine and excused myself to go home to sleep because Jolene and I are going surfing in the morning.

I said my thanks and kissed Jolene at her door and walked back to my house where all were in bed.

I was sound asleep when I woke to find Jolene sliding into my bed, having come into my room via my window. I moved over and took her into my arms and after kissing for a few minutes we both fell asleep and didn't wake until the sun was beginning to make streaks in the sky. We got up and went into the kitchen where I put on the coffee. We drank our coffee quietly in the kitchen and after putting our empty cups into the sink we walked to the shop to get our boards. The waves were okay but nothing to write home about, so we mostly rode a little and spent our morning lying on our backs on our boards outside of the break where the kelp beds grew, holding hands and catching some sun. We saw Terry's wagon pull up in front of the shop and knew it was time to go to work. We went in to the beach and walked up to the shop. We walked in and Terry took me into the shaping room with him. He asked me a hundred questions about what I liked about the board I was riding and then asked me another hundred questions about what I thought would make its performance better for me. After about an hour he seemed satisfied with the information he had gotten. He pulled a new blank foam board with two stringers of wood in it and put it on his bench. He began to scrape away at the foam with one of his tools and then after demonstrating for a minute he handed the tool to me and let me try. I was careful not to take too much material off at each stroke and together we shaped out what I thought would be great on the water, it was longer than the board I was riding and the edges or rails, were sharper, to make the board turn quicker in the waves. By noon the shape was done and I went to have lunch with Jolene after signing my name on the tail of the board in large enough cursive to be easily read by anyone who might take even a short look. I went to have lunch with Jolene who had been in and out of the shaping room during the morning offering suggestions here and there. We ate at the counter as usual while Terry went to the bank and make his deposit from the weekend. Jolene was excited as Terry had told her she too was to get a new board for the contest and they would shape it that afternoon while I watched the counter and spoke to the customers. I sold my first surfboard that afternoon and I was pretty excited by it. Terry was happy about the sale and when it came time to close the three of us went across the street to ride the afternoon waves and relax in the water. I rode home with Terry and Jolene that day for the first time and it was nice to have another ride in Terry's wagon. Jolene got off with me and we walked into my house to see what was for dinner that night. Jolene began to help

Maw with what she was making and I went about the salad at the same time. We told Mombo about our day when she came in and she was very happy for us. We spent the evening watching TV in my room until it was time for me to walk Jolene home. I went back home and went to bed and slept until I felt Jolene climb into bed with me very early in the morning. We did as we had been doing, kissing for a few minutes and then falling asleep until it was time to get up and go surfing. We had our coffee and walked to the beach to get our boards watching the waves as we walked along the highway. We rode waves until we saw Terry pull up in his wagon and then we went across the highway to go to work.

CHAPTER FIVE

Terry was pleased to see us as usual but this morning he said, "Hold on you two, I want to talk to you."

"What about Terry?" Jolene replied. I figured Terry was going to call us down for our amorous activities and was expecting this when instead he said, "Training, that's what. You two are going to represent this shop in the contest and I want you to train for it. From now on, like it or not, you two are going to start working out in the morning before you go surfing. I want you two to start running five miles a day on the beach and doing all of the sit-ups and pull-ups and the other ups you can think of that will make you strong. Jolene I'm going to stop buying you your weekend whiskey until after the contest. You will surf better if you're strong and surfing better will be the difference out there."

I just nodded and looked at Terry. Jolene said, "Okay Terry is there anything else?"

"Yes there is. I'm going to start taking you two to every beach we can drive to on Sundays so you two can get some variety in the waves you're riding. Part of it is for me and part of it is for you. I've decided I need to go surfing like I used to do and you're going with me. And one more thing, Jolene I think it's cute of you to sneak over to David's in the mornings early. I'm not going to say anything to the parents because I was doing about the same thing when I was your age. I think you two are great and I want you to know I'm on your side. I presume a couple of smart kids like yourselves will know how to stay out of trouble but Marcy said she'd like to have a talk with you about girl stuff and I advise you to talk to her. David I just want you to keep doing exactly as you are and above all you take care of my sister or else. Now you two get to work and remember I want to see you two running to work from now on okay?"

Jolene and I got up and Jolene smiled at me and hugged Terry.

I said, "Thanks Terry. I'll take good care of Jolene," and went to the itch room to get to work. I worked until lunch when Jolene came and said that food was here and it was time to eat. Terry was off on another errand and Jolene and I got to discuss what Terry had told us that morning.

She said, "David can you believe Terry? I never believed he would be so great to us. I guess we're going to have to stop sleeping late and do the running Terry want's us to do. What do you think?"

I said, "I think it will be good for us. It certainly can't hurt for us to be in great shape for the contest and I'm happy Marcy will talk to you about all of the girl stuff. It makes me feel great Terry is on our side."

Jolene said, "I know. He's the perfect brother but I'm going to miss my Saturday night drinking though."

"It doesn't matter," I said. "We'll have plenty of time for that kind of fun after the contest. The most important thing for me is you go out and beat every one of your competitors in your division. I know you can win."

Jolene said, "Do you really think so?"

"Absolutely! I don't think you know how good you look out there because you can't see yourself. I'm sure you can win."

Jolene said, "I wish I was that confident."

I said, "If you ride like you did the other day you'll be on top and taking home the trophy at the end of the day."

"Okay," she said, "I'll work hard for this because you think so. I know I'm good but if you think I can really win I'll go for it all of the way."

I said, "I'll do the same. If we both give it a hundred and ten per cent we'll have nothing to feel bad about even if we lose."

We both finished lunch and went back to work until it was time to close and we went across the street to the waves. We put our boards away at the end of our fun and Jolene and I went running on the beach in the hard sand. We ran for two plus miles and then ran back to my house on the beach. We were both tired from our run when we got inside and Jolene said, "David, I didn't realize I was so out of shape."

I said, "Neither did I, my legs are killing me. I guess we really do need to get into shape."

Jolene said, "Okay, before we surf tomorrow we'll run again and do our exercises."

I said, "Do we have too? This is harder than I thought."

Jolene said, "David you'd better be kidding me after what you said at lunch."

I said, "Of course I'm kidding you. I think it will make a real difference in our surfing. I want to do well in this contest. It would be a major embarrassment to let you down."

Jolene said, "David you would never let me down. I don't think you have it in you to let anyone down. Have I told you today I love you?"

I replied with a smile, "Not since this morning. I love you too. Where is everybody? I think we're the only ones here. What would you like to eat?"

We kissed and went into the kitchen and found a note saying Mombo and Maw had gone to Claire's house to visit with my cousins we first stayed with. I told Jolene where they were and she rolled her eyes at the ceiling and said she was happy we weren't there. We made and ate dinner and went to my room where we perused some of the old surfing magazines I had while the TV flashed pictures at us. I walked Jolene home as Mombo and Maw were coming back and we waved to them as they pulled into the driveway. I was back home in a few minutes and was anxious to hear if they had any new thoughts about my cousins.

Mombo said, "David I'm so disappointed your cousins are nothing like you. I can't remember when I've been around children who are so devoid of personality.

I said, "I guess you didn't have an exactly fun evening then?"

Mombo said, "Oh, it wasn't bad, just boring. I guess all of those years in New

Orleans changed me. I'm really not the same person who left here with your father. Oh, before I forget there's a letter for you from him. I'll get it for you."

Mombo left the room and came back a minute later with the letter. It was nice to hear from my dad and he sent me a check to buy some new clothes for California and school. I was pleased with the check and the amount. I thought I'd have to make arrangements to go clothes shopping soon and decided I would definitely have Jolene go with me. I kissed Mombo and Maw and went off to bed to get some sleep before Jolene and I had to go in the morning.

I woke again to Jolene getting into bed with me and we fell back to sleep as soon as our bodies touched under the covers. This morning was the first morning she had taken her clothes off before getting into bed with me. She wasn't naked but she stripped to her sexy bikini. I liked the way her skin felt against mine and told her so before we dozed off.

Jolene kissed me awake before dawn and we left the house for our morning run. We ran the same course as we did the day before and ended at the pier where we did our exercises on the beach in front of the shop. When we were finished we looked at each other acknowledging the way we felt and then went to get our boards. The waves were good that morning but the exercises had taken a lot out of us. We both were tired when we came in to work and Terry said, "Did you two run this morning?"

Jolene said, "We're tired as hell, don't we look it?"

Terry laughed and said, "Yes you do. Are you finding you're out of shape?"

I said, "Unfortunately yes. This is hard but we both know you're right about being in shape. We'll be in great shape by contest time."

In the afternoon the man from the invitation committee came into the shop and I had to stop sanding to sign the forms and pay the entry fee. Terry signed as our sponsor and it was done. The posters advertising the contest looked great and we were promised good attendance from the area surfers and spectators. We surfed and ran that evening and as we got back to my house and went in we were both breathing hard. We went inside and there was dinner already done for us. We ate like we were starving and when we were done we did the cleanup and went into the living room. As we sat down Mombo got up and left the room and came back shortly. She handed a key to Jolene and said, "Jolene dear, I think the front door would be much more convenient than David's window don't you?"

Jolene looked a bit embarrassed and said, "I'm sorry. I hope my climbing into David's room didn't bother you."

Mombo smiled and said, "Not at all dear. You two are very cute but I want you to use the front door unless you particularly like David's window."

Jolene said, "Thank you Mombo, the front door will be just fine. Thank you very much."

Maw sat smiling and when Jolene looked at her she got a nice wink in return. We excused ourselves from the living room and I went to walk Jolene home and was back in my bed not much later.

We worked hard during the week training and on Sunday Terry took us up to Rincon point north of Los Angeles. The drive was long and we talked on the way about all of the spots we wanted to go to. Rincon point was great and it broke off of the point in a beautiful left which was very fun. The locals were not too nice until they realized who Terry was and everything was fine afterwards. We rode the uncrowded waves until one o'clock and then loaded the boards up for the drive back to Huntington Beach. We stopped at Marcy's house to get her for dinner at the Boyer's and she and Jolene made arrangements to have lunch the next day and have some serious girl talk. I declined dinner that night as I was very tired and knew we would be up and running early the next day. Our usual routine took place the next morning and Jolene said she liked having a key to my house very much. We went to work when Terry got to the shop and at noon I was pulled from my work to watch the front of the shop while Jolene and Marcy went off together. They didn't get back until it was almost time to close and Jolene had an odd smile on her face when she returned. I said nothing until that night when we were in my room and asked, "Are you going to tell me about your day with Marcy?"

Jolene said, "Yes it was wonderful. She and I talked about everything I've always been afraid to ask my mother. She told me everything about making love and I'm not afraid anymore."

I said, "That's great. What else did you find out?"

Jolene said, "She took me to a place called Planed Parenting and I saw a doctor who gave me a prescription for birth control pills. I have them with me and I want to leave them here so my mother won't find them."

I said, "That's fine with me. What else?"

"Marcy told me all about what it's like to make love and now I can hardly wait. She said it's the most wonderful thing in the world and told me you and I need to spend more time together getting to know each other's bodies. She highly recommended we do this without our clothes and said we should learn to bring each other to a climax. I knew what it was from touching myself and she said everyone does it. It's perfectly okay and I want to start right now."

I said, "If that's what you want to do then let's do it."

Jolene looked down said, "I'm still kind of shy, can we turn off the light?"

I turned off the light and we undressed each other and got under the covers of my bed where we spent the next two hours giving each other the most extreme pleasure I'd ever experienced. When we were tired and it was time to walk Jolene home she said, "David, now I love you more than ever, I know what it's all about now and I can't imagine what making love will be like. If it's better than what we've been doing I think I'll just explode."

I walked Jolene home and came back home knowing what I'd be doing in the morning and feeling just incredible.

Jolene woke me the next morning getting into my bed. She was completely naked and she felt fantastic next to me. We didn't get back to sleep that morning but loved each other until it was time to get up and go do our morning run and surf stoke. We were completely in love with each other now and we both thought it was great. I felt like telling the world and so did Jolene. We kept the secret to ourselves and couldn't wait to get home that night. Our new boards were done by the weekend and we liked the way they performed. I felt mine was much more maneuverable than my old board which was now for sale in the used rack at the shop. Jolene loved hers as well and it improved her brilliance on the waves. I was certain she would win the contest but kept it to myself not wanting her to get over confidant. Terry took us south on the weekend and we went to surf at a spot called Salt Creek which was a point beach break but big and fast. The waves were tubing overhead and it was fantastic. There were lots of surfers on the beach watching and we paddled out to the big powerful waves. I was nervous but it ended the minute I took off on my first wave. I dropped in and the thrill was fantastic as the wave broke behind me and the sound was tremendous. I was blown forward by the force of the blast but kept my balance as the wave came up and poured over my head. I was screaming along faster than I'd ever been before and I was glad for my new board under my feet. I got to the end of my ride and dove off my board in celebration. When I came up I was covered with chicken skin. I grabbed my board and paddled back out to the line up. On my way back out in the rip I watched Jolene take off and make the drop into a huge wave. She crouched as the wave curled and streaked the side of the wall of water with her hand as she sliced through the water on the face of the wave. She worked the wave top to bottom and in the tube before kicking out at the end. I met up with her on the outside and I said, "That was some ride you had."

She shook her blond hair and said, "Don't I know it? That was great!"

We paddled to the take off spot again and just as another set was coming in. Jolene took off first and I watched as the top of her blond head, hair flying disappeared behind the wave. My second wave was bigger than the first and my ride was even better. The thunder of the surf almost was deafening and it blanked out every other sound when the wave broke. I paddled back out and Terry was outside when I got there saying, "David that was a tremendous ride. Just unbelievable."

I said, "Did you see Jolene's? She's just fantastic. I can't believe what she's doing out here."

Terry agreed she was just what I'd said, fantastic. We rode until we were tired from paddling and fighting the soup to get back outside. We headed to the beach and the sand together. We attracted a lot of attention from the spectators and there were a lot of questions about who we were, especially Jolene who just smiled and let Terry answer all of the questions. We carried our gear to the wagon tired from all of the exertion we'd had and we drove off thrilled but individually quiet from the experience. We drove most of the way home with out speaking much and were happy to put our boards away and go home to nap before dinner.

The weeks flew by and I watched as Jolene's body got hard from the training we were doing. By the end of a month she had beautiful muscular definition and she was sexier than I could believe. Our strength was wonderful and we both became able to do things on our boards we weren't able to do a month before. We were both surfing to the height of our abilities and it felt great. During this time we made ourselves available to every spot in Huntington we could get to without

Terry's help. We surfed at Tin Can Beach just north of the cliffs, Black Pipe and Five Wells both other parts of The Huntington Cliffs. All were great surf spots and we took our boards in the mornings and put out our thumbs and got there through the benevolence of other surfers. Sometimes we would work our way back down the beach and would stop off at Gordie's shop, which was located at the cliffs near Five Wells. Even though he was a competitor of Terry's shop there was a great camaraderie between us as we all had the same goals. Gordie was completely pleasant to us, as he knew of Jolene's abilities and was one of her fans along the coast. Our visits there were always wonderful and we liked the company there and the stories that would be told when we would stop by to get a soda after a morning on the water before we went back to our shop. We were both very confident in ourselves as we never had been before. Jolene was amazing and seemed completely unafraid of any wave or condition. The biggest difference in her was the way she walked and moved. She was perfect and attracted great attention everywhere she went. I loved the change in her and in myself as well. I became much more muscular than I'd ever been before and I felt completely great. My family could see it in us too and Mombo commented frequently about how great Jolene and I looked together.

Before we knew it the contest was on us and we were definitely ready for it. The day it began the waves were breaking big and fast at the pier. We smiled at each other as we got to the shop in the morning to get our boards and we knew our favorite spot would be good to us that day. When we registered for the contest we were given numbers to wear while we surfed our heats and we both were able to advance all day long to the finals which were to be held on Sunday. Our families were on the beach for the Sunday finals with the inclusion of my cousin Claire and her daughter's family. The waves on Sunday were breaking bigger than we'd ever seen the pier break without closing out and the surfing was treacherous because the waves were so large. The two of us handled our favorite break well all day and I won my first heat and advanced to the next. Jolene did the same in hers and advanced to her next heat. This went on all day long and the waves kept getting bigger to the point of almost closing out by the time the last heats were announced. I lost in the last of my heats and managed third place in the junior division of the contest. I was congratulated by everyone and felt I'd done great for a new guy. Jolene turned out to be the star of the afternoon as I had predicted. She won her division on the last wave of her heat, which was almost double overhead. She dropped in and made an incredible bottom turn that swung her body almost horizontal to the water before her board spun back under her. That alone brought cheers from the crowd and we watched as she sped up the wave to the crest and sliced down into the curl. She disappeared into the wave and we lost sight of her for what seemed an eternity. Jolene was blown out of the tube by the air compression which happened when the wave closed out behind her. She held on barely and the wave broke over her head again and we lost sight of her for another minute. When we saw her next she was flying out of the tube and screaming across the wave working it up and down in complete control. I wish she could have been on the beach to hear the crowd she was dazzling out there. I was so proud of my girl I felt like exploding when her ride was over. She kicked out and over the shoulder of the wave for her ending and we waited for her to come in when the horn sounded signaling the end of her heat. Jolene received perfect scores for her last ride and totaled the most points of any surfer that day except for some of the men. She finally got to the beach and Terry and I were the first to get to her. She knew she had done well and she had a smile a mile wide on her incredible face. She walked up to the judge's stand carrying her board and showing off the logo which told the world where they could get one like it. Terry was grinning as much as she was and the three of us walked together through the crowd and the applause. The trophies were presented as soon as the points were totaled up and Jolene was given a trophy which was almost too big for her to carry. We stood around as she signed autographs for the crowd giving all of the credit to Terry who she said was her greatest supporter. She put her arm around me while we stood on the sand with the thunder of the waves breaking in the background. It was over after awhile and we walked back to the shop with our two families. She carried her trophy and I carried mine while Terry and his friends brought our boards. Terry must have had as much confidence as I did in Jolene and we found a case of iced champagne in the shop. The popping of a cork started the party and we all were jammed into the shop with family and friends not to mention a number of manufacturers who wanted her attention. My cousins were amazed at what we had accomplished and they stood back as we both received the onslaught of guests offering congratulations to us both. In an hour the champagne was gone and we were riding back to her house with Terry where her parents served dinner to us, my immediate family included. It was late when Jolene came to me and kissed me deeply by the pool where we were drinking beer away from the group. She said in my ear, "David I love you and I want to make love with you tonight. Is that okay?"

I said, "I love you too and yes I think tonight would be perfect."

Jolene said, "Then go home and go to bed and I'll see you as soon as I can."

I kissed her in agreement and went to find Mombo and Maw so we could say goodbye and thank Jolene's parents for their hospitality. We drove the few blocks home and we all went to bed when we got there as it was much later than usual. I was asleep when Jolene slid into my bed and kissed me to wake me up. I said, "Hi my love."

Jolene said, "Shush my darling. I love you so much."

Jolene slid on top of me and we began to experience what we had waited so long for. We both had tears in our eyes when it was over and we fell asleep holding each other until the morning coming through my window woke us and we looked at each other for the first time in the daylight as lovers.

We got up and I said, "Jolene what would you like to do today?"

She surprised me by saying, "I want to go shopping. I'm taking the day off from the beach and the shop and I'm going to call Terry at home and tell him we're not coming to work today."

I said, "Good, we could use a day off from all of the work and excitement."

Jolene said, "I'm really taking the day off because we made love last night and I feel like a different person today. I want to spend the day just with you. I feel so completely different from yesterday I feel like everyone can see it on my face."

I said, "Well you are different. Today you're a champion."

Jolene said, "You're my champion. I'm sorry you didn't win yesterday."

I said, "I feel great about yesterday. I was beaten by two of the best surfers on the coast. I was pretty good for a new guy don't you think?"

Jolene kissed me and said with a big smile, "Not bad for a new guy. There's one thing though."

I said, "What's that?"

Jolene said, "After I call Terry, will you make love to me again? I liked making love better than winning the contest yesterday."

She got out of bed and went to call Terry. When she came back we made love again and slept until ten and woke together smiling at each other. My mother had gone to work and my grandmother hugged Jolene knowingly when we walked into the kitchen to make breakfast. We cleaned up our mess when we were done and changed our clothes to go to the shopping center on our bikes. We spent the day buying clothes and just being together. I spent all of the money my dad had sent me and Jolene helped me with all of my purchases. She had a pile of new things as well and it was difficult for us to get it all back home on our bikes. We took our new things to our respective homes and ate dinner separately. I would see Jolene later and knew we would go surfing in the morning. We did without our training run and it was nice to leave the exercise out for a change. We went to the shop when we saw Terry and were both surprised when the shop had a steady stream of customers all day long. Terry said the day before was just as busy and we spent all day waiting on customers and sold most of the boards that were left from the day before. We took a lot of orders for custom boards as well and a lot of them were to be from the signature series Terry was selling. Jolene was also visited by several manufacturers' representatives who wanted her to endorse their products. She took all of the paper work to read and in the afternoon she grew tired of talking with the reps and pronounced me her manager, which made Terry laugh like I'd never seen him. They wanted her to endorse everything from wax to wet suits and some of them were offering really good money to her. We ended the day just going home and eating dinner with her family. We spent the evening with Terry going over all of the offers she had gotten and found I had gotten two myself. I was pleased at this and we talked about them as well. No decisions were made and we went to work as usual the next morning. Terry fired me first thing in the morning from the itch room and hired a kid who had been after him for a job every day for the last six months. I was promoted to shaper and he and I would be working hard for the next few weeks just to keep up with the orders for boards which came from Jolene being a champion. Jolene and I finished out the summer surfing every morning and night and were blissfully happy with our lives. This went on until we were thrown a curve in the last week of August when Jolene got a letter from the high school saying registration for school would be in two weeks. Our wonderful carefree world was about to come to an end and we were very sad to see school starting. Terry was sad as well as the three of us had become a wonderful team which would soon have to get together only before and after school. We would continue our jobs at the shop but Terry would have to hire replacements for us when we weren't able to be there.

CHAPTER SIX

It all ended on a Tuesday morning when instead of surfing and going to work we surfed and put our boards in the shop, hugged Terry and walked to the high school to register for classes. We had decided to take our required classes together and our electives were chosen in the same manner except we each got to choose one of them. Our electives were art and home economics as we thought of eating the things we would get to cook for lunch. We took Spanish for a language and Algebra for math. The only classes we didn't have together were our physical education classes. These we had to take separately but didn't mind. We started school on the following Monday and we were faced with having to not go barefoot anymore. Wearing shoes alone was enough to make us quit school and we suffered from the socks we had to wear with them. We longed for the slippers we usually wore and wearing pants and skirts was just ridiculous. We thought seriously about quitting but we couldn't by state law. We were trapped but we still had our mornings and Jolene's parents still did not know, or at least had not confronted us about our early morning activities. They assumed we were surfing every day and we were. What they didn't know about was what was happening before we went surfing.

We were both called into the vice-principal's office at the end of our first month of school for being tardy so much to our first class of the day. This caused our parents to become involved and Jolene's parents were not very pleased. Mombo simply told the vice principal they should make the school more interesting and I might want to be there more. We were warned we had to improve our attendance and quit being tardy and we did for at least a while. We were still chronically late for school and often rode up on our bikes dripping from the ocean. We kept towels in our lockers for this purpose and most of the other kids thought us to be very eccentric. Our grades were okay as Jolene could get an A from just sitting in class and paying attention. She and I did our homework together and my meager grades actually went up some. We hated school together and waited for summer to come again. Socially we were almost outcasts at school because we spent our time together and had few friends other than our surfing friends we saw at the pier everyday who went to school with us. Our status as surfers and Jolene as a champion made our separation from the other students seem snobbish to some of the other students. It wasn't snobbism but we liked our own company and we were always decent and polite to anyone we interacted with. Jolene and I considered the others in school to be immature or at least uninteresting to us. We kept to ourselves and waited for it to be over. We just had no desire to participate. Our peers at school considered us to be married and there were several rumors about to that effect. We didn't care and continued our eccentric ways.

An odd thing happened that November as Jolene and I were doing our homework in my room and listening to the radio when a new song came on the radio. It was very different than what we were used to and Jolene commented it was a great song. It definitely wasn't surf music and when the song finished the DJ said it was a new song by an English band called The Beatles. The new song fascinated us and we looked forward to hearing more of the new music. This happened soon enough because there were more songs by the same group on the radio as well as songs by other bands from England. The whole of the school and our friends began to dress like the members of the new bands and there was a big deal about the length of the hair on the band members. Long hair was common for surfers and it didn't excite us very much. Surfers had always grown their hair long and I was always being called down by the school saying I needed to get my hair cut. The style of dress changed some and Jolene and I went along with some of it. We were surfers and we intended to stay surfers despite the new trends at school. It gave us something interesting to think about and we did enjoy the new music.

We turned fifteen in November and celebrated our birthdays together with our families. It was nice to be a year older and we felt much older because of Jolene's notoriety. When we went surfing the cameras were always present and Jolene began to be paid for her likeness when we were on the water and it was used in publications. I had my share of attention as well and all of the money we earned from the shop, endorsements and publications went into a joint account for our future.

The November of our birthdays was something to remember as an assassin in Dallas killed President Kennedy one morning while we were in school. We considered him to be a great man and we were saddened by the event. We did get two days off from school and we used our new free time for riding waves at the pier and we hoped America wasn't falling apart.

By Christmas we considered ourselves pretty rich for a couple of kids. I had to go to Alabama for Christmas with my father in December and it was the longest week of my life and for Jolene too. We missed each other terribly. We spoke on the phone each day and she even made Terry bring her to the airport to get me on my return. She wept when I got off of the plane and held on to me for dear life all of the way home. I felt so loved. It was wonderful but I was very sorry to have caused her so much pain by leaving. In a few months I would have to tell my father I would be staying with Jolene in California for the next summer instead of coming south.

It was after I returned from Christmas with the other side of my family that we got our biggest surprise. Jolene and I were invited to a big surf contest in Hawaii. We were thrilled by the invitation and wanted very much to see the islands and be in a summer climate again. We had kept up our training and with a little extra work we were in good shape for the contest. It was to be in the last week of January and we definitely wanted to go. Jolene being the champion would have her airfare paid by the contest but I would have to pay my own way there and back. It didn't matter as we had more than enough money to go. Mombo was all about the trip but Jolene's parents were on the cold side of things. They loved me dearly but were not very willing to let us go alone. We went to Terry to bail us out of the situation and after some convincing he agreed to close his shop for two weeks and go with us because he had always wanted to visit Hawaii. Business was terrible for him in the winter so he decided to give his one employee the two weeks off and close the shop. This convinced Jolene's parents and before we knew it we were stepping off of a jet in Oahu, Hawaii.

Hawaii was tremendous and we loved being where we could wear our summer clothes and surf without our wet suits. We were in paradise and we knew it the minute we got off of the plane from the smell of the Plumaria and the other flowers. Terry liked it there too and we all began to talk about living in Hawaii and opening a surf shop there. The contest was to be held on the north shore of the island where the winter surf came in big and strong. We stayed at a nearby hotel splitting two rooms with Terry and Jolene and I got to stay together under Terry's liberal supervision. We had a rented station wagon and went to all of the surf spots we could before the contest. We surfed Ala Moana, the famous beach in Wakiki, Sunset beach and all of the others. We watched at the Banzai Pipeline where the waves were incredible but didn't surf there as the waves were treacherous. The spot had only been conquered a year before by the famous Phil Edwards and there were few who dared to go out to the perfect break which had razor sharp coral just under the water's surface. The contest went very well. Jolene got second place in the young women's division and I placed third again in mine. We were very impressed with the way the Hawaiians rode the waves. They were incredible surfers and we discovered a culture we could identify with completely. Jolene and I made up our minds we would move there as soon as possible. Terry was right with us about the move, as he wanted the same thing as we did which was a summer that just wouldn't go away. It was all over too quickly and we flew back sadly to the homes we occupied with our families. It was nice to be home in a way but we had to go back to school again and we didn't enjoy being there very much. We had been back for about a week and were reading in my room one night when Jolene said, "David, something has to change."

I said, "I understand but what?"

Jolene said, "We need to get out on our own. We have to find a way. We're like a married couple still living with our parents. I want to be with you as your wife would. Not that I think we should get married, but I want our own house where if I want to cook dinner naked I can do it."

I said jokingly, "You could do it here but Maw might get the shock of her life."

"David please be serious with me about this. I love you more than anything and I want to live with you. How can we convince our parents we need to do this?"

I said, "What about school?"

Jolene said, "We both hate going to school. It's only because of the dumb state law we both haven't tested out. Hawaii doesn't have that law and if we were there we could be out."

I said, "Jolene you've been doing your homework again."

She said, "Yes and it's a good thing. You are entirely too complacent sometimes. I'm not at all sure I can stand dealing with another year of school after this one."

I said" I'm sorry for making light of what you want to do. You're right though, we're not learning a thing in school. It's just wasting our time."

Jolene said, "It's getting so bad I've been thinking of getting pregnant so we can get married and get away. When I start getting foolish ideas like pregnancy, I know it's time to act."

I said, "What do you have in mind?"

She said, "Well, we have more than enough money to move to Hawaii and start a surf shop. You make boards as well as Terry does and we both know the business. I'm sure we could make a living there."

I said, "What about our parents? They might have something to say about what you're thinking of."

Jolene said, "What if we just packed our bags and boards and left?"

I said, "They'd find us. As soon as your picture was in one of the magazines we'd be caught."

Jolene said, "But what would they do if they caught us?"

I said, "Take you away from me and out of my life most likely. Your folks would make you come home and go back to school here."

She said, "Damn, you're just too sensible. You're right though, my folks probably don't know we make love every day. David how are we going to do this?"

I said, "What if we went to them and told them about our lives and begged?"

Jolene said, "That's no solution. I want to be with you and live in Hawaii. I can't wait until I'm eighteen. I want this now."

I said, "One thing I can think of is us flying to Hawaii. Declaring residency there, getting our GED's and coming back to California and at least not having to go to school. We could get our jobs back with Terry and things would be better."

Jolene said, "Better yes but that's not good enough. I want to live with you."

I said "I want to live with you too but we're sort of stuck being fifteen years old and living with our parents."

Jolene said, "There's got to be a way to do this. I'm going out of my mind having to go home every night, waking up and coming over to sleep with you early in the mornings. I just want to reach up and turn off the light after we make love and go to sleep like we did when we were at the contest in Hawaii."

I said, "I think we should talk to your parents and try and reason with them."

Jolene said, "I think we should just leave."

I went and put my arms around her and said, "How about if I make love to you for now? I promise I'll put my brain to work and figure out what to do."

Jolene said, "Making love will work. I just get so frustrated sometimes and I love you so much I don't think I can stand it anymore."

I said, "I know, I love you too."

I thought and thought for the next few days and was no closer to figuring out what to do than before. I said one night to Jolene, "Jolene, let's talk to my mother about this."

Jolene said, "Are you sure? Once we let the cat out of the bag we might not be able to get it back in."

I said, "You're right. That's not really an answer. I'm beginning to think the best thing to do would be your first idea of just leaving and getting Terry to deal with the parents."

Jolene said, "Maybe so," and went back to her book."

Two days later Terry announced that he and Marcy had gone to Las Vegas over the weekend and while they were there they had gotten married. Jolene was ecstatic for them both and especially pleased for Marcy whom she had developed a great friendship with. When we were told I asked, "Well what comes next for you then? Children? A house with a backyard?"

Terry said, "We thought we'd move to Hawaii and start a surf shop there. Want to come along?"

Jolene said, "Terry don't even joke about this. Are you serious?"

Terry said, "Yes I'm serious. You told me several weeks ago about what you want to do so I'm going to help you to do it. If you hadn't won the Huntington contest I wouldn't have enough money to do this. I owe both you and David one."

Jolene jumped up and hugged her brother hard with tears in her eyes saying, "Thank you, thank you." Over and over again.

I said, "What will you do about your folks. It will take some convincing to get them to let Jolene and I come along."

Terry said, "That's just it David. You're not coming."

Jolene said, "Then I'm not coming either. I love David and I'm not going anywhere without him."

Terry laughed and said, "Of course not. Listen to me, this is what we're going to do. I'm going to make arrangements to move my operation and my life to Hawaii. I'm going to keep the shop here and sell boards but they'll be made in Hawaii instead of here. I'll convince the family you need to be there because of your surfing career and you'll move there with Marcy and me. You will break up with David to move to Hawaii because careers are more important than boyfriends' right? We move and David moves a week later. Parents don't check on old boyfriends and I'm sure Mombo will have no problem with David moving to Hawaii to be with you."

Jolene said "Terry you are a genius and my hero. How can we ever thank you?"

Terry said, "Easy, you two will just have to become my surf shop slaves for five or ten years and I'll be paid back."

I said, "Terry this is indeed wonderful. I'll be happy to be your surf shop slave for as long as you wish."

We went home that night and when I got home I pitched the deal to Mombo and Maw. I said, "Mombo you have always been wonderful to me but it's time for me to leave home."

Mombo said, "Like I didn't know this was coming? Let me guess. You're going to run off with your love Jolene. Am I right?"

I said, "Pretty much. We're not going to run off though. Jolene is going to move to Hawaii with Terry and I'm going to move there and meet her without her parents knowing. We'll fake a breakup before she moves and nobody checks on old boyfriend's right?"

Mombo said, "Pretty good plan. What am I ever going to do without you around here? Oh well, you have your life to live and the right to live it. I'm happy Terry will be there and you have your delightful Jolene to love. David I think it's a good plan and I want you to know I'll keep up appearances around here. When I'm asked I'll just say that you were so upset about breaking up with Jolene that you went to live with your father. Out of sight out of mind."

I got up and went and hugged Mombo saying, "Thanks mombo, I knew you'd play." Maw just lit another cigarette and smiled while she gave me a wink.

The stage was set and a month later with a lot of convincing, Jolene and I broke up for the effect. She missed me tremendously and I missed her but it would only be for two weeks. Terry, Marcy and Jolene left for Hawaii on the first of April in 1964. I left a week later. I was taken to the airport by Mombo who kissed me goodbye and told me I always had a home with her. I kissed her back and went to get my flight. Five and one half-hours later I was landing in Oahu and being met by the love of my life and my best friends in the world, Terry and Marcy Boyer. They had rented a temporary house for all of us there. It was small but would do for all of us until we could find separate homes which were close to each other. Mombo would have some of my things sent to Hawaii by slow cheap boat and I would see those things in a month.

It was wonderful living there and Jolene and I were completely happy. After looking for two weeks we bought a house up in the canyon behind the band shell in Wakiki in the Japanese/Hawaiian neighborhood which was old but wonderful. We were five minutes from Wakiki beach where Terry opened his surf shop. There was already one there near the beach but we all figured another one wouldn't hurt. We were right and we had good business from the start. Sales were good and we loved the neighborhood we lived in. Our home was a small one-bedroom place having no screens or glass in the windows, which was typical of all houses in the village. The temperature was so perfect all of the time none were needed. Gecko lizards lived with us in our house as in all of the homes in Hawaii. They were good about eating the few insects they found in the house and our neighbors told us they only lived in houses where good people lived. The people who lived in the neighborhood were very friendly to us and no one in the village locked their houses. It was like being in heaven. Jolene and I immediately took our GED's and we were done with school forever unless we wanted to go back and that wasn't very likely. We spent our free time fixing up our house and making it ours. Jolene went to every garage sale and thrift store on the island she could get to and I would repair or restore whatever she brought home. In another month our place was great and we added the furnishings as they came out of the shop I'd built for fixing things. Terry and I were turning out boards at a fierce rate at the beach and Jolene's surfing got them noticed at the local spots and they began to sell in Hawaii as well as in the states. Marcy went to work as a clothing buyer for one of the department stores in Wakiki and loved Hawaii as much as we did. She loved her new job and we all were getting along great. Terry and I worked long hours at the shop making boards with Jolene at the counter. We surfed every day at Wakiki beach in the mornings as we had done in California and little by little the locals accepted us there. I went back to the itch room to save money for the company and Jolene continued to attract attention on the water and she was quickly becoming a celebrity on the waves there as she was in Huntington Beach. Each night I would get dropped off with Jolene and we would go into our home and make dinner. There was little TV there so we would read and play games with each other at night for the most part or we would work on something new for the house. We were never bored and we loved being together. We surfed each morning before we went to work and our lives were as good as it could get.

We had plenty of money in the bank and the business was doing well. Terry decided he wanted some business partners so Jolene and I bought into the surfboard business and then we were part owners of a company. We were very comfortable and deeply in love.

The summer came and went and we hardly noticed as winter came to us. The tropics were perfect and we loved not having to use our wet suits as we came towards our birthdays in November. We turned sixteen that month and Terry and Marcy took us out to celebrate another trip around the sun. We went to one of the fantastic Japanese restaurants in our neighborhood and had a wonderful time. We knew most of the people in the village by then and they all celebrated with us. Terry and Marcy dropped us off after dinner and we stumbled to our door and to our bed where we celebrated being sixteen by making love. When we were finished Jolene looked at me with her head on my chest and said, "David can we get married?"

I said, "Sure if you want to. I even think we're old enough to do it here. What brought this on? I thought you were against marriage."

Jolene said, "I suppose we're too young and I would like to have my parents there when I get married, but I just love seeing Terry and Marcy together and I guess it makes me want to be married like they are."

I said, "I like them too and I'll marry you anytime you wish. Remember you're the girl of my dreams and I love you very much. Are you having some kind of nesting instinct going on? Are you thinking about having children?"

Jolene said, "How did you know?"

I said, "I read once that girls do that sometimes. What kind of children are you thinking of?"

She smiled and said, "Well children are completely out of the question right now, but I've been thinking of a boy who looks just like you."

I said, "Well that's flattering. I would hope we'd have a little girl who looks just like you."

"Stop that!" she said. "I feel like you're patronizing me and I don't think it's funny."

I said, "I wasn't being funny or patronizing. I was being serious."

"You were?" she said. "I'm sorry my love. I'd like to have a girl too. A boy and a girl but I think we should wait for awhile. We're only sixteen but I feel like I'm twenty. Do you think we'll be burned out by the time we're twenty? That's four years away."

I said, "I don't think so. We have a lot to do here and the time will pass quickly for us. We'll be old before you know it."

She said, "I still think something is missing but I don't know what."

I said, "I know what's missing. It's the rest of our childhood. We're living like adults when we should be living at home and having an interactive social life and being miserable like the kids we went to school with."

Jolene said, "I think you're right. What do you suggest?"

I said, "Maybe we should go back to school."

Jolene said, "Back to school? David we hated school. Why are you saying this?"

"Not high school. We could enroll in junior college and go there instead."

Jolene said, "You know school might be good. We could try it at one of the junior colleges near here and see if it would help."

I said, "We'll look into it tomorrow. It might be just what we need."

The next day instead of going to work, Jolene took some time from the shop and went to the local junior college and found out about enrollment there. She came to the shop at noon with all of the applications and information and said, "David it's wonderful. The campus is beautiful and there's no tuition at all when you've been here for six months. Everyone dresses like they have been at the beach all day and they give PE credits for surfing. Can you believe that? Can we take a couple of classes there in the spring semester? It starts in January."

I said, "I don't know why not. Maybe it'll fill the void we've been feeling lately. I like they give credits for surfing. That will make it fun. Do you think a class will improve your abilities?"

Jolene laughed and said, "I don't know. I guess we'll have to take the class and find out."

We discussed the idea with our partners Terry and Marcy that night when we were over at their house. They were all for the idea and they understood our feeling of something missing. Marcy mentioned our sneaking around in Huntington Beach was something which kept life interesting for us and we thought back and realized we did miss our running around. What it really came down to was that we were too young to be adults, but we had no notions of returning to what we were doing two years before. Reliving our past was out of the question and we decided to see if we could fill the void until school started by surfing more than we were. We had been used to going morning and night and we decided to do more of it again. We started to wake up at dawn and head for the beach every day before work like we did at home. We had gotten lazy about getting up early so we started the practice again and the extra waves were good for us. We were both sixteen and could get drivers licensees at that age in Hawaii. One day I bought an old Jeep station wagon that didn't run, and to Jolene's amazement I had the old thing running in a couple of days. After a few driving lessons for Jolene we had transportation and it opened the whole island up for us. She went to work on the Jeep's interior and a few days after

I got the thing running she had decked it out surfer style with bamboo curtains, Pendleton seat covers and a hand painted blue and white paint job. It was the envy of Wakiki and Terry had the shop logo painted on the side so all would know who we were. We would leave our boards strapped to the top of the wagon which was semi-open air and go. We drove somewhere every morning to surf and our feelings of something missing started to disappear. The Jeep was good for our surfing after work, as it was convenient to jump in and drive home in seconds when we got out of the water. Terry loved going surfing with us and he stayed with us after work on most days and we rode the waves together. We were also designing some of the more radical boards on the island. We experimented with channels on the bottoms of our boards and I have to say Jolene was responsible for an innovation the whole of the surfing world began to use. We took out a patent on the device and had them mass-produced in the states. They sold everywhere and Jolene and I got richer.

We were in the shop one day when one of our customers, who was a very good surfer, came in with the skeg broken on his board. This is a fin which keeps the board going straight and acts like a rudder when the board is put on its side in the water. We were going about the difficult repair when Jolene looked at what we were doing and said, "Why doesn't someone make a skeg you can replace in five minutes with a screwdriver? You could have different skegs for different conditions too."

Terry and I looked at each other at the same time and the light went on in our heads at the same time. When the friend's board was repaired we sat down and drew plans for just what Jolene had described. We got some estimates on manufacturing the product and with the help of a patent attorney we were in business. Our boards were the first to have the interchangeable skeg devise and it increased our sales. Before long other manufactures wanted the invention for their boards and we were selling it to them. The money wasn't great but it was steady. It went into our account for the future, which was getting to be substantial. Later that month Jolene had a stroke of genius again. We were sitting around talking when the subject of automobile racing came up and we were discussing the factory teams that raced each year for the Formula One championship. Jolene said, "David, why don't surf board manufacturers have teams like they do?"

Terry and I looked at each other and the light want on again. Terry jumped up and began to hug Jolene, who was saying, "What? What did I say?"

"Terry said, "Your right! Why don't we have a Boyer Boards surfing team? We could have them do all of the contests and exhibitions. It would be great for advertising and we could have the best surfers on our boards. Jolene you're a genius!"

Jolene was given the job of putting together the team and she was to be the head of it. It took her no time at all to find several of the best surfers to be on the team and I took the job of having special shirts and shorts made for them. The idea caught fire and soon all of the board makers followed our lead. There were special team competitions and under Jolene's guidance ours was the top team.

We were doing well in Hawaii and it was coming up on Christmas and the holidays. This time of the year was not always good for business in California and we had heard the holidays in the islands were especially good. We built boards in advance and hoped for serious sales during Christmas. We had planed on staying in the islands for Christmas and my family was okay with the idea. My dad knew what was going on with Jolene and me but Jolene's parents didn't have a clue. Terry and Marcy had announced they would be spending the holidays in the islands and Jolene would stay with them. We all thought everything would be fine until three days before Christmas Jolene's mother and father walked into the shop in Wakiki to surprise her. Jolene was behind the counter when they walked into the display area we had. She said later she was so stunned her heart stopped for a full second. She was just thinking of something to say when I walked out of the back and behind the counter where Jolene was standing. Her parents looked at me and their mouths fell open in disbelief. I was as shocked as she was and stood there unable to speak. Laura was the first to say something and she said, "Well David, we thought you were with your father in the south. Jolene would you explain this to us please."

Jolene said, "Well mom there's definitely something to explain but I'm going to tell you now you're probably not going to like it very much."

Stan said, "What aren't we going to like? Should we wait for your brother to hear the explanation? Hello David. It's nice to see you I think."

I said, "It's nice to see both of you as well and I'm sorry the circumstances aren't better."

Jolene said, "Mom and Dad, we'll tell you what's going on but first I want to tell you I'm happy to see you despite the circumstances. This was really all my idea so please don't be mad with David. Here, you'd better sit down. David, please get us all a soda." Jolene went on, "Mom, David and I have been very much in love for a long time and it's time you knew about it. He's been my true love since about a week after I met him in Huntington Beach. It was just like you said it would be and I couldn't help falling in love with him. We've been serious lovers since I won the contest at home and I couldn't stand it any more and I had to be with him as his lover. I know we were too young, but things are good with us and please don't be too mad at us. I'm sorry we lied to you when I moved here but I knew you'd never give me permission to come here and live with David."

Her mother said, "You two live together?"

Jolene said, "Yes we live together, and Terry and Marcy know all about it. We have our own house in the village behind the band shell and we'll be happy to take you there when we leave here. It's very nice and you might like what we've done to the place if you give us a chance. I know we're only sixteen but we own our house and have a car and a big bank account as well. We work hard here every day and we love what we're doing. I suppose we'd be married if we had even remotely thought you would have given us your permission. We came to Hawaii to be together and I'm asking you to please try and understand."

Laura said, "Jolene I'm shocked but I'm not particularly upset with you and David. It's going to take me awhile to understand all of this and I wish I had known what was going on. This explains what we couldn't figure out when you left. We knew you and David were very much in love and I was pretty sure you two were making love together. We had the hardest time with the thought of you and David breaking up. He's a wonderful boy and we couldn't figure out why the two of you broke up. It was what worried us the most."

Jolene said, "You mean you're not angry with us?"

She smiled and said, "No dear, I'm not. Now would you please come here and give me a hug. I've missed you both terribly."

Jolene got up and tears came into her eyes and her mother's as well. They hugged in the shop and Jolene said, "Mom the hardest thing I've ever done was to leave you and dad but I had to have David. He's everything to me and I wouldn't know what to do without him. I love him so much. Please don't take me away from him."

Laura said between tears, "No Jolene we won't take you away from David. If you had to do this to be with him like you wanted I could never do that to you."

The two of them stood hugging and crying in the shop and Stan came over and hugged me. He said, "You two are the damnedest pair I've ever seen. Hello David, it's good to see you."

I sat back down and Laura and Jolene did as well while they were wiping the tears from their eyes. Terry walked in at this time and I heard him say "uh oh!" when he came into the shop. His parents turned around and said, "Hello Terry. Yes we've discovered the secret and you're not in trouble. Where's Marcy?"

Terry said, "Marcy is at work and what are you doing here?"

Stan said, "Your mother and I came for a surprise Christmas visit and I guess we're the ones who are surprised. Come and give your dad a big hug. How's business you trouble maker."

Terry went to hug his dad and after we all stood there looking at each other until Laura said, "Terry will you watch the shop while David and Jolene take us and show us where they live?"

Terry said, "Sure you guys go ahead I'll call you at their house. Would you like to come over and eat dinner at our house tonight?"

Laura said, "Not tonight. I think I want to have dinner with David and Jolene tonight."

We left the shop and used the Jeep as her parents had taken a cab to the shop from the airport. We piled them all in and drove the short distance to our one bedroom house we had in the village. Laura loved the place from the start and loved the inside even more when she saw what we had done to it. She said, "Oh this is wonderfully romantic Jolene. Where did you ever find all of the furniture for it?"

Jolene said, "We bought everything at yard sales and thrift stores. David can work miracles on old furniture. That's why everything looks so new and clean. Look what he's done with the kitchen mom."

Laura went into the kitchen and said, "Honey it's wonderful. David I'm very impressed."

I said, "It's all Jolene's taste and decorating. She picked everything out. I just fix what she brings home or restore it. I think she's very talented."

Laura said, "I think you're both wonderful. You've done all of this at your age? I can hardly believe it. You two are fantastic and you deserve to be together. I want to see the rest of the house."

Jolene and I took them on a tour of what was ours in the village including the small shop I built to fix things in. They were amazed at all of it and their acceptance of it and what we had done made us feel better about them being there. We stopped looking around after awhile and sat them in the living room while Jolene went to the kitchen to make some drinks for us all. We had started on our drinks when Stan said, "David how are your finances?"

I said, "They're good, we make a lot more than we spend and we keep it all in an account we started before we left California."

Jolene said, "We're in great shape dad. I keep getting money from endorsements and we get money from the shop we now own half of as well as the products David and Terry make and sell."

I said, "Jolene's invention makes the most for us though. It was her idea to begin with."

Stan said, "What invention is that?"

I said, "Jolene thought of the replaceable skeg for surfboards. Terry and I were the first to manufacture one and we sell them to all of the other board makers. They're very profitable."

Stan laughed and said, "Jolene you invented this? That's amazing."

Jolene said, "I just thought of it and the boys did the making. We have them made for us on the mainland. We have a patent and everything."

Stan said, "You have a patent on this invention?"

Jolene said, "Sure, we hired a patent attorney and he did all of the work for us. Now everyone who makes something similar pays us a royalty."

Stan said, "Jolene would you mind telling me just how much money you two have in your bank account? I'm just curious about it."

Jolene said, "It's been quite awhile since I looked closely at the balance but I think it's about one hundred thousand dollars. It would be more but we bought this house and bought into Terry's business."

Stan said, "One hundred thousand dollars! My God Jolene I had no idea you two were so successful!"

Jolene said, "We're just saving for the future. You never know when the money might stop."

I said, "We don't spend much. Our biggest expense is food."

Jolene added, "We were thinking about going back to school in the spring."

Laura said, "You haven't been going to school?"

Jolene said, "That was one of the reasons for coming to Hawaii. David and I hated high school so as soon as we were here we both tested out with the GED. When we talk about going back to school, we mean we're going to go to college at the local junior college. It's free and we think it will help with what we've been missing."

Stan said, "What have you been missing?"

Jolene said, "Our childhood's. We're living like adults and we're not that old. We should be in school for the experiences."

Stan said, "You two figured all of this out by yourselves? I'm amazed at the two of you. You have a beautiful home, a couple of businesses and surfing careers and now you've decided you're missing part of your childhood's so you're going back to school so you can experience them? Laura, I'm sure we'll never have to worry about these two. They're fine and I think doing better than we are. Congratulations to you both I think someone should write a book about the two of you. I'm very proud of what you've done."

We finished our drinks and Jolene went to the kitchen and began to cook an early meal for us. We were pleased her parents were impressed with our lives and it was fun to show them we were doing well. We were a great team but we had always known that. We finished dinner and drove her parents to the Royal Hawaiian Hotel where they had reservations booked. We waited while they checked in and said good night in the lobby and went back to our home in the village. We were lying in bed when Jolene said, "I think that went pretty well. David I can't tell you how much my parents mean to me. It was so good to see them. I've really missed them."

"Jolene why didn't you ever tell me you missed them so much?"

She said, "I didn't want you to think I was weak. We both needed to be so strong for what we've been doing. I didn't want you to worry about me."

I said, "Well you should have told me. At least you could have called home more often."

She looked me in the eyes saying, "I feel so vindicated. I feel wonderful. Will you make love to me so I'll feel perfect again?"

I said, "Of course and reached to turn off the light."

We drove to the shop in the morning and went surfing while the winter sun was coming up. We opened the shop and went about our jobs until Terry came to work after dropping Marcy off. He called me out of the shaping room and we sat to talk about yesterday afternoon and Terry said, "Okay tell me what happened."

Jolene said, "Well the parents walked in yesterday afternoon while you were gone and caught us together red handed. I explained things to them and spilled the beans. They're not mad at any of us. We took them to our house and they loved it. We told them about everything and they accepted what we're doing and they were pretty impressed and mom said she wouldn't make me leave. They're going to let us stay together."

Terry said, "I'll be damned. You managed to convince them to let you stay. Jolene this is good news."

"I'll say, my greatest worry yesterday was they'd make me go back to California without David."

Terry said, "I wish you were back in California sometimes. It's really hard to keep the shop there going from here. You know as well as I do how much trouble it's been."

I said, "You bet. Keeping good people there has been a pain."

Jolene said, "So what are your plans tonight?"

Terry said, "I thought Marcy and I would have everybody over for dinner tonight. Is that okay with you and David?"

"No problems here," I answered.

Jolene said, "That's fine with me."

Terry said, "Well then why don't you two come over at seven after you go surfing."

We both agreed seven would be fine and we went back to what we were doing. Stan and Laura came to the shop that afternoon and said they had been sightseeing all day and they loved Hawaii. Jolene and I were happy they were having a good time and Terry invited them to dinner that night. Terry's house was much bigger than ours and we had a great meal. Jolene was very happy to be with her parents again. We stayed up late and then drove the parents back to their hotel where we left them and then made the drive home. We were getting undressed when Jolene said, "David what would you think if we went back to California for awhile?"

I said, "I wouldn't mind as long as we're together. I really don't care much where we are."

Jolene said, "I miss my mom and I need her. It's taken me a long time to realize she and my dad mean a great deal to me. I'd like to be able to see them more."

I said, "When would you want to do this?"

Jolene said, "If we could I'd like to go in the spring when the weather gets nice there. Remember what Terry said about the shop in Huntington and the problems with the staffing there? I was thinking if we went there we could run that shop and you could make boards through the summer. It would make the shop more profitable and I could run the surfing team from there."

I said, "How long have you been thinking of this?"

Jolene said, "Since this afternoon. I wouldn't want to spend the winter there though, I would want to come back and spend the winter here."

I said, "Do you think your parents would let us live together there?"

Jolene said, "I think the only thing we have to do is ask them."

I said, "Well Mombo always said we can live at her house anytime we want. If we lived there you could see your parents whenever you want and they wouldn't have the annoyance of having us making love in front of them."

Jolene said, "Could we really?"

I said, "I don't think there would be a problem with that now. To tell you the truth, as much as I love it here I miss the action there at the pier sometimes. If we came back every winter so we could have a perpetual summer that would be great. We could just leave the Jeep and the house and go. Our favorite surf spots don't break here in the summer anyway."

"David you're simply the best! What you've just said has made me very happy. I love you so much sometimes I just can't stand it."

I said, "Well then let's go to bed and you can show me how much you love me."

Jolene said, "Gladly, come on my dear we have things to do."

Jolene took me by the hand and led me to our bedroom where we made love to each other until almost morning."

The next day was Christmas Eve and we had extra shopping to do. I took Stan out for awhile and Jolene took her mother out in the afternoon. Stan and Laura took all of us out to dinner that night and we had a wonderful time. We were to meet the next morning at Terry and Marcy's house to open presents and I went to bed that night thinking of how much Jolene was going to love the Christmas gift I had gotten for her.

We woke up the next morning and after coffee we took the Jeep and went surfing at Ala Moana. The waves were great and we stayed longer than usual because we didn't have to open the shop. We finally got out of the water and after changing at home, we drove to Terry and Marcy's where Jolene's parents were. We went inside and Terry handed us drinks and we sat down and began to open our presents. It was great fun and I gave Jolene two things she had been wanting. She was pleased to have the clothes I gave her and I loved the new shorts and shirts she had given me. Her parents gave us a couple of sets of fantastic new sheets we could really use and the same to Terry and Marcy. When it was over and there was wrapping paper everywhere Terry said, "Well that was great, this is wonderful, what a great Christmas."

I said, "It's not over yet," and reached into my pocket and pulled out a small wrapped gift box and handed it to Jolene. Jolene looked at me funny and started to get through the wrapping and into the box. She took the top off of the box and looked inside. When she looked inside she stared and one-second later tears flooded her eyes. She took out the engagement ring inside and put it on her finger as she crossed the room to where I was sitting. When she got to me I was grabbed and held so tightly I was sure I would be hurt. She said into my ear, "This is just what I wanted. I love you so much I just can't stand it!"

Jolene got up and crossed the room to show her parents her engagement ring. Her father looked and nodded to me his approval while Jolene's mother began to cry. Terry came over to me and gave me a hug signaling his feelings and Marcy had tears in her eyes as well. Jolene came and hugged me after showing her parents and said, "What on earth did you do this for?"

I said, "Because I love you and I want everyone to know there's more going on between you and me than just going steady."

The whole family laughed at this and Jolene said, "It's just beautiful. It's just what I've been wanting. I haven't said anything but you always manage to read my mind."

Stan got up and raised his glass and toasted, "To David and Jolene. The finest couple on the planet!"

Everyone in the room raised their glasses and Jolene began to weep again as she hugged me around the neck very tightly. We stayed for a few more hours and then went home with Stan promising us all an engagement dinner that night. We drove back to our love nest in the village with Jolene looking at her ring every other second while I drove. When we got home I asked if she wanted to go surfing and saying nothing she led me to our bedroom where she gave me the most wonderful present I could imagine.

CHAPTER SEVEN

We went to a very fancy dinner that night and there was a great deal of champagne poured for us. After dinner Jolene said, "Mom, what would you think about David and me coming back to Huntington for the spring and summer?"

Laura looked shocked and said, "Jolene what brought this on?"

Jolene said, "Mom and dad, I really miss you and I miss where I grew up. David and I have done a lot, but when it comes down to it engaged or not, I'm still a kid and I do need my parents. The shop there needs us for the summer and if it's okay we'd like to come home until the fall."

Laura said, "Jolene this is shocking. I don't know what to say. Where are you thinking of living?"

Jolene said, "At David's house if it's okay with his mother and Maw."

Laura said, "Yes I suppose it would be all right. Stan what do you think?"

Stan said, "What does it matter. These kids are going to do what they want regardless. Personally I'd like to have my daughter around."

Terry said, "Well we could sure use you two at the shop there. It would solve the problem of shipping boards there and I know you two will be great for business."

Jolene said, "Then it's okay?"

Laura said, "Yes it's okay. I'll just have to get used to my daughter living two blocks away. God what will my friends say? They'll hate the example you two will set for their kids."

Everyone laughed at this and Jolene hugged me from her chair at the table. Stan toasted us again and we knew we would be going home in a couple of months. Laura asked, "What will you do with your home here?"

Jolene said, "We'll just leave it until we get back. Tom-Tom the neighborhood guy who lives everywhere will most likely live there and look after things for us. He lives in everyone's houses all of the time. He's kind of a fixture in the neighborhood and watches everything for everybody."

Laura said, "When will you go back to Hawaii?"

Jolene said, "When the water starts to get cold of course."

This made everyone laugh again and the subject was done and we felt like we were set with Jolene's plan. We drank the rest of the champagne and all went to our respective beds. Jolene and I were lying in bed and I said, "Jolene, I have to hand it to you. You have done the impossible and I'm amazed and completely in love with you."

Jolene said, "Thank you my dear fiancée. Things have worked out pretty well. It wouldn't have happened if you hadn't given me my fabulous engagement ring. You were the one who made it happen."

I said, "I hardly think so but I'd better call my mother in the morning and tell her she's going to have company for the summer."

Jolene said, "I would hope so. Now come and make love to the girl you've chosen for the rest of your life."

We got up the next morning and I called Mombo the first thing. She was happy to hear from me and was even happier when I told her of our engagement. She was still happier than when I asked if we could come and live there for the summer. Her answer was yes and Jolene and I began to pick dates for leaving the islands.

We spent the next several months doing as we wanted in Hawaii. We surfed every day and kept fixing up our house at night and on the weekends. We had enough money to go out to the local restaurants in the village where we lived when we wanted. We rode the winter waves on the north shore and by the time spring rolled around we felt like we had lived in the islands our whole lives. Business was great at the shop and we loved the money coming in. Terry was great to us and neither of us had to work very hard. The locals considered us to be like they were after a couple of months in the big winter surf and we had friends we liked at almost every spot on the island.

Four months later Terry dropped us off at the airport and we boarded our plane with a couple of suitcases apiece and our favorite surfboards. We flew to Los Angeles where Mombo met us and drove us to Huntington Beach. I have to say it was great to see my Mother and Maw. Jolene and I moved our things to my bedroom as soon as we arrived home and went about settling in. We were tired from our flight but we went over to her house and were welcomed by her mother and oldest brother who just happened to be visiting. It was wonderful to be back and Jolene was right. With all we had done and as good as we were at being adults, we were still a couple of kids when it came down to it. We stayed for awhile at her house and went back to our quarters at my house for dinner. We ate with Mombo and Maw and went and climbed into the bed where we had first made love. Tomorrow we were going surfing and then we would go and fire the help at the shop and take it over.

Dawn came early for us the next morning and we climbed out of the sack and went to the kitchen to make coffee. We drank what we wanted and took our boards and walked down to the pier where we went into the edge of the Pacific Ocean. We paddled out to the break and we were immediately recognized by some of our old surfing friends who were delighted to see us again. We told them stories of the surfing in Hawaii and of our engagement between catching waves. When it became time we took our boards and went to the shop across the street. We opened the place and the help was late getting to work. The place desperately needed our care and we went about putting the place right for the whole of the day. Word got around fast and we had a steady stream of our old friends' coming in to see us. I ordered supplies to start making boards and Jolene went over the books to see what had been going on. No one had been stealing from us but the shop lacked the life it had when we both met there. We finished the day surfing the afternoon glass off and after locking the shop we headed for home and dinner at Jolene's house with her parents. Dinner was great and it was interesting to see Jolene kiss her mother good night and go to where we were living. The next day would come early and we knew we had a thousand things to do at the shop after we surfed our favorite spot.

Our second day at the shop was wonderful. Our friends continually stopped off to see us and there was life on the corner again. Terry always had people hanging around the shop and the practice started again as soon as word got around we were back in town. We immediately had sales of everything we stocked especially the clothing line which went along with our surf team. By the end of the day Jolene was placing an order for more stock and I was taking delivery on the supplies I would need to begin building boards in Huntington Beach. Even Ralph who owned the sandwich shop on the other corner was pleased to see us back. It was wonderful to eat his food again and sit with Jolene behind the counter while we ate. School was still going on for those who went so the nighttime scene wasn't what it was during the summer. We knew it would pick up as the days grew longer and the weather became warmer at night. In the early afternoon the representative from the company we bought the foam blanks we made our boards from came in along with the truckload of blanks I had ordered. He was happy to see us and began to tell us about a new high density, high flotation foam that had been developed recently. He told us about all of the properties of the new material and left us with several of the blanks which were made from the new product to experiment with. We were the first shop to get the new material and it promised smaller more maneuverable boards which would float the same weight as larger ones did. This excited us, as it would definitely give us another edge over our competition. We made plans to build the first two new boards from the shop out of the new foam and they would be custom made for us. We went home after surfing excited and exhausted by our day and made dinner with Mombo and Maw. We told them about our new plans for our line of boards and watched TV with them after dinner, which was nice, as we saw little of the tube in Hawaii. We went to bed talking about the possibilities for the smaller boards until we fell asleep.

We were awake before dawn the next morning and we rode our bicycles to the shop where we locked them in and went across the street to surf as the sun was coming up. This was our favorite time of the day and the waves were good. When it came time to open the shop we put our boards away and Jolene said, "David, I have an errand to run. Please don't start shaping the new foam until I get back."

I said I wouldn't and went about cleaning the new boards in stock as she rode away on her bike. She was back two hours later with several books on the subject of hydrodynamics and I suddenly figured out where her lovely mind was going. She said, "We have to learn what the other board makers don't know about the way things move through the water."

I said I understood and we went about learning what we could from the highly technical books. I got no shaping done all day but by the time we went out surfing in the afternoon we had a much better idea of what we needed to make. We stayed with the books until we went to bed and all of the next day. By the end of the next day we were sure about what the new boards would look like. They were to be much shorter and the same width but they would have a flatter profile and harder edges. Jolene thought the big center skeg which was typical should be eliminated in favor of two or three smaller "fins" as she called them, each on opposite sides of the board. This would facilitate the board always being stable even on the steepest waves. I had the plans and went about shaping all afternoon. By the time we were to close, the new boards were shaped and ready to glass. We could hardly wait until the next day but we managed to go for our afternoon surfing and then home to dinner. We ate with Jolene's parents and all was very comfortable. They were delighted to have their daughter back and seemed to like having me back as well. The biggest difference was Jolene's mother was treating her more like an adult person than someone she had control over. Jolene loved this and said so when we left the parent's house to walk home holding hands with the smell of the Pacific Ocean in the air.

As soon as we got to the shop the next day I went about glassing the new boards. I had Jolene sign them both, as she had thought of going to the library and getting the proper information to learn. They of course had our biggest decals on the board's front and back to advertise and when the glass was dry they looked great. I managed to get them sanded during the day and when the bits of glass were cleaned off I gave them the shiny gloss coat of resin all boards get. We left them in the shop until the next morning when they would be dry and could be waxed to use on the waves. We were so excited we almost couldn't stand it that night. We went to bed early so morning would come quicker for us. It came soon enough and after coffee we practically ran to the shop. The new boards were beautiful and almost two feet shorter than anything which was on the waves with the exception of boards made for kids. We got to the water and after kissing for luck we paddled out to the take off spot. The boards floated as well as what we previously used and they paddled very nicely. Jolene was first to take off on a wave and I watched as she dropped in and disappeared behind the wall of green that was foaming at the top. I was next and caught a five footer which was moving fast. It took a little longer to catch the wave but when I had it and stood up my new board took off like nothing I'd ever experienced. It was like riding lightning and it turned so quickly it almost lost me. It was completely stable on the steepest part of the wave and was incredibly maneuverable. I finished my ride and paddled back out where Jolene was waiting for me with a huge smile on her face. She said, "I think we've made an incredible breakthrough."

I said laughing, "To say the least. These boards are incredible. They'll do anything."

"They certainly will," she said. "I've never experienced such freedom on a wave. They make these five-footers seem tame. I can't wait to get them into some real size. They're just fantastic."

We surfed away the morning and each time we paddled out to the line up we were asked a hundred questions by the other surfers who had been watching us do the impossible all morning. We gave out very little information about what the new boards were made of but told all of those interested they would be available soon at our shop. We finished one of the most fun mornings ever and went to open the store. When we were inside I called the rep for the new foam and then and there told him to come to the shop when we closed and he could see what we'd done with his product in the afternoon on the waves. I also asked him to send a truck to pick up half of the foam blanks of the old type and bought all of his stock of the new foam. He was thrilled with what we told him about the way our new boards performed and he swore to us he'd keep the new foam away from the other manufacturers if we'd promise to purchase all of his stock during that time. The deal was done and I went into the shaping room to begin a board for Terry while Jolene buried her fantastic head back into one of the books on hydrodynamics. Terry's new board was shaped by noon and I glassed it immediately. It was done by the end of the day and I planned to ship it by air freight the next morning. Terry would be astounded by what we were going to send him. The end of the day arrived and just before we closed the rep walked in and Jolene began to show him our radical new board design. He was completely amazed by what we'd designed and built and went with us across the street to watch us use them. The waves were breaking as they were in the morning, but the off shore wind was blowing and holding the waves up nicely. He watched from the beach and when we came in he had dollar signs in his eyes. He was completely amazed at not only the way the new boards looked but he couldn't believe the way they performed. We shook hands on our deal and we walked back to the shop with him. He left from there and I called Terry at the shop in Wakiki from ours. He answered the phone and I said, "Terry, Jolene and I are sending you a new board and it will be there day after tomorrow. I want you to promise to use it the minute it gets to you okay."

Terry said, "What have you two been up to? What could be so important that you have to send it by air? Air's expensive."

Jolene was on the extension by this time and said, "Terry just trust us. You're not going to believe what we've made for you. You're going to love it and we're all going to be rich."

I spent the rest of the conversation trying to assure Terry we had not lost our minds and told him when to expect the delivery. We went home and explained our breakthrough to both sets of parents. We took our new boards with us and they were impressed by what Jolene and I had done. We made it an early night again and after some excited lovemaking we went to sleep anticipating the next day.

We almost went straight to the shop the next day but we just had to surf our new boards again. They performed as they had the day before and we were as happy as two kids could be. When we got to the shop after surfing I went right into the shaping room and began to build new boards for the general public as fast as I could. Jolene helped and by the end of the day we had ten of the new boards ready for glassing. We skipped surfing in the evening and stayed very late to glass and clean up our mess. It was a great day and the day after we had ten of our discovery on the rack in the shop. All carried Jolene's signature and the biggest of our decals. We surfed that night and got the same hundred questions we'd gotten each time we went out with them. The next morning Jolene sold two of them and two more in the afternoon. It was about four o'clock when the telephone rang and Terry was on the other end screaming, "Fantastic! Just Fantastic! You two are the greatest. How did you ever come up with this? I've never ridden anything so great. I can't believe it. How did you do this?"

Jolene was on the extension and explained the whole thing to him step by step. Terry was incredibly happy we'd made a deal for all of the new foam and was pleased a large quantity of the new material was already on its way to him. He was as thrilled as we were and we laughed at his excitement. We rode our new boards again after work and the next day we sold two more of our new stock. It quickly became clear to us we wouldn't be able to keep up with the demand without hiring help. We put a sign in the window advertising for help and hired a girl two hours later and put her to work in the itch room. She didn't know much about surfing but had worked with fiberglass on numerous boats with her dad. Her experience was good enough for us and we showed her the ropes and she spent the afternoon sanding for us.

By the end of the week we had sold all of the original boards we had made and were putting out new stock when Jolene's brain came up with another great idea. She said, "David, these boards are special so why don't we date and number them?"

I said, "I don't know, why don't we?"

Jolene said, "We weren't but we are now. I think the numbering of them will make them more special."

I said, "It certainly can't hurt. I'll start numbering and as soon as we figure out what number we're on, you call Terry and tell him so he can keep in sequence with us."

Jolene said, "Everytime we make a new shape we should start a new edition don't you think?"

I said, "I didn't but I do now." And Jolene laughed until there were tears in her eyes.

Jolene recovered and then said, "We need to capitalize on this breakthrough. What if we come up with a new line of surfing apparel to go along with the new boards?"

I said, "Jolene would you stop coming up with these fantastic ideas please. I'm going to work myself to death if I have anything else to do."

Jolene said, "Okay, okay, I'll stop. Tonight we'll design some new stuff and I'll deal with getting it manufactured for us. I wouldn't want to kill my fiancée would I?"

I said, "I would hope not but I'll tell you what, tonight is Thursday and we've got a lot to celebrate. Can we leave the new designs 'till tomorrow and take some of this cash we're raking in and go out for a fancy dinner together?"

Jolene said, "You mean get all dressed up and go to that fancy place in Newport?"

I said, "Sure, why not?"

Jolene said, "Yes, why not?"

We closed the shop and went home to change our clothes. We borrowed Mombo's car and drove to Jolene's house so her parents could get a look at us all dressed up and successful. We walked in and Laura said, "My God! I don't believe it! Jolene you're all dressed up and David too. What's going on here?"

Jolene said, "David and I are going out to celebrate what we've done. We've borrowed his mother's car and we're going to the Fancy Pelican in Newport for dinner."

Laura said, "Well I guess you've grown up. I don't believe it. You two look so nice and you look so sophisticated. Wait for your father to come and see you."

Laura went and got Stan who walked into the room and said, "Wow, you two look great! Jolene I can't remember the last time you wore a dress. You two look fantastic. What's the occasion?"

Jolene said, "Money dad. We're making a lot of it from our new boards and there's more to come we just know it. Our new boards are just flying out of the shop. David and I are having a wonderful time and we're very happy. I think we owe it all to you for coming to Hawaii and then allowing me to stay with David and to come home."

I said, "I think so too. This wouldn't have happened if we hadn't come back here this spring. Did I ever tell you that you have the smartest daughter on the whole coast?"

Stan said, "No, I don't think you have."

I said, "Well you do. Jolene tell them about today's ideas."

Jolene and I sat while Jolene told them about what was going on and what she thought was going to happen. Stan and Laura were impressed enough to make Jolene happy so we excused ourselves after awhile and drove down to Newport Beach to have a nice dinner. We were the only ones our age there and we both had big lobster dinners. We stuffed ourselves with food until we could just sit and look at each other at the table. Jolene smiled and said, "You know I could get used to this."

I said, "So could I. This is really fun. If you keep coming up with new ideas I'm pretty sure we'll be rich by the time we're twenty."

Jolene said, "Do you really think so?"

"I certainly do. We're selling five times the number of boards we used to sell and they haven't even caught on yet. I'm shaping as fast as I can and I'm barely keeping up with the way they're going out of the shop."

Jolene said, "Well we'll just have to skip a few of these expensive dinners and hire you some help. It looks like you're going to need it."

I said, "How about you? If your clothing line takes off you'll be up to your ears just like I am."

Jolene said, "I didn't think of that. Maybe we should hire a professional to help with the marketing?"

I said, "No way. If we hire a professional we'll never go surfing again because we'll be too busy working. Besides, everyone wants one of our boards, not one someone else has made. I think we need to raise our prices and be more exclusive."

Jolene said, "Who's being the genius now. That's the smartest thing I've heard all week. I'm certainly engaged to the smartest man on the coast."

I said, "Who just happens to be engaged to the smartest woman on the coast. Aren't we lucky?"

Jolene agreed and we paid our check and drove the short distance back to Huntington Beach. We were so full we went straight to bed and woke up at sunrise.

We walked to the shop when we got up and got our boards and headed for the water. The waves were small but our new boards performed as well as we thought they would in the smaller conditions. The new boards were great and we were still getting used to them. On one wave Jolene almost collided with another surfer and lost her board. The wave took it into the beach and she had to swim in to get it. She paddled back out and met me in the line up and we continued surfing. We rode the small waves until it was time to go to work and we each rode one more wave in to the beach. We went to work and Jolene began to design the new line of clothing which would advertise our shop and the new boards. I came out of the shaping room at noon and Jolene had lunch from Ralph's waiting. We sat down to eat when two of our surfer acquaintances came in and picked two of our new boards from the rack. Jolene got up and took their money and wrote them each a sales slip. We talked for awhile and found our new boards were the talk of the town and they had both ended their savings accounts to buy one. They told us if the new boards could make them look like us on the waves, we'd surely be rich. We thanked them for their business and Jolene said, "You know David, this is really fun."

I said, "You bet it is. Everyone loves what we've done."

Jolene said, "You told me not to come up with any new ideas but I'm afraid there's one more."

I said, "Oh no! What's that?"

Jolene said, "Are you sure you want to know?"

I said, "Might as well. You can't keep these ideas bottled up. What's the new one?"

"Are you sure?" she teased.

I said, "Give it to me and end the suspense. By the way, are you in a hurry to get rich?"

Jolene said, "No, not particularly, but here's my new idea. Do you remember this morning when I lost my board and had to swim for it?"

I said, "Yep, you weren't happy about it either. I'm surprised you didn't say something to the kook who cut you off."

Jolene said, "What if we designed a strap that was long enough for a person to move around on their board and would keep their board from getting loose."

I said, "Where would you think it should be attached?"

Jolene said, "What about if it was around the ankle?"

I said, "That would be good I guess. How would you attach it?"

She said, "What's that stuff that goes back and forth together and makes noise when you pull it apart?"

I said, "I think it's called Velcro."

Jolene said, "That's it. The strap could connect from the Velcro to the board. These new boards are so light when you wiped out they wouldn't yank your leg off."

I said, "I'm sorry I asked to hear it."

Jolene said, "Oh it's not a good idea?"

I said, "That's not the problem at all. It's a great idea. I'll get right on it. Will you put the help wanted sign in the window and find someone who can shape boards please. I'm afraid I'm in love with a girl who wants to get rich and retire before she's twenty. Now come here and kiss me so I can remember why I'm working so hard."

Jolene got up and gave me a big kiss and said, "I love you and you are my only hero."

I said, "And you are mine my love. And don't get any more ideas unless they're as good as the one you just had."

Jolene laughed and said, "All right I promise."

I went into the office and started to figure out how to attach the strap to a surf-board and make her wonderful idea work. By the end of the day I had a solution and went to share it with Jolene. She was pleased with what I'd come up with and I explained, "It attaches to the board with a plug that's made of hard plastic and steel that gets glassed into the board. Then it goes to the surfer's leg and wraps around with an ankle band that's made from wet suit material but backed with Velcro. It will be soft and won't hurt your leg. I thought some elastic material would be good so I think if we use clear plastic tubing which stretches we'll be in business. Can I go surfing now? It's time to close and I'm tired."

Jolene said, "You are the smartest man alive. You're just wonderful. Yes let's go surfing and then we can go home and I'll make you dinner. I'll get a company to make these things for us on Monday."

I said, "What are you going to call them? We can't call them straps or things. You have to think of a name for them."

Jolene thought for a minute and then said, "What if we called it a leash?"

I said, "Fine, can we go surfing now?"

Jolene said, "Yes let's go. I'm afraid I've overworked my fiancée."

We went for our evening with the waves and I forgot all about being overworked and tired. We were walking home and Jolene said, "David, if I promise not to come up with any new ideas tomorrow will you take me to the dance at the Pavilion?"

I said, "Sure who's playing?"

She said, "Dick Dale and the Del Tones from Newport. It's the first dance of the season."

I said, "Yes but only if you promise to kiss me where we first kissed."

Jolene said, "That's what I had in mind."

We walked the rest of the way home holding hands and Jolene telling me how much she loved me.

We were up early the next morning and after coffee we went to the pier for our morning wave riding. Our new boards even did well on the mushy waves breaking that morning. The surf wasn't very good so we went to the shop early and started work. The girl who was sanding for us was there and doing well at her task. At ten a guy about three years older than I was came to the shop and asked for work shaping boards. I quizzed him on his experience and found that he had worked for Hobie Alter shaping boards but was fired for coming to work late too many times. I hired him at a fair rate of pay and warned him about coming to work late for us. He said he understood and I put him to work in the shaping room and began to teach him how to go about making the shape of our new boards. I also swore him to secrecy and told him if he breathed a word of what we were doing I would fire him and sue him for corporate espionage. He looked at our new boards and understood immediately we were on to something important. His name was Dale and he seemed quite nice. He caught on quickly and Jolene was pleased I had some help in the shop. She came into the shaping room and asked if I could watch the shop for awhile as she had an errand to run. I told her to go and she walked towards our house. She was back in a couple of hours but wouldn't tell me what the errand was. I left her in the front of the shop with her secret and went back to work with Dale. We shaped a number of boards during the day with Dale doing the rough work and me putting the final shape on them. We worked until five and then said goodbye to our help and went across the street to ride the waves which had substantially improved during the day. We found Dale out in the crowd surfing with the regulars and he asked to try our new shape. I switched boards with him and he went for a ride. He came back smiling and really understood why I had been so adamant about him keeping secret with the information he was learning. He was very happy to be part of something new and I could tell he was serious about what we were doing. Jolene and I went and put our boards in the shop when the sun was almost down and walked home where Mombo was cooking dinner. We helped with the meal and did the cleaning up afterwards. We got to tell all about our day and the excitement which was building for us. Mombo and Maw were very pleased with our success and loved hearing the stories about what we were doing. We showered after dinner and when I went to the closet Jolene said, "Here's a present for you to wear tonight."

She handed me a box from the shopping center and after thanking her I opened it to look. Inside was a new pair of slacks and a new shirt and tie. They looked great when I'd put them on and Jolene asked me to wait for her to dress in the living room. I kissed her and went to wait with Mombo and Maw. Twenty minutes later Jolene appeared and she looked fantastic in a new outfit. She had a miniskirt on which was very short and showed off her beautiful legs and that had a matching off the shoulder top. She looked fantastic and she said she had gotten her outfit that day at the shopping center when she bought me my new clothes. We said good night to Mombo and Maw and began our walk to the pier and the Pavilon. It was the first dance of the new season and everyone in town was there. We walked up to the box office and bought our tickets and went inside. We walked around the inside of the big building and as we did I noticed people were pointing and seemed to be talking about us as we moved through the room. I said to Jolene, "Do we look that nice in our new clothes?"

Jolene said, "I don't think we do. We're certainly getting a lot of attention though."

I agreed and just after I finished speaking the band started to play. They were loud and wonderful and we began to dance and didn't stop until their set was over. When we could hear each other again Jolene said into my ear, "Want to get drunk?"

I laughed and said, "Of course I do."

With that she turned and walked to the doors and with people noticing us we walked out and down to the end of the pier. When we got there Jolene opened a bottle of scotch and took a drink. She handed me the bottle I swigged as well. We were standing where we had first kissed and she said, "David do you remember our first kiss?"

I said, "Of course I do. That was the night that my life changed."

Jolene kissed me and said, "It was the night that changed my life too. I fell in love with you on this very spot and I'm very glad we're here again."

I said, "That was a pretty scary night. I was hoping you wanted to kiss me but I was scared to kiss you first. I'm glad you had the nerve to kiss me."

Jolene said, "I know, I was scared too. But I had to find out if you wanted me so I kissed you and it was wonderful."

I said between drinks, "Almost as wonderful as the night you had me touch you."

Jolene said, "That was scary too. I'd never let anyone touch me like that before. I was really scared but I loved the way it felt when you put your hands on me."

I said, "I'd never done it either and I loved it as well."

She said, "It feels like that night was a hundred years ago. Everyday with you has been wonderful."

I said, "It's gone by pretty fast don't you think?"

Jolene said, "Almost too fast. David I love you so much I can't imagine what I'd be like if I hadn't met you. Everyday is just great."

I said, "Well I can't imagine being without you either. You are my true love."

We kissed again and went about drinking scotch and watching the stars on the water below us. We began to get cold and after a few more kisses and we went back inside and danced some more. We were still attracting attention when a girl who knew Jolene from school came up and said, "Hi Jolene I heard you were back in town."

Jolene said, "Christine, I haven't seen you in years. How've you been?"

Christine said, "Fine, I'm in school at Marina and hating it. Jolene I've been hearing all kinds of things about you. You disappeared from school and town and everyone said you'd moved to Hawaii. Now I hear you and David are engaged and living together and running your brother's shop and making the most radical boards anyone has ever seen. Is it true?"

Jolene said, "Every bit of it. I moved to Hawaii with my brother and David followed me there so my parents wouldn't know. We own a house there and we own half of the surf shop with my brother and we got engaged last Christmas."

She held up her ring for Christine to see.

Christine said, "Jolene it's beautiful. You are so lucky. Everyone is talking about you and David. You two are heroes and people are saying you've designed an incredible new surfboard that's going to change everything about surfing."

Jolene said, "Is that why everyone is pointing at us like we're somebody special?"

Christine said, "Yes you are someone special. People speak of you two like you're movie stars. You two are famous!"

Jolene said, "Christine you're kidding."

Christine said, "Oh no I'm not, look around. Everyone is watching you and David while I'm here talking to you. I'm really happy for you. You've inspired every girl in Huntington Beach. I hope you think it's wonderful."

Jolene said, "Christine I'm amazed. We had no idea."

Christine said, "Well believe it or not you're famous and you both look gorgeous tonight and I'm very happy for you."

Christine excused herself back to her date and Jolene said, "David can you believe it? Is this really why we're being stared at?"

I said, "I guess so. Either that or it's the new clothes we have on."

Jolene said, "I can't believe we're famous. Come on let's go and dance."

We showed our hand stamps and went back inside to the buzz of surf music. People looked at us while we walked and during the intermission the announcer called for a spotlight and had the operator shine it on us while he told the crowd our names. When he was finished the crowd gave us a good round of applause which had us amazed. The band came back on after their break and we began to dance to the music. We danced until the band stopped and we were on our way out of the building again when several young girls and boys came up and asked for our autographs. We laughed and signed what they wanted and then walked to the end of the pier to kiss and finish the bottle. We drank together and Jolene said, "I think what Christine said is true. This is very weird. We shouldn't be famous, we haven't done anything."

I said passing the bottle back, "I don't know what's going on but we're getting a whole lot of attention. Is it okay with you?"

Jolene said, "I guess it is. I'm just surprised that's all. Who would have suspected this would happen?"

I said, "All we did was run off together and then come back to run the shop and make boards."

Jolene said, "I know. It's kind of fun but it means we'll be watched constantly by everyone."

I said, "True but it might be good for business."

Jolene said, "That would be good."

I said, "And how many kids our age get to go home and make love after the band quits?"

Jolene laughed and said, "Not many. Now would you take me home and make love to me?"

I said, "Of course I will. Do you want to leave right now?"

Jolene kissed me on my cheek and said, "Yes, right now."

CHAPTER EIGHT

We left the pier and walked home to get to our bed and made love. We went to sleep holding each other and woke the next morning to a foggy coast and cool air. We were up in a few minutes and after bouncing into our shorts we went to the kitchen and I made coffee while Jolene made cinnamon rolls for us to eat while we drank from our cups. She was quiet this morning and I was pretty sure what was on her mind as we walked to the shop to get our boards and have fun on the water. We hit the water in the fog and paddled out to where the sound of the waves were coming from. We got to the outside together and Jolene said, "David I'm going to do something silly. I just have to know."

I didn't have a clue as to what she was up to but let her go without question. She paddled out near where three boys were sitting on their boards and waiting for bigger waves. I was right with her when she paddled up to the three of them and said, "Hey you guys, this may sound stupid but do you know who I am?"

The boys laughed and one of them said, "Of course we do. You're Jolene Boyer and he's David Parish. Why? Did you suddenly forget who you were?"

Jolene said, "No I didn't forget, but last night someone told me I was famous and I wanted to know if strangers to me knew who I was."

The boys laughed and one said, "Well you're only the best surfer in town and you and David build the best boards we're all saving for, yeah, I'd say you were famous. Will you give us a discount for knowing you when we come to your shop for our new boards? We're all dying to have one of your new short boards."

Jolene said, "Sure why not. It won't be much but when you're ready come in, we'll help you out."

The boys said their thanks and Jolene and I went to get into some waves. After a few apiece we were sitting on our boards together in the fog when Jolene said, "Well I guess it's true. Do you really believe they think I'm the best surfer in town?"

I said, "I know you're the best surfer in town. How come you don't know it?"

Jolene said, "I guess I never thought I could be. I grew up watching my brother and his friends and I always thought they were much better surfers than me."

I said, "That does it, you need to enter some more contests and when the trophies pile up maybe you'll believe it."

Jolene said, "Okay. I guess it's true. This is going to be hard to deal with."

With that she went and took off on another wave and I followed on the next one after her. We surfed until the sun began to come out and went to put our boards up at the shop. We had stashed them and were coming back out when two guys much older than us came up and said, "Are you open for business?"

Jolene said, "Sure why not? What can we help you with?"

The blond one said, "Surfboards. I'm Phil Edwards and this is Mickey Munoz. We've heard you two are making some very advanced boards and we want to see them."

I said, "Hi, I'm David Parish and I'm pleased to meet two of my surfing heroes."

Phil looked at me and said, "Well it's a pleasure to meet you. And we already know you're Jolene Boyer. You're a great surfer. We knew your brother a bit, how's he doing?"

Jolene said, "You two know who I am? That's amazing! I never thought you'd know me. You two are really famous. I've been looking at pictures of the two of you since I was little. Come on in and by the way Terry's just fine."

We went inside and showed the guys our new design they raved about the shape and the way they looked. Phil said, "How did you think of this?"

Jolene said, "Books. We read about hydrodynamics and this is what David made and came out of the shaping room."

Mickey said, "How do they perform?"

I said, "Like riding on a stick of lightning. They're very fast and extremely maneuverable."

"They'll really hang onto the steepest part of a wave." Jolene said excitedly. "We still can't believe how great they are."

Phil said, "Jolene if you say they're great, then we'll each buy one. Is cash okay?"

Jolene said, "Cash is fine and I still can't believe the two of you are in my shop."

Phil said, "We have some promotional pictures in the car, can we give you one or two? We'll autograph them for you."

I said, "Pictures would be great. It's wonderful you want to ride our boards."

Mickey said, "If they're as good as you say they are, we'll be back and let you do a custom board for each of us."

Jolene said, "Great. We're sure you'll be back."

Phil said, "Jolene, do you have any pictures? We'd love one of you."

Jolene said, "No I don't but maybe I should get some made."

Phil agreed and went off to his car and came back to the shop with the photographs in hand. They both autographed the photos and Jolene said, "Phil, we have a house in Hawaii. What's it like to ride the Pipeline?"

Phil said, "Scariest thing I've ever done. The first time made the hair stand up on the back of my neck. It's fantastic. Mickey's done it. Why? Do you want to be the first woman to surf the Pipeline?"

Jolene said, "Yes. I'd kind of like to be the first woman to surf it."

Mickey said, "Well if any woman can do it that would be you. I saw you win the Huntington contest and if you can ride your last wave you can definitely surf the Pipeline."

Jolene said, "You were there?"

Phil said, "We both were. You were fantastic. You really ripped on your last wave."

Jolene said, "Thank you very much. That's a great compliment coming from you two."

Phil said, "As you know we both live in the islands. Why don't you call us when you're back in the winter and we'll take you there and teach you how to get into the break, I'm sure you can handle it. We want to be there when the first woman rides it too."

The guys paid for their new boards and after getting their addresses and phone numbers in Hawaii we locked the shop and went home. It was still a crappy day for the beach so we stayed around the house all afternoon talking and watching TV. It was a good afternoon and Jolene still could not believe two of her oldest surfing heroes knew of her. She was finally getting the idea she might really be famous and we both thought our lives might change some.

The next morning we went for our morning surf stoke and Jolene was quiet as we walked to the pier. We got our boards and went to the water where we slid in and paddled out and to what was breaking for us that day. The waves were nice at three to four feet and moving fast. Without speaking we each caught a couple of waves and when Jolene had made a couple of rides she said, "David, am I as good a surfer as people say?"

I said, "Yes you're the best."

Jolene said, "Well if I'm that good, maybe I'd better enter the contest in two weeks at Windansea in La Jolla. I need to find some surfers for the shop team and that would be a good place to look for them."

I said, "I think that's a great idea. We're still in good shape and if we run for a week or two we'll be fine. Do you think I should enter too?"

Jolene said, "Most definitely. I think you're brilliant on the waves."

I said, "Well then it's settled. We'll call this afternoon and see if we can advance register for the contest. Either that or they'll mail us the forms."

Jolene said "Excellent," and put her attention back to the sets that were rolling in.

We surfed until it was time for work and went across to the shop and opened up. Our two employees were there and after we entered they headed for their jobs while Jolene and I did the front of the shop. When it was done I disappeared into the back to shape and Jolene manned the counter putting away new stocks of wax we'd gotten in. We had our sandwiches for lunch and Jolene sold two more boards after I'd gone back to work in the shaping room. I was pleased with the sales and smiled at her as we finished our day at the shop and went across the highway to surf before we went home for dinner. Mombo and Maw were there when we walked in and Mombo said, "Hello my darlings, are you hungry?"

Jolene said, "I'm starving, what should we make?"

Mombo said, "It's already done. Maw made her rice casserole this afternoon so all we have to do is make a salad and heat up the casserole."

I said, "Wonderful," and went to the refrigerator to get out the things I'd need to make the salad. Jolene got me a beer and we stood in the kitchen talking while the food heated up. I said, "Mombo how are things at the hospital?"

Mombo said, "They're fine except for the doctor who keeps hitting on me."

Jolene said, "Why don't you go out with him?"

Mombo said, "Because he's fat as a pig and I hate fat men."

"Enough said." Jolene chuckled, "I wouldn't go out with him either. I like men who are shaped like David."

I said, "Good thing for you. Would you have fallen in love with me if I was fat?"

Jolene said, "Never. How many fat surfers have you ever seen?"

I said, "I'll give you that, not too many."

Mombo laughed and said, "Work is fine. I like the hospital and the rest of the staff are very competent. It's good there and they pay me very well compared to my last job here. By the way, when are you two planning on going back to Hawaii?"

I said, "Probably not until October when the water starts to get cold. Why, are you trying to get rid of us and rent out our room?"

Mombo laughed and said, "No my darling I was just curious. I love having you and Jolene here with us. We don't see enough of you two because you get up so early but I love having you around in the evenings."

Jolene said, "Well I love being here and I'll miss you when we go back to the islands."

Mombo said, "Well I'll certainly miss the two of you."

Maw nodded her head and lit another cigarette. The casserole was hot so we served salad and rice and went about filling ourselves. When we were done Jolene kissed Maw for such a wonderful dish and the two of us went to the sink to do the dishes. When we were done Jolene said, "Let's go to my parents house and watch TV. I haven't seen them for a few days. Is that okay?"

I said, "Sure let's go."

We kissed my mother and Maw and walked up the street holding hands. Jolene said, "David, can we get a car?"

I said, "I don't see why not. I guess I just haven't gotten around to it yet. What kind would you like?"

Jolene said, "You pick it out and remember we need to carry the boards with us and advertise the shop."

I said, "Okay if that's what you want, I'll get us a car. It was convenient having the Jeep to run around in. I guess we need one here too."

By this time we were walking up to Jolene's door. She turned the knob and we went inside. Her parents were just finishing dinner and invited us to have desert with them. We declined the sweets and sat on the couch close to each other and watched the tube as a movie began to come on. We watched the film with her parents and I was falling asleep by the time it was over. Jolene pulled me up off of the couch by my arm and we said good night to Stan and Laura and walked back to my house and our bed. The next morning we were up before the sun and we went running to get in shape for the contest at Windansea. Our run was fine and we didn't breathe very hard after we finished our five miles. We got our boards and went surfing. The waves were not particularly good and we decided to open the shop early that morning. Jolene got on the phone and began to try and find a company to manufacture her leash idea and I went to the shaping room to check on stock and supplies. The week was typical of what we did each day and the following week Phil and Mickey came in raving about the boards they'd bought from us and placed an order for two custom made boards. I made notes from their suggestions and began to formulate what I thought would be great for them.

We visited for awhile with them and when they left we went back to work. The next day I was watching the classified ads for suitable transportation for Jolene and I and I found a '53 Chevy woody for sale and the ad said it was in excellent condition. I went to see it the next day and it was perfect. It had a small Chevy V8 in place of the original six-cylinder motor and a four-speed transmission. It was a bit of a hot rod and I liked the power it made under the hood. Its custom exhaust system made it sound great and the headers helped it produce more horsepower. I paid for the Chevy and took it straight to our sign painter to get the shop logo painted on the doors and the back. It was done the next day and I went and picked it up and drove it to the shop where I gave the keys to the Chevy to Jolene. She said, "What are these to?"

I said, "Your new ride. It's parked outside. Go and take it for a spin."

Jolene said, "David you're wonderful," and went outside to take a look. I stayed with the shop and she drove away from the shop past the windows. She was back in a half-hour and I said, "Jolene, will that do you?"

Jolene said, "It's just perfect. We'll use it this weekend when we go south to Windansea."

We both went back to work and stopped at five to go surfing.

Before we knew it, it was Friday and we were driving south to the contest. We had packed up forms for those who would be invited to be on our surfing team and Jolene made sure we had plenty of promotional T-shirts to give away. We checked into a motel when we got to La Jolla and went to sleep after we got hamburgers from a stand down the street. The contest was the next morning and we went to sleep early to be fresh for the competition the next day.

The next morning at Windansea was fantastic. The weather was just right and the waves were breaking on the outer ledge at about five to six feet and almost tubing. We registered and were given our numbers. There were photographers by the dozen and I thought this might be a good chance for Jolene to get a good picture for promotions like Phil and Mickey had. We spent the day riding perfect waves and we were both able to advance to the finals the next morning. During Jolene's heats I took the time to go around and tell the photographers I needed a good picture of her and they understood. Most of them said when the film was developed, if they had anything good, they would send it to us at the shop as long as we promised to use their byline. We made some acquaintances with some great young surfers that day and spoke to them about our surf team. Most thought it would be a good idea and we promised them if they did well in the contest we would talk further.

We went back to our hotel room tired and hungry. We changed our clothes and went to dinner at a good restaurant down the street. Its parking lot was full of cars with racks of surfboards on top and we knew we were in the right place. We went in and were immediately recognized by a lot of the people there. We had a nice dinner and when we had finished our meal two guys walked up and introduced themselves as being from Surf magazine. We invited them to sit with us and they joined us at our table. They had heard about our new boards and wanted to do an article about them and one about Jolene as well. We arranged to meet with them after the finals the next day and Jolene would be interviewed along with me. We went back to our hotel and went to sleep to rest for the next day and the meat of the contest.

Jolene was up first and was ready by the time I got out of the shower. I dressed quickly and we loaded the woody and headed for the beach. We were early and went out to ride some waves and warm up before the contest started. The break was better than the day before as the angle of the waves coming in was better and helped the wave shape. I considered it to be a perfect day and we went back to the beach at contest time to get our numbers and register for the day.

We spent the day waiting and winning our heats all day long. I placed second late in the afternoon in my division and was on the beach getting compliments as Jolene's final heat started. She was up against a woman from Hawaii and one from Australia and both were incredible surfers. Jolene would have her work cut out for her today I thought as I stood on the beach watching. I was distracted as her heat began by a pat on the shoulder and there were Phil and Mickey. We spoke for a minute and turned our attention to the water to watch. The three girls were very equally matched and the girl from Hawaii was riding one of our new boards Terry had built for her in Wakiki. The heat was going well but the points were very even up until the last waves of the day. Jolene took off on her last wave and dropped in from the crest. She made a beautiful bottom turn and pulled off a wicked cutback as she raced in front of the breaking wave. I knew she was going all out to win this contest when she did something I had never seen done before. She dropped back to the waves crest and dropping back down the wave she did another radical bottom turn and sped back up like she was going to kick out of the wave. She swung her body to kick out but instead of going over the shoulder of the wave she held onto what she was doing and swung her board three hundred and sixty degrees and dropped into the wave again. The crowd on the beach went wild as she recovered from the drop and disappeared into the tube. She was inside for about thirty seconds and then was blown out by the compression. It was the ride of the day and as she finished and kicked out, the crowd on the beach went crazy and I was smiling from ear to ear for my girl. Phil and Mickey we punching each other's shoulders and shaking mine they were so excited for her. The three of us headed for the shore where Jolene was coming out of the water and she had a look on her beautiful face which told me she knew she had done well. We walked her up the beach to the judge's stand and when the points were totaled she was the winner of the event. It was her 360 that made the difference and her opponents came and congratulated her. The trophies were given out and I thought ours would help the look of the shop as we now had several to display. When things quieted down some, Jolene and I went to find some of the surfers who were local and invited the ones she liked to be on our surfing team. They were pleased when they found they would all get custom boards and plenty of shirts and shorts from our shop. We had them sign contracts and told them we would have a meeting the following week about the up-coming Huntington contest. We went to find the guys from Surf magazine and they were looking for us at the same time. Jolene did her interview at the same time I was interviewed about our new boards. In another two hours we were finished and loading our things into our wagon. While we drove north on the coast highway, Jolene sat close to me and glowing from her day on the water. She said, "You did wonderfully today. This was the best finish you've ever had."

I said, "Thank you my love. You were just amazing out there yourself. What possessed you to do the 360 maneuver?"

"I have to tell you it was an accident," she said. "I went to kick out of the wave because I thought it would close on me. I was going so fast when I got to the top of the wave when I kicked my board around it just kept going. I was lucky to stay on and when I found I still had my balance I decided to drop in again. I was just lucky."

I said, "Luck or not it won the contest for you. Do you think you could do it again?"

Jolene said, "I think so. I suppose I could practice at home. It's all because these boards are so light I was able to do it at all."

I said, "Well you're a champion again and I love you tremendously. What do you want to do when we get home?"

"The same thing I did the last time I became a champion. I want to make love to you. You're my champion and I wouldn't be able to do any of this without you helping me."

The rest of the way back home we cuddled as we drove along the highway. When we got to the shop we unloaded our gear and the boards and after locking it all in the shop we drove home and went inside to make love.

We slept late the next morning and skipped surfing that day. We went to the shop and began to put things away where they belonged. It was about ten when the customers started coming in and there were lots of them. We sold six boards that Monday and it was a store record. I took orders for another four custom boards and it seemed like the crowds would never go away. There were lots of locals who came in just to congratulate us and it was nice to see our friends. The shop looked positively bare when the day was done and I asked Jolene to remind me to make extra boards for the Huntington contest. She promised she would as we crossed the highway to the waves we loved in the afternoons. Our friends on the water who hadn't come to the shop were all about congratulations and I was pleased Jolene was getting so much attention. She was smiling and saying thanks when some decent sets started to roll in and we stopped talking to ride some waves. The afternoon was good and we were tired when we got out of the water. We went to the shop and got our wagon and drove the short distance home for some badly needed rest. We lay down for a while and then got up to go and tell Jolene's parents about our weekend in La Jolla. They were thrilled Jolene had won another contest and we barbecued with them in the evening by the pool. We excused ourselves when it began to get late and went home to make love and sleep. We woke up the next day and after surfing and getting some new boards out of the back of the shop and onto the rack for sale, we went about our jobs until Jolene called me from the back to help with another onslaught of customers. There was another steady stream of them all day and I was happy to know Dale was working hard in the back making product for us. One of the photographers from the weekend who was local to us came in with a great shot of Jolene which would make a fine promotional photo and we bought it from him on the spot. He gave us the number for a place that made big 8 x 10's and we sent it to them the same day. Jolene wanted to order a hundred and was shocked when I got on the phone and ordered five hundred instead. I knew she would give them away when the article on her in Surf magazine came out the next month. I was right about the order because customers and the curious deluged us when the articles were published. The article on our boards made sales soar but I had anticipated this and we had made lots of boards for stock. It was a good thing because by the end of the first week we had sold everything off of the rack and Dale and I were staying late to get more products done. The volume fell off in a couple of weeks and we were happy to hear Terry was having the same kinds of sales we were. We were thrilled to hear Marcy was pregnant and Jolene was excited to know she was going to be an aunt. I could tell by her face she would want to do the same thing in a few years and I smiled at the thought of being a father when the time came.

We had our meeting with our new team and passed out all of the swag to them including enough for them to give to their surfer friends. They were excited about the idea of trying for wins in several of the divisions and we demanded they begin to exercise to get ready for the event. They took it pretty well and promised to be in great shape by contest time. The contest was a month away and we were prepared by the time it rolled around. We hit the beach the morning of the contest with our team and found there were two other shops that had teams as well. Both Hobie and G&S surfboards were there and we hoped we could dominate the event. Jolene won the women's division and I placed another second to one of the guys on our team. Two of our other team members won as well in their divisions and all in all it was a fantastic weekend for the shop and us. The next few days were very full for us as we were hit by dozens of customers at the shop. We had introduced the leashes Jolene had thought of and most were of the opinion they were a great idea. Our sales were way up as expected and Terry found the same thing in Wakiki. We happily surfed away the rest of summer.

As the summer came to it's end, we began to make plans to get back to our home in the islands in another month. We promoted Dale to head shaper and manager, which he was delighted with and hired a friend of his to shape for us under his supervision. The girl we had originally hired for the itch room had been long gone because of the nature of the work, and we had been through two others since. Dale got his younger brother to take the spot and we were comfortable with the condition of the shop when we left. School started again and we were glad we didn't have to go. We left a month later for the islands and the peace we loved there. Terry was very happy with our return and Marcy was happy Jolene would be there to help with her pregnancy. Jolene planned to learn all she could about having babies from Marcy and I knew it would be only a couple of years away for us. Our home behind the band shell in the village was perfect and Tom-Tom had made sure of it for us. Our neighbors were very glad to see us back and we were asked a hundred questions about our summer on the mainland. Jolene's parents had given her several tickets back and forth to the islands so she could fly and visit them and we were pleased she would not only see her parents but she could check on the shop monthly.

Being back in Hawaii was great, as we had really missed the place and all of our things there. We both went and registered at the local junior college and we liked the classes we took at night. Jolene had us both take a beginning engineering class to be able to design better surfboards and her brilliant mind kept the both of us passing. We took a history class as well and we enjoyed learning world history at night when we were in class or at home in the village. Terry was happy to have help with the shop again and we gave him time to go to another island for a get-away with Marcy. They went to Maui for a week and loved their time off together. We had our Jeep and it was serving us well. The four-wheel drive made it possible for us to drive on the sand and it was nice to pull practically up to the edge of the water and park. The first month we were there we hit all of the spots we had missed and when we were satisfied we went back to surfing the spots close at hand in Wakiki. We sold boards like crazy and Terry said it was all due to the articles written about the new boards and us. As Jolene and I learned engineering we were able to redesign the new boards and stay ahead of our competition. We made faster more maneuverable boards and they seemed to perform better and better as we developed their design in stages, which we had learned from school. We noticed that Wakiki was growing and there was a lot of construction going on there this year. Terry was well aware of what was happening and it seemed we had gotten in just before things had gotten too expensive. We had our little house and Terry was looking for a bigger place to hold his family which was on the way. He found a place two blocks from us in the village and we were delighted to help him fix the old place up before he moved into it. He kept the place a secret from Marcy until it was done and she loved it when she saw it for the first time. They moved in the first week of November and Jolene went back to California to see her parents and check on our shop while she was there. I missed her terribly when she was gone and she missed me as well. We celebrated her return by going out for a nice meal with Terry and Marcy when she came back and it was great to have my girl with me again. We surfed the next morning and had a wonderful time on the waves before going to work at the shop. There was to be a contest at the break in Ala Moana and Jolene said she'd like to enter. We went and signed us both up and we did well there. Jolene won the women's event and I had third place in my division. The Hawaiian's were tough to beat as always and we both had to work hard to get our trophies. The crowds came to the shop afterwards and Jolene spent a couple of days signing pictures for her fans while she sold surfboards. We loved the islands but still missed the action of Huntington Beach and the pier. Another two weeks and we had adjusted to being alone with each other at night. In the evenings we read and played games together when we weren't doing our home-work and going to school. Each day we would get up happy to be together and after a small breakfast we would head for the beach and our friends we saw each day on the water. They were great but they were surfers like us and usually went to bed early to get up before dawn and surf until they had to go and deal with their jobs which supported them the same as ours did. Jolene would usually be the first to wake in the morning and her comment each day would be, "Get up my love another day in paradise awaits."

With this I would open my eyes and kiss my girl good morning. We would get out of bed together and put on our shorts and head for the kitchen to make coffee. Jolene would turn on the radio and we would listen to the weather and hear the surf reports which were broadcast on the station we listened to. If they were promising we would get in the Jeep and drive to where the surfing seemed it might the best. The shop opened at ten and we would generally be back by then to get the day go-ing and clean before Terry got there. Life was pleasure and pleasure was life in the islands. We had Mango and Papaya trees on our piece of property and we would bring our homegrown fruit with us to work to munch on during breaks or offer to our customers who would come in from the beach. Wakiki was always crowded and the tourist business was fun for us. We met all sorts of people there and it made things interesting for us to speak with the different people who would come in during the day.

There was the big wave contest coming up at Sunset beach where the waves broke on a reef half a mile out. I asked Jolene if she wanted to enter and try the giant surf with the pros. She thought about it for a few days and decided to enter the contest. I built her a new board for the big waves and she went to Sunset a number of times before the day of the contest. Phil and Mickey were surprised to find her there one day practicing and they loved that she was going to enter. As far as they knew she would be one of two women in the contest and there was no specific women's division. She would be competing with the men for the first time and she was very nervous about it. She held her concentration for the time before the big waves and I hoped she would do well there. Phil and Mickey were great and gave her almost daily instruction on the giant waves. The three would go together and with their coaching she became proficient at handling the moving mountains. The day finally came and Jolene was ready. She was silent as we drove to Sunset Beach in the morning and I could tell she was nervous. Phil and Mickey were there and they welcomed us while we were parking the Jeep. This seemed to make her feel better and I watched as she began to loosen up. There were many people in the crowd of spectators who asked her for autographs before the event even started and she signed for all who came asking. The contest began and I watched through my binoculars. Sunset was breaking big that day with swells almost twenty-five feel tall crashing as they broke. Her first ride was good and I watched as she streaked down the face of the huge wave. It was impressive to watch any of the contestants and I was specifically watching my girl. She did great but finished out of the points in fifth place. She was beaten by Phil and Greg Knoll and two others I hadn't heard of as they were Australians and were not familiar to us. Mickey placed right behind Jolene and even having a bad day himself he was very happy for her. She rode into the beach and after getting through the treacherous shore break which was fifteen feet high she was pleased with what she'd accomplished. The other woman placed far behind her and a great bond formed between Jolene, Phil and Mickey. One of the photographers came to us later in the week with an outstanding shot of her riding one of the huge waves and we bought it from him to use as a new promotional photograph. She was pictured in the pages of Surf magazine on one of her rides and it was great for us. We began to get calls for big wave boards and the extra business was good. Christmas was coming and we decided to go to Huntington Beach for the holidays. Terry would hold things down for us and we flew away from Hawaii three days before Christmas after we both celebrated our seventeenth birthdays. Our families were happy to see us and our shop there was doing well. Dale was keeping the place in great shape and was turning out boards at an incredible rate. We were pleased things were going so well and we had a wonderful time seeing all of our friends there. Jolene was quite the celebrity by now but one would never know it to talk to her. She rarely offered information to others but was happy to answer questions from anyone who asked about her career. Mombo and Maw were doing fine and we moved into their home for our stay during Christmas. We were seventeen years old and had grown up considerably by then. Jolene looked more like a model than a surfer and her face looked great with a little age on it. We had been together since we were fourteen and it was difficult to believe we had been together for almost three years. Jolene's parents were great to us and we were never treated like we were our age by them. They regarded us as adults and we loved being around them. Our Christmas was wonderful and we mostly stuck to clothes for presents to each other. We went back to Hawaii before the New Year and spent it with Terry, Marcy, Phil and Mickey and their families. It was a great night and the party at Phil's house was fantastic. There were a number of other surfers and promotional people there and it was great fun to meet more of our heroes. Jolene was a hit that evening and the number of guests who came up to meet her was wonderful. We left at one o'clock with champagne in our hair and Jolene was finally getting the idea she was indeed someone very special. We were driving home when she said, "David, I'm finally beginning to really feel like I'm famous. All of those fantastic surfers knew who I was and it was really great. All of the years you told me I was special I never really believed you. I do now and I want to thank you for always telling me what I was."

I said, "I was just telling you what you couldn't see yourself. You're doing great and I'm very proud of you. You have been fantastic throughout it all and I don't think many people could have done what you've accomplished. I have thought you were fantastic ever since I first saw you on the water in Huntington Beach in the summer of '63. The first time I saw you on a wave is something I'll never forget ever. It was the day I first surfed and those two things seriously changed my life."

Jolene said, "I don't think I've ever thanked you for being there for me always. You have constantly been there for me and I love you for it. Thank you so very much I love you dearly and I really wouldn't know what to do without you in my life."

We drove home holding hands and fell happily into bed after washing the champagne out of our hair and having something to eat.

We woke up late the next day and went to the shop for the tourist business which was always happening on Wakiki. We both just watched the shop together and in the afternoon Jolene said, "Are we going to spend the rest of our lives doing this?"

I said, "I don't know? Is there anything else you want to do?"

She said, "I don't know. Other than eventually getting married and having children, I would like to travel more and see the world like in the film The Endless Summer. I think I'm missing the excitement we had when we were younger."

I said, "I miss it sometimes too but I don't know how to go about getting some of it back. Huntington Beach is nice during the summer but here in Hawaii life is pretty slow. Maybe if we think about it together we can come up with something."

Jolene agreed and we began to think on the subject. A week later the question was answered for us when a man walked into the shop and introduced himself as Bruce Brown who was the maker of our favorite surf films. They were always brilliantly edited and his commentary was completely hysterical to the audience. Jolene and I were invited to be in his next film and he wanted Jolene to be a major part of it. It was to be mostly about women in surfing and there were to be six of what he called the best in the world. The film which was not to exclude men was to take place all over the Pacific and we were thrilled by the news. We were going to travel and get paid for it. The film was to begin shooting in February and it was going to start in Hawaii. The filming would take us from Hawaii to the mainland next. Then it would go to Australia and some of the Indonesian Islands that had good surf and then on to Japan and back to Hawaii. It would be two whole months of traveling. The money wasn't great but all of our expenses were to be paid and our boards were guaranteed to be featured in the film. We said yes immediately and were very excited after Bruce left the shop. We told Terry in the afternoon and he was very excited for us. He was proud of his younger sister and his pride showed on his smiling face.

CHAPTER NINE

Marcy was due to have her baby in a few weeks and Jolene definitely wanted to be a part of it. The day came and Marcy called Terry at the shop from their house saying she was taking a cab to the hospital in Wakiki and Terry should meet her there. He and Jolene left the shop quickly and I was told to call Marcy's parents and Jolene's and tell them what was happening. I did as I was instructed and they said they would be on the next plane flights to Oahu. I closed the shop early and went to the hospital and caught up with the two of them. I got there just when Terry was headed for the delivery room dressed in hospital scrubs to be with his lovely wife for the delivery. Jolene and I waited about an hour and a half until Terry came out of the delivery room to tell us that Marcy had a beautiful girl and her name was Teresa for her grandfather. Marcy was in the recovery room asleep and Terry had been told she would be out all night. We left the hospital and went home to celebrate Teresa's birth. We got Terry stinking drunk and he was so proud all he could talk about was his new daughter. Jolene promised him she would take the responsibility of teaching Teresa the ways of the beach and the waves when she could get Terry to stop talking for a minute. Terry passed out soon enough and

Jolene and I walked back to our house hoping to get to see and hold Teresa the next day. It happened the next morning at about ten and it was a wonderful sight. Teresa was beautiful and very alert for such a young baby. When it came to Jolene's turn to hold her niece the look on her face was wonderful. She looked perfectly natural holding the little girl and I could tell by the look on her face we would be doing the same thing sooner than either of us thought.

The film was to start shooting soon and we were excited to leave on a wonderful adventure. We were talking about the film one morning surfing, when a familiar car pulled up in front of the shop and Phil and Mickey got out and came inside. We both said hello and then Phil said, "The Pipeline is breaking want to go?"

We stopped what we were doing and grabbing the boards they suggested we bring, we loaded the Jeep and followed them to the Banzai Pipeline. There were dozens of people on the beach and lots of photographers. The Pipeline always attracted spectators even in the days before Phil rode it. The four of us paddled out and Phil began to coach us when we got out past the break. He was very careful to describe in detail what we should and should not do to get into the treacherous waves. Jolene was the first to take off in the huge surf and had a very successful ride and became the first woman to ride the famous walls of water. I went next and dropped in down the almost vertical face of the wave. I made the drop and turned my board to be in the tube. I was taken by surprise and wiped out going over the falls and hitting the water hard. I brushed the razor sharp coral while I was under but was lucky and was only scratched by the dangerous bottom. When I recovered my board I paddled back out and Jolene was waiting for me on the outside. She was very concerned for me and looked at the scratches on my shoulder. I said it was nothing and with my assurance that I was okay, she went with Phil to get another wave. She took off on the biggest wave of the next set and made the drop fine. I saw her from the side and she was standing tall in the huge tube that made her look small in comparison. She was having the ride of her life and I hoped one of the photographers on the beach was getting good shots of her with a telephoto lens. I paddled back to the take off spot and Phil picked a good wave for me. I paddled as hard as I could and got into the wave. I was careful not to make the same mistake twice and played the wave well. The next thing I knew I was completely locked in and the wave was breaking ten feet over my head while I was almost standing straight up. It was the most exciting thing I'd ever done and by the end of my ride I was seriously stoked. I paddled back to the outside and Jolene was there to meet me. She said, "David isn't this just the best! I can't believe how exciting this is. You were fantastic. Are you ready for another?"

I said I was and we both paddled out to the take off. I went first this time and dropped in on another huge wave. I made the drop and had a replay of the wave I'd taken before. This ride was more fantastic than the first and I had another great experience. Jolene followed on the next wave and from my vantage point I watched as she had another great ride. When we got back outside Phil said, "Well how do you like being Pipeline surfers? Jolene how does it feel to be the first woman ever to surf the Pipeline? I'm very proud of both of you."

I said, "It's fantastic! I can't thank you enough for your help."

Jolene said, "Phil, I'm forever in your debt. I've always dreamed of surfing here and now I've done it thanks to you. Thank you so much for everything. You're the best!"

Phil said, "No problem. It's a pleasure to be here with you two. Jolene this is where it really gets dangerous."

Jolene said, "How's that?"

Phil laughed and said, "Because now you have to go and talk to the reporters who are on the beach. It's going to be like a shark attack. I only hope someone got some great pictures of you."

We all laughed and when we calmed down we took one more ride and surfed in to the beach. Just like Phil said Jolene was surrounded by reporters and had to talk for hours to them. She was having quite a time with all of the questions and was very patient with them. It was over after awhile and when they left her alone we walked to the Jeep with our boards. We were both exhausted by the day and Jolene stayed quiet for the ride home to Wakiki.

The day before was as thrilling as one could expect from life and Jolene and I had both accomplished goals we had had for several years. It was major for both of us and especially for Jolene. She had a calm about her the morning after we rode the Pipeline as if she had finally achieved a satisfaction she had been striving for. We surfed that morning as always and went to open the shop at ten. We had a beautiful silent morning and our thoughts were with the extreme waves we rode and left the day before. It was noon when a crew from the local television station came into the shop and asked if Jolene was the woman they'd heard about who had ridden the Pipeline the day before. She answered she was and they asked to be able to set up and do an interview with her at the shop. Jolene agreed on the condition the background be the surfboards in the shop. The producer agreed and the crew went about setting up for the filming. Jolene went and brushed her hair and came out wearing a clean new T-shirt with the surfing team logo on the front so all who watched could see it. They started the interview and Jolene was right with all of the questions put to her. When she was asked how she felt when she was riding the waves at the Pipeline, she responded by saying, "It was fantastic, how would you have felt out there?"

The interviewer was surprised by this and then asked what she liked about being the first woman to ride the waves there. She answered, "I liked being an example to all of the women out there and the little girls who have great dreams. You should never give up your dreams no matter how many people tell you they're impossible to accomplish."

When the interviewer asked her what she expected from her conquering the waves at the Pipeline Jolene said, "I expect all of the girls to get up and get off of the beach and go surfing. It's there and it's really fun. I've always wanted more women and girls to get off of the beach and have fun."

There were a dozen questions about where she was from and how old she was. Jolene handled it all perfectly. When the interview was over, the crew packed up their gear and left the shop. Before they finished loading their remote truck the local newspaper was there and Jolene told them the same thing she had told the television people. It was that way all day long and we went to Terry's house that night to watch Jolene on the news. Jolene held Teresa through the whole newscast giving her back to her mother only when it became obvious Teresa needed to be fed. Jolene looked great on TV and Terry loved the way she handled the interview. In addition to her interview there was film of one of her rides at the Pipeline and the footage was fantastic. Jolene came off as very intelligent and wonderfully casual to us and we wondered what the exposure would bring her. We found out the next morning when we went surfing and there were people waiting for us when we got out of the water to go to work. There were lots of women who had seen her on TV the night before and they continued to arrive through the day at the shop. We sold a dozen boards during day to young women and Jolene was great about encouraging them to go out and go for it on the waves. The crowds went on for longer than we expected and the business was great for the shop. Jolene was pleased she was the catalyst for more women surfing and she was asked to speak to several women's groups on the islands. She did this willingly and was pleased by the chance to go and inspire others. I was as proud as could be when she returned from one of her lectures and came home with the latest issue of Surf magazine. There she was on the cover of the magazine locked into the tube at The Pipeline showing perfect form and a beautiful example of how it's done. When the magazine hit the stands the phone at the shop didn't stop ringing and Jolene had to deal with most of it by herself because Terry and I were really busy making boards for the young women Jolene had inspired. She was invited to lecture all over the place and especially in the states by almost every woman's group who had heard of her. She put them all off until she was done with Bruce's film, which was to begin shooting in a week. We were pleased when the filming began and Jolene could get away from the phone. We shot film all over the islands and there were some fantastic days at the break wall on the island of Maui. Jolene was absolutely spectacular there and the printed film really showed her abilities on mid-sized waves. We filmed at Sunset beach on a huge day and back at the Pipeline when it was breaking good on another day. Jolene was the only woman who would go out at the Pipeline and she got all of the footage shot on one fine morning when the pipe was doing its favorite double overhead trick. We finished with Hawaii and went to California where they filmed on a big day at Steamers Lane in Santa Cruz and another great day south of Carmel. We went from there to Rincon Point and then down to San Pedro and up to Palos Verdes, Long Beach and Lunada bay. Huntington Beach was next and it was good to be home for two days. Jolene loved being at our favorite spot and they got fantastic footage of her riding the pier and surfing through the pilings on a big day. Jolene made it all look effortless and it showed on the film. We went further south to Salt Creek and the crew got permission for us to ride what some considered the best break on the whole coast, The Trestles which was on the marine base at Camp Pendleton in Oceanside. We ran the beaches all the way to San Diego and stopped at Katy M's, Mile Zero, Doheney State Park, Dana Point and Windansea before we went to Mexico and went to Ensenada, 100 K and

The Blow Hole. Then it was back to L.A. for long flights to Australia where we spent a solid week surfing near the Great White sharks which plagued the coastline there. A week in Indonesia and it was on to Japan and the waves there. When we finally returned to Hawaii we were exhausted but pleased with all of the stamps in our passports. It had been an incredible two months and Bruce had been a total gem to us both. He promised that Jolene would be the star of the film and we waited for all of the film to be edited and the first screening to take place. A month went by and we went to the screening at a small neighborhood theater Bruce rented for the big night. The film and the footage were spectacular and Jolene really got to see her abilities in her face for the first time. We were both impressed with what Bruce had accomplished. Along with the fantastic surfing footage and Bruce's, wit there were parts of his narration so funny we wept with laughter until we couldn't see the screen. When it was over there was champagne and Bruce toasted the cast and the audience present broke into applause for the girls in the film. Jolene was flattered by the applause and hung tight to my arm as we left the theater. We drove home where we went to bed and Jolene still held me very tight all night long. When we got up in the morning I asked why she was feeling like being so close and clingy she said, "Last night was really emotional for me. I had an hour and a half of watching myself on film and to tell you the truth I didn't know I was so good. I've never watched myself and I looked like all of my heroes up there on the screen."

I said, "So what's wrong with that?"

Jolene said, "I've just realized I've grown up. My childhood and all of the difficulty of being a teenager is behind me. I feel calm and good and confident and I'm not afraid of anything anymore. It's a difficult feeling to describe but it's going to take some getting used to."

We finally got to the shop and while Terry and I worked, Jolene set about contacting some of the women's groups who had invited her to speak. Most were on the mainland and we knew in two weeks we would be leaving for home and the pier we knew so well. Terry took us to the airport and we boarded our flight to L.A. We were met by Mombo who was very happy we were home. She drove us to Huntington Beach and we loved moving back into our room there. We relaxed for a while, and then taking our favorite boards with us, we went to the pier for an afternoon at our favorite surf spot. Most of our friends were there and we heard from them the film we did was to show at the local theater the coming weekend. Jolene decided to go and we wanted to take our parents with us. Jolene's parents hadn't seen her surf since the first contest at Huntington and she was anxious for them to see what she had become. We went Friday night and the place was full as could be. We had spoken to the owner of the theater and he reserved seats in the audience for our families and us. It was a great night and the crowd loved their local girl being there to see the film with them. Jolene got a big round of applause when the film was over as Bruce brought her up to the stage and introduced her to everyone. She spent the next hour signing autographs and after we went to her house to visit with her parents and mine. Her mother was very impressed with her and so was her father. They couldn't stop talking about how great she was on the waves, as they really had little idea of her abilities. They were beginning to completely understand who their daughter was and were very proud. Jolene and I went about our daily routine of surfing and working except for her schedule of lectures for the women's groups she had arranged before we left Hawaii. Her talks went well and she was usually quoted in the newspaper the next day. I was always pleased when she would come home and we would be together again as many of the dates were out of town. I loved my girl and missed her when she was gone. The speaking engagements were done soon enough and we got to settle in at home. We got to go to the dances at the Pavilon and we drove to our favorite spots to surf when we wanted. We had become very financially secure and Jolene was good with investing our money and making it grow for us. Our businesses were doing very well and at times we thought of retiring but thought we'd be bored in a month if we didn't have the shop to keep us busy. It was always a great place to see all of our friends and it was very much like home to us. Jolene decided to turn pro that summer and I went pro along with her. It would keep us out of all but a few contests and Jolene was all about giving others a chance at the trophies. We went to all of the contests with the team but we coached and stayed on the beach for the interviews and promoting our surfboards. It was actually more fun for us and I could tell Jolene loved the notoriety she had. She always included me in everything and I was pleased to be a part of her success.

Jolene's talks or lectures to the women's clubs were during an interesting period in America. We were both seventeen years old and the year was 1966. There was a war in Vietnam, the feminist movement, poverty, free speech issues, free love, the pill and the strife for civil rights. Lyndon Johnson was our president and it didn't matter much because Jolene and I were too young to vote. We had hidden in our surfing basically ignoring what was going on in the world until Jolene decided to talk to the groups inviting her to speak. She was asked a number of questions regarding the afore mentioned topics, and she really had no comments to the questions put to her about these subjects. That was fine for small groups, but Jolene was conscientious about what she was doing so she read about what was going on and was horrified to find the condition of things had really gotten out of hand. We were fourteen when John Kennedy was killed and although we mourned his death and thought it to be a terrible thing, we had stayed in the surfing world where we only had to look towards the next wave. We never read the newspaper and TV for the most part was uninteresting to us with the exception of movies we liked to watch. Jolene was awakened by the groups she spoke to and began to take an interest in the world in general. I did as well and the two of us began to become politically aware at the age of seventeen. A month after she had finished with her talks she got a call from a feminist magazine who wanted to do an article and interview with her. She agreed to the interview and had them come to Huntington Beach. The interview took hours and Jolene put up with all of their questions that afternoon. I was working in the back with Dale but would occasionally come to the front of the place to see how things were going or to see if Jolene wished something to drink. The interviewer didn't seem to like my presence there so for the most part I made myself scarce in the back of the shop. Jolene was asked a thousand questions and some were difficult for her to deal with. The interviewer couldn't believe she had never finished high school and she only had very limited college experience. She did say what she knew of the Vietnam War, that it was completely stupid, but all wars are stupid and she said so. She was correct about civil rights and some of the other pertinent questions but when it came to feminism the interviewer troubled her. The interviewer was perplexed by Jolene's comment she never could have been the person she was without me in her life for support. This wasn't at all what she wanted to hear and the questions went deeper. Jolene was adamant there was nothing wrong with men and insisted she most likely would have made all of her accomplishments without them in her life and she questioned the interviewer as to why some women felt It was necessary for women to have license to be themselves. Jolene had notoriety from competing with men as the interviewer said but Jolene insisted it was healthy and couldn't imagine not having goals to accomplish without high standards to rise to no matter who set them. Jolene then reminded the interviewer she was part owner of two successful businesses and she had done this simply because it needed to be done. The interview was finally done and when it was time to close and go surfing, we took our boards across the street and went surfing before we went home to eat.

When we were at home I asked, "So my darling, how did you like your interview?"

Jolene said, "Not too much. I don't mind helping to inspire other people, but the interviewer really wanted me just to inspire women. I don't mind inspiring women, as you know because I've tried to get them off of the beach for years. I'd like to inspire everyone to go out there and do something."

I said, "Well I guess you're different. You have always just done what you thought you needed to do in life."

Jolene said, "Sure why not? You do the same thing. There are a lot of people out there who just go and do what they wish without worrying about getting permission. I felt like the interviewer wanted me to give out permission for other women to be like me."

I said, "Well some might need it. I guess you never did. You're a strong personality and I personally love you for it. Some men have problems with women being better at things than they are, that's why there are still women's divisions in the contests we used to enter."

Jolene agreed and we left my room to join Maw and Mombo in the kitchen where they were making dinner.

Two days later we were asked to be judges for the Huntington contest and we accepted the jobs. Jolene was to be part of the invitation committee as well and she was pleased to be a part of inviting good surfers. She went far out of her way to find and invite dozens of people she thought were great surfers but had never been in any contest or invited to the event which was in our town every year. I thought she really put out extra effort and the day of the contest it really showed. Jolene had invited large numbers of women to the contest and their division really was a battle. Everyone loved the intense competition and it made both of us feel great. It was a fabulous weekend with great surfing for us to judge. Everyone was happy with the turnout and our team did well in the standings. It was somewhat difficult for us to be impartial when it came to judging time, but we did our best and no one complained about any favoritism what so ever. A week after the contest when our business had died down a bit, Jolene's magazine article hit the stands. Right away she got invited to be part of a speaking tour which would take her away for a month. She was torn between staying with me or going to do what she considered important. I urged her to go and she ultimately decided to leave with the group. I was proud of her decision but knew I would miss her terribly. She left a week later and I was left to my own devises for the first time in years. I decided to get back to my roots some and scoured the newspaper for a hot rod to buy. I found a '32 Ford roadster with a Chevrolet motor which was being sold in a half-finished state because of financial problems its owner was having. Mombo took me to where it was parked and after seeing the car and haggling some over the price I bought it and drove it home. I spent the next month putting it right and buying chrome and fuel injection and making it into a vision of street rod beauty. It was incredibly fast and very fun to drive. Mombo loved her turn behind the wheel and Maw really liked it as she had one of the same year model when she was much younger. It was a great way to spend the evenings without Jolene and it was perfect when she returned. It was painted a very deep red with white leather interior and everything on the motor that could be chrome plated was chrome. It had lightweight wire wheels in front and racing slicks in the rear on the aluminum wheels. When Jolene was done with her tour I picked her up at the airport in Mombo's car because I had left the roadster as a surprise present for her. I had decided it was to be her car because I thought she would love it and also look great driving it around. Jolene was so happy to see me at the airport she jumped into my arms and I practically had to carry her to the baggage claim. We kissed the whole time we were waiting for her bags. After they were retrieved, I took her to the car where she was all over me. We drove home where I was dragged into the bedroom and Jolene showed me how much I had been missed. This went on all night with her telling me repeatedly she was never ever going away again. We didn't even get up to go surfing the next day and I was lucky to get her to let me out of our bed by noon. I got up and made her brunch and she was very glad to be home. After we had eaten she decided she wanted to go to the shop and after she dressed and was ready to go, I tossed her the keys to the roadster and said, "I bought you a car while you were away and I think you'll like it. Why don't you drive and we'll take it to the shop?"

Jolene looked at me oddly and said, "What happened to the woody?"

"Nothing," I replied, "it's in the garage. Let's go and get your new ride."

I went and opened the garage with Jolene and she went completely off when she saw what I'd made for her. She said, "David it's beautiful. You built this for me to drive? I absolutely love it. It's just fantastic. Why did you do this?"

I said, "Well I missed you and I had nothing to do at night so I built this roadster for you. It was a way of feeling close to you while you were away from me."

We went to the car and climbed in over the sides, as there were no doors. Jolene sat on the white leather and said, "It's just fantastic! I can't believe you made this for me."

I said, "Do your feet reach the pedals okay. It was a major concern to me you could drive it effortlessly."

Jolene checked and said, "Yes it's perfect. Show me how to start it."

I said, "It's a four speed just like the woody, but I want you to be careful. It's really powerful. All you have to do to smoke the slicks is step on the gas hard. It's a real rocket. I think it will do the quarter mile in about ten and a half seconds and well over a hundred miles an hour."

Jolene said, "That fast! This is going to be fun."

She started it up by turning the key and the motor roared into life growling as it settled into an idle with the engine loping from the extreme camshaft I'd installed. Jolene got a big smile on her face as she put the roadster into reverse and backed down the driveway and onto the street. She put it into gear and started away from the house chirping rubber as she shifted into second. The acceleration pushed her back into her seat and she smiled as it happened. She stopped at the stop sign at the coast highway and when the traffic allowed she turned south. She went straight through Huntington Beach and didn't stop at the shop. I said, "Honey, what about the shop?"

Jolene said, "What about the shop? This is almost as good as riding waves and I'm going for a drive."

She was smiling the whole way during the two-hour drive. We went all of the way to Laguna Beach and then back. She loved the way people looked at us and the custom roadster and I had to admit she looked fantastic in the beast. When we got back to Huntington Beach she parked in front of the shop and when she cut the motor she turned to me and said, "David thank you. Next to my engagement ring, this is the most fantastic present I could ever imagine. You must have missed me terribly and I'm sorry but I promise I'll never go anywhere without you again."

Jolene turned and kissed me before we got out of the roadster and went into the shop. The help there were interested and they went out to inspect our new ride while we went inside and started to get some work done around the place. Jolene loved her car and made several excuses in the afternoon which required the running of errands and I loved watching her drive away in the roadster. We closed the shop and went surfing in the afternoon as usual and had a wonderful time on the waves. Jolene was missed while she was gone and the locals came up to us on the outside and welcomed her home one by one. It was a great afternoon and she loved being back. We went to her parent's house for dinner and Jolene insisted driving the four blocks there in the roadster. She wanted to show it off and took both her mom and dad for rides in it while I stayed and paid attention to cooking dinner. We had a wonderful time with her folks and they were as glad she was back as I was. We stayed late after dinner and then drove home where she wiped the entire car clean before coming in and to bed. When we were finally together she said, "Thank you again. I love my present."

I said, "Not at all it was a pleasure to do it for you."

She said, "David, when are we going back to Hawaii?"

I said, "Whenever you want. It's the last week in August now and school will be starting in a few weeks. As you know business will fall off and we won't be needed here."

She said, "I'm missing Terry, Marcy and my niece. I want to go and be with them and surf the north shore. I'm done with interviews and all of that stuff forever. They can have the politics. I'm a surfer and that's all I ever want to be."

I said, "Well that's all I ever wanted you to be. We'll go a couple of weeks after school starts if that's soon enough for you."

She said it was and we began to make love.

A week later I came back into the shop after running an errand in the roadster and when I saw Jolene behind the counter I said, "Jolene my darling, how would you like to see how fast the roadster is?"

She said, "I'd love to but what about the police?"

I said, "Tonight is Wednesday and they have time trials and grudge races at Orange County International Raceway in Irvine. Would you like to go and run the roadster?"

Jolene said, "I'd love to. How do we do it?"

I said, "All we have to do is drive there and pay our money. You just need a helmet."

Jolene said, "But I don't have a helmet."

I pulled one I'd just bought from a box and handing it to Jolene said, "You do now. Do you think you can handle things?"

Jolene put the helmet on and said, "Oh I think yes. You'd better tell me all about it on the drive down there. I don't know much about this."

We finished the afternoon and Jolene was getting excited about running the roadster at the drag strip. I gave her all of the information I thought she'd need on the way there. When we got there we registered the roadster and it was weighed and we were given a class, which was 'B' altered and a number was painted on the side of the car with white shoe polish. We readied the car in the pits and when all was right and the exhaust headers were opened I strapped Jolene into the car and with a few last minute instructions she fired it up and pulled it into the staging lanes leading to the starting line. Jolene waited her turn creeping to the starting line and when it was her turn I got in front of her and directed her to the staging lights. When she was properly staged, the linesman started the descending lights of the Christmas tree and when the final light turned green, Jolene stood on the throttle hard and dumped the clutch. The slicks immediately started to smoke and the front wheels came up a few inches off of the asphalt. The car started to get sideways and Jolene corrected by turning into the slide. She never took her foot out of the throttle and when the engine's revs got high she shifted hard for second gear. She made the shift perfectly and the front wheels came up again. She stayed in control and I heard her get third and fourth gear. She broke the lights at the finish and the timing clock told that she had run the quarter mile distance in 11.03 seconds and 124 miles per hour. I waited for her to drive back to the pits where we would prep the roadster for another run. Jolene was grinning ear to ear when she pulled into our pit and said, "That was great! I want to try it again! How fast did I go?"

I said, "11.03 seconds and 124 miles per hour. Was it fast enough for you?"

She said, "Hell yes! That was really exciting. I think I can go faster though. I think I was slow off of the starting line. I'm sure I can do better."

We let the roadster cool down and went about the preparations for her next run. While we were working several people came by our pit and complimented us on the roadster and Jolene's run. When the car was right we went to the staging lanes and she lined up again. Jolene got a better start this time and her time was 10.81 seconds and 128 MPH. Damn good I thought for a small block Chevy roadster. When Jolene got back to the pits she was smiling big and was pleased to have gone faster. We prepped the roadster again and changed the spark plugs. Jolene insisted I should have the next run and I put on the helmet and with a good start along with some serious power shifting I broke into the mid tens at 10.58 seconds and 131 MPH. When I drove back to our pit Jolene was bouncing up and down and clapping her hands. I was pleased with my time and Jolene made me tell her about full power shifting. I told her how it was done and when her next run came she made the quarter mile in the same time as I did. 10.58 and 131 MPH. We called it quits after her run as the slicks were just about toast. This was normal as the tires weren't new to begin with and the slicks had been burning each run that we made. We drove home while we still had rear rubber to run on and were back in Huntington Beach before one a.m.

Jolene parked the roadster and after she wiped it clean, we went inside and went to bed. We were under the covers holding each other and Jolene said, "Thank you for a very exciting evening. I can't remember when I've had more fun and excitement."

The next several weeks went quickly and soon enough we boarded a jet for the islands. Jolene's only regret was her roadster would have to stay behind in Huntington Beach. I was sorry to leave it too. Terry and Marcy picked us up at the airport in Oahu and drove us to our home in the village. Jolene was surprised at how much Teresa had grown and was somewhat sad she'd missed part of her niece's life. We went back to Wakiki and loved being there as Jolene's summer had been too much of life in the fast lane and she said it was great to get back to a slower pace. I agreed and we settled into the routine we had been doing for years now. It was comfortable and slow and it was great to be home again. We surfed and worked our way to November when we turned eighteen. This was important to us because it brought us closer to adulthood. It was also important to the United States Government, as I had to register for the draft. I hoped I wouldn't be called up, but with the Viet Nam war going on, there was little chance of not being called. Jolene was not happy at all with my registering for conscription and gave me her input before I went to my local draft board to sign my name and take my chances. Terry had registered years before but had been called and had evaded conscription with his naturally flat feet. They were fine for surfing but the army considered him 4-F and unfit for service. We celebrated our eighteenth birthdays at our house with a few close friends and Terry and Marcy and Teresa. Jolene loved Teresa and was always happy to baby-sit or take her niece to the beach. I loved seeing them together and one night after our birthdays, when we were lying together after making love, I said, "Jolene my love, I have something important to ask you."

Jolene opened one eye and looking at me said, "What's that?"

I said, "Jolene, will you marry me?"

Jolene said, "Is this for real?"

I said, "Yes it is."

Tears came to her eyes and she said, "Yes David I'll marry you. Marrying you is all I've ever wanted to do."

We kissed and when her tears slowed she said, "When do you want to get married?"

I said, "I was thinking about Christmas when there's time to have our parents come over to the wedding."

Jolene said. "Where should we get married?"

I said, "I think you should decide, but I'd like to be married on the beach somewhere."

Jolene said, "Yes I definitely want to be married on the beach. What would you think if we were married in the little palm grove there by the shop in Wakiki?"

I said, "If that's what you want then that's what we'll do. I think it would be the perfect place and we can see the ocean while we're being married."

"David, do you care what kind of a ceremony it is?"

I said, "No I'll leave that up to you."

She said, "I want to wear a simple white dress and you to wear a white linen suit without a tie and I want it to be a civil ceremony and I want us both to be barefoot."

Smiling I said, "Barefoot is good for me. You know how we both hate wearing shoes."

Jolene said, "Is it okay if we get married on Christmas day? It will be the anniversary of our engagement."

I said, "If that's what you want we'll do it. I guess we'll have to call and tell everybody the date and let them make plane reservations."

She looked at me and said, "David, have I told you lately how much I'm in love with you?"

I said, "Only every time you look at me. I love you the same way."

Jolene said, "Where should we go for a honeymoon?"

"I don't care as long as it's with you."

Jolene said, "I don't either. I'll think of something wonderful. I'm so lucky, I have the best man in the world. I'm absolutely sure of it."

CHAPTER TEN

The next day we woke up and Jolene was very excited about getting married. She called Terry and Marcy right away and they were excited for us as well. We went to ride the waves and to the shop and when we got inside Jolene called her parents and told them the news and that they should make reservations for Christmas. I called home and told Mombo and Maw and it seemed they were more excited about coming to Hawaii than our wedding. I didn't care and called my father next. He had been out of the loop for a long time and thought I was too young, but I knew he would understand when he got to Wakiki and saw what our lives were like. I called my sister who I hadn't seen in a couple of years and she was happy for us and said she'd be there too. I made arrangements for Mombo and Maw to stay at a friend's house which was vacant near us in the village and all of the others would have to get hotel rooms. Jolene shopped with Marcy until she said she found the perfect dress and I spent a lot of time trying to find a suit that would compliment what Jolene would wear. That month passed quickly and all-too soon our families were arriving on the island. It was fun to have them there and

Mombo and Maw loved the place we'd borrowed for them. My sister shared with my dad at the Surfrider hotel and Jolene's parents and oldest brother stayed at the Royal Hawaiian. My mother and father hadn't spoken for years but managed to get along for the time they had to be near each other that December. There were lots of preparations to be made and it was an effort to get everything done on time. We spent Christmas morning at Terry's house opening presents until it came time to go and dress for the ceremony. Jolene and I dressed separately and I didn't see her until she came to the palm grove with her father where everyone had assembled for our wedding. There were about three dozen of our friends from the islands as well as family, and I was waiting with Terry whom I'd asked to be my best man. When I saw Jolene she was a picture of island beauty and I thought my heart would stop from the way she looked. She was more beautiful than I'd ever seen her and I loved how this gorgeous woman was going to be my wife in a few minutes. Her father walked her up to where Terry and I were standing and the ceremony began. We held hands during the ceremony and watched the waves in the background when we weren't looking at each other. All I can remember of the ceremony was Jolene's face and the words "Do you David Parish take Jolene Boyer…"

The ceremony was over before we knew it and we went back to our own home for a reception. It was wonderful and Jolene was so beautiful and glowing from the ceremony she seemed to light up the whole room. We ate our wedding cake and had champagne poured on us and after two more hours and the guests began to leave. I said, "Well my lovely wife where are we going on our honeymoon?"

Jolene said, "That starts tomorrow. Today we have something else to do."

I said, "What's that?"

Jolene said, "It's nearly time to go surfing. We fell in love on our surfboards and I couldn't think of anything finer than us going out and riding waves on our wedding day to start our marriage."

I said, "I couldn't agree more." And we went to our bedroom to change and get ready for the waves. We surfed all evening until the sun was gone and walked to the shop where the Jeep was parked. We got in and drove home. After we ate something for dinner, we went to bed where we made love until the sun was coming up again. We woke up and got out of bed and I found that Jolene had packed a bag for each of us the day before. We went and got our surfboards and took an inter island flight to Maui where Jolene had rented a cottage for us in Kanapalli. It was beautiful and incredibly romantic and there was good surf right out of our front door. It was perfect. We spent the week surfing and eating out in Lahina and lying in the hammock which was attached to the big Banyon tree on the side of our cottage. The week went all-too quickly and we were sad to go back to Wakiki at the end. We got our Jeep at the airport and drove the short way to the village where we settled back into our home delighted to be married.

We woke the next day and surfed Ala Moana before we drove to Wakiki and opened the shop. We were cleaning when Terry walked in and said, "Welcome newlyweds. How was the honeymoon?"

I said, "Thank you it was wonderful."

Jolene said, "It was lovely and something I wanted to go on forever."

Terry said, "That's great. I missed you two around here. What are your plans now?"

Jolene said, "We're going to stay right here and live like we've been doing for the past two and a half years."

Terry said, "Thinking about having children soon?"

Jolene said, "Thinking about having children, yes, but I think I'm still too young for kids."

I said, "I agree, children would be hard for us right now. I'm content to wait awhile."

Terry said, "Well I think you're right. I still can't believe how much work they are. I'd be dead if it wasn't for you two letting me sleep late. Marcy and I are up all of the time at night with Teresa."

Jolene said, "And how is my darling little surfer girl?"

Terry said, "Oh she's just fine and getting bigger all of the time. Marcy is thinking about going back to work as soon as she stops nursing. What would you two think of having Teresa here at the shop all day with us?"

Jolene said, "Perfect, I can't think of a better place for her to grow up. As long as I can take her in the water every day, I think it'll be wonderful."

"So you wouldn't mind helping me take care of her?" said Terry.

Jolene said, "Heavens no. I wouldn't mind at all. This is the perfect place for her to grow up and become a famous surfer."

Terry grinned and said, "Good, I'll tell Marcy tonight. She'll be delighted."

I said, "Terry remember we owe you one for getting us to Hawaii and helping us stay together."

Terry said, "Oh you two belonged together from the start. The only problem was you were just young in age. I think it was the best thing I ever did other than give David a job that day."

"Terry why did you give me a job anyway?"

Terry said, "I guess we never talked about it did we."

"No we didn't."

Terry said, "Well you walked into the shop with your lip busted and I thought you showed so much character by wanting to go back where you'd just been beaten up, I had this feeling you were someone I wanted to get to know. So I gave you a job and the rest is history."

Jolene said, "Did you think David and I would fall in love?"

Terry said, "Truthfully I didn't even think of you when I hired David. Hiring him was something that just happened. You should thank Marcy sometime because she's the one who convinced me to leave you two alone when we figured out you were going to David's house very early in the morning to get into bed with him."

I said, "How did you find out?"

Terry said, "I was coming home with Marcy after being out all night doing what you two were doing, and as we drove by in her car I saw Jolene going into your back gate. It wasn't hard to put two and two together and see what was happening. Marcy thought you two were so great together and reminded me we were both doing the same thing at your age. Then when I saw how much you two loved each other I couldn't break it up."

Jolene said, "Terry I'll never be able to thank you for helping me find the perfect man. You're the best brother a girl could ever have."

Terry smiled at the compliment and I said, "Thanks Terry. I owe you one forever."

Terry and I went into the shaping room to get on the day's work and Jolene stayed behind the counter to wait on the customers. All through the day Jolene went about changing her name on the identification she carried. It was no easy task and she had to run errands with our marriage certificate all day to accomplish the change. When she came in at the end of the day she was tired and wanted a cold beer. She showed me her new drivers' license and I saw her name for the first time as Jolene Boyer Parish. It looked great to me and I was pleased she wanted to use my name. Jolene was tired when we closed, so we drove back to the village and got Japanese food at one of the restaurants to take home with us. After dinner Jolene said, "David, you'll never guess how rich we are."

I said, "Do you want me to guess or do you just want to tell me?"

Jolene said, "I went to the bank today to change my name on the bank accounts and I was surprised to find out from our banker that we're worth almost three hundred thousand dollars."

I said, "That's fantastic. How did that happen?"

Jolene said, "Well, we're making quite a bit from the shop and the inventions and when they get put into the mutual funds we invested in, it adds up pretty fast. Besides the economy has been great and our interest rate is very high. Our money is being good to us."

I said, "I told you that you were going to be rich one day before you were twenty."

"You did at that but I never believed you," she replied.

I said, "How long will it be until we have a million and can retire?"

She said, "Funny you brought that up. Our banker said it will happen in about ten years if it all goes the same and we keep recycling the interest into principal."

I said, "No kidding. We'll only be twenty eight years old then."

"That's right. Would you like to retire at twenty eight?"

I said, "I'm not sure, ask me when I'm twenty eight."

We went back to working at the shop everyday and Marcy stopped nursing the next month. When she did, Terry brought Teresa to the shop with him each day and put her in the playpen we'd bought for the store. Jolene made sure the things around her were surf related and Teresa had an amazing array of toy surfboards around her playpen and Jolene was very serious about taking Teresa swimming at least twice a day. Sometimes she would take her surfboard with her and the two of them would just paddle around and play in the shore break. Teresa loved the water and quickly began to develop a tan we were all proud of. Jolene had such a great time with Teresa, I knew we would be having children before we knew it.

One afternoon I was watching the counter when a man and woman from France came in and bought two boards. One for each of them and I was told they had been dying to learn how to surf but there was no place on the coast of France to buy a board. The man was very nice and he suggested to me if we were to open a shop there we would have plenty of business. I thanked the man for his purchase and his advice and helped them to the cab with their boards. When I came back into the shop Jolene was behind the counter saying, "Isn't that interesting, no surfboards in France? David I have to run an errand, will you watch the shop while I'm gone?"

I said I would and sat on the stool and picked up the newest Surf magazine to read while Jolene was gone. She was back in an hour and from the books in her arms I knew she had been to the library. I said, "That was quick. What are we reading about?"

Jolene said, "France. I have an idea, why don't you help me with it?"

I sat with Jolene behind the counter and she opened the first of the books to a page where there was a map of the Atlantic coast of the country. There before us lay a coastline which was at least a thousand miles long. Below the French coast was a coastline of Spain and Portugal which was at least another thousand miles in length. I looked at Jolene and instantly understood what she was up to. I said, "You're thinking of opening surf shops in France aren't you?"

Smiling she said, "Smart boy. I just love how you figure things out."

I said, "Three or four shops selling our regular boards on the French coastline might make a lot of money."

Jolene said, "And a few more on the coast of Spain and Portugal should make even more. Look at this picture. It's the town of Biarritz and look at the waves. They look pretty good don't they?"

I had to admit from the pictures in the book the waves looked completely rideable. I said, "Jolene this is a great idea. I think we should go to France and see."

Jolene said, "I think we should go to France with a lot of surfboards and open shops there."

I smiled and said, "When do we leave?"

Jolene said, "Not until summer. It's cold there and we need to make and ship extra boards there first."

I asked, "What happens then?"

Jolene said, "Then we go there with part of the team and surf. A few days at each beach and we'll sell everything we bring with us. I think we should fill a container and send it. Then we'll have stock to open shops with."

I leaned over and kissed my wife saying, "And don't I have the smartest wife in the world. Wait until we tell Terry."

I went into the back to shaping room while Jolene read about French beach habits and their seasons. Terry got back in the afternoon and Jolene said, "Terry we're going to be rich."

Terry said, "Jolene what have you thought of now?"

Jolene said, "A trip to France and listen to this."

Jolene went into depth about her idea and Terry loved it. The three of us got into a huddle and decided we should acquire a small building in addition to the shop in Huntington Beach to produce the boards we'd need for the venture. After a call to Dale in California we had pretty much solidified the idea. Jolene and I would fly to California and rent the property we would need and put Dale to the task of making the stock we would need for what we were going to do. Then at the first of summer we would fly with the team members to the south of the French Atlantic coast and begin from there. Jolene speculated the towns that attracted the richest tourists would most likely be the best places for the shops, and after her research she knew exactly where to put the three shops she planned on. One month later we flew to California to start the plan. We arrived at the airport and Mombo picked us up and drove us home. It was late when we got there and we went straight to bed to get up early the next morning and go surfing at the pier before we went to the shop. When we woke the next day the first thing Jolene did was to go and clean her roadster which we drove to the shop. Our friends on the waves were very happy to see us so early in the spring and we had fun seeing them. It was exciting to find Dale had done his homework and had already located a place to build what we would need. I thanked him for his great advance work especially when I found he had tentatively hired two more shapers to help with the workload. Things were definitely in motion and I was pleased at how easy it was. I went to work finding the best way to ship what we wanted to send and found it was much easier and cheaper than I expected. In a month we had three hundred new boards built and carefully wrapped to put into the container we were going to send to France. The whole month was nothing but fun as Jolene and I only had to be there to supervise and go surfing. It was great to be home and it was difficult to get Jolene away from her roadster. It was something she definitely enjoyed and we went out to dinner a lot so she could drive us up and down the coast to different restaurants. It was tremendous fun and I loved seeing my wife behind the wheel of her red hot rod day and night. The team was all about traveling with us, and when we were ready we shipped the boards and waited for our turn to go after them. We shipped it all to Biarritz and we met our shipment there four weeks later. Jolene and her more than ample mind had been studying the language and it was a good thing for us. She made arrangements for us to place our container in a transfer yard where we could get to it when we needed to. Our first day there we went to the beach with our boards in a rented van and found the waves were breaking at three to five feet so we unloaded the van and headed for the water. As we walked to the waves with the team and our boards the whole beach stood up and watched us. When we went into the surf the people on the beach crowded to the edge of the water to see what we were doing. Jolene was the first to take off and caught a good wave. She slid down the front of it and began to work the swell up and down. I could hear the crowd yelling on the beach and I knew we were already a hit. The rest of the team took off on the waves and as they rode Jolene and I could hear the crowds on the beach. The Frenchmen loved what we were doing and before an hour was up the local TV was there and was filming us on the water. We rode waves for the French twice that day and gave out flyers advertising the shop opening in a couple of days. I spent the next day looking for a store front while Jolene and the team rode the waves. With the help of a real estate salesman, I rented a small space before the day was out. We moved a bunch of our stock into the shop and were open for business the next morning early. When the crowds came to the beach it was time for another surfing demonstration. The Frenchmen were thrilled again and before the team was done we had sold three boards. This went on for the whole afternoon and our shop was packed all day. The customers bought our stock and immediately took them to the water and tried to learn. They dealt with being beginners and we watched as they emulated what we had been doing and they learned pretty quickly. By the end of the day some of them were getting decent rides and we were pleased at how much of our stock was gone. We called Terry that night and caught him just as he was coming to work half a world away. He was excited at our success and we told him we were having a wonderful time. After our phone call we met the team in a restaurant which had been suggested to us and found the girls and boys on the team surrounded by fans. They were being treated like stars and it seemed they were thoroughly enjoying their stardom. Each had at least two of the opposite sex on each arm and as soon as the crowd recognized us, Jolene and I were surrounded as well. It was all I could do to keep a hold of my wife and we were nearly swept away from each other several times in the restaurant. We found ourselves the next morning with bad hangovers and we woke up late and went to our shop. There was a crowd waiting for us and we opened and let them in. We had sales from the first minute we were open and found out surfing had become the thing to do almost overnight. Surfing was cool and it was a great status symbol to have a surfboard whether or not you used it. By the time we closed and after the team was on the waves twice that day, Jolene said, "David we have a problem."

"What's that?"

Jolene said, "We don't have enough surfboards to sell. If we do this kind of business for three more days I think we'll be sold out. What should we do?"

I said, "Go and call Dale and tell him to send everything we have at home as fast as possible."

Jolene laughed and went to place the call. She was back in a few minutes saying. "He's already on it. Dale anticipated our sales and he's got an air express company standing by in case of an emergency like we're having."

I said, "Will it be expensive?"

Jolene said, "No he's got a good price and he's sending two hundred boards. We'll have to meet them at the airport though."

We were close to selling out and our sales were still strong in Biarritz when Jolene and I went to the air cargo terminal in Bordeaux to meet the boards Dale had sent us. We collected them in the van and went back to the beach where we unloaded them into the shop. Sales were continuous for another week and we were happy when they tapered off some. The team was having the time of their lives and were living like celebrities. They fought to stay in Biarritz and run the shop while we went to the next spot Jolene had selected for us. We went to Arachon and the result was the same as in Biarritz. We were selling boards the minute we got out of the water on our first day. As each shop was opened we filled it with boards and later with our apparel that went along with the boards. The French were mad for all of it and we began to look around for someone to run things for us while we went back to the states. When we opened in La Rochelle, a young girl with blond hair walked in and said, "Hi, I'm Wendy. I'm from Newport Beach and I've been living here for two years and I think you two are fantastic. Do you think I could work for you?"

Jolene said, "Great. We're from Huntington Beach."

Wendy said, "I know, you're Jolene Boyer and he's David Parish. It's a pleasure to meet the two of you. I've been a fan of yours for a long time Jolene."

Jolene said, "Amazing you know who we are!"

Wendy said, "Of course I do. Who in southern California doesn't know who you are?"

Jolene said, "I love this. Ten thousand miles and I meet someone who knows us. David this is just the best. I'm not Jolene Boyer any more. David and I got married at Christmas and my last name is now Parish."

Wendy said, "Great, that's wonderful news. Congratulations to you both. Now what can I do to help?'

Jolene said, "Wendy get behind this counter and sell boards as fast as you can. You're hired and tonight after we go surfing we're taking you out to dinner. You do know how to surf don't you?"

Wendy said, "Of course I do. Did you think I was one of those girls that just stayed on the beach and tried to look pretty? You're my greatest hero and I never dreamed you'd come to France. This is fantastic. I love your being here."

With that Wendy got behind the counter and began to sell surfboards all the while speaking in perfect French to the customers in the shop. When it came time to close, we pushed the last of the customers out of the shop with Wendy's help and went to the van where our boards were stashed. I opened up and Jolene reached in and handed her own board to Wendy and said, "Here, you ride mine today. I'll take one of the others. You've been a tremendous help to us today. How can we ever repay you?"

She smiled and said, "A good meal and a job would work."

Jolene said, "Those things you've already got. What else can we do for you?"

"Nothing. I'm content just to ride your board. This is a dream come true."

We headed to the waves and paddled out with the crowd on the beach watching us. Wendy was a very good surfer and Jolene took notice of her abilities. We rode until it began to get dark and then started in to the beach. We got out and carried our boards to the van and Wendy said, "Jolene are we still going out to dinner?"

Jolene said, "You bet. Where do you want to go?"

Wendy said, "How about the restaurant Irene's up the block if it's not too expensive."

Jolene said, "Not at all, should we go now?"

"No. I'd like to go home and change first. Can we meet there in half an hour?"

Jolene said, "Half hour then. We'll see you there."

We parted company and Wendy walked away from us on the street. Jolene and I went to our hotel and changed into something suitable for the restaurant. We went and got a table for three and were waiting when Wendy walked into the place and seeing us, she bypassed the line and came to our table and joined us. When she was seated we ordered drinks and Jolene said, "This is incredible luck to find you here in France. How did you ever get here?"

Wendy said, "Well two years ago I had to leave Newport and everything I grew up with because my parents moved here. My father is in the Foreign Service and was transferred here."

Jolene said, "Do you like it here?"

Wendy said, "Yes and no. I wish I was still in California, but I have to admit that France has been a great experience for me. I'm seventeen and it can be great here. I finished high school here and I don't much want to go to college. I would rather go back to Newport and be a beach rat. It's all I really ever loved."

Jolene said, "You sound just like David and me. We've always been on the beach and we don't plan to leave."

Wendy said, "I would have left but my parents wouldn't let me go. I've been sort of stuck here but I think I'll like it better if I'm surfing and running your shop."

Jolene said, "We don't want you to run our shop."

Wendy said, "I thought you hired me to do just that?"

Jolene said, "No, we hired you to run all of our shops here in France and whatever we start in Spain and Portugal."

Wendy said, "Really! I never dreamed you would hire me to do all of those things. Thank you very much, but do you think I'm capable of it?"

Jolene said, "Of course you are. I'll be just a phone call away. I'm only a year older than you are and I can do it. It's easy and you'll be fine."

Wendy smiled and said. "If you think so. I'd be happy to give it my best."

I said, "Good then it's settled. You'll be our manager here and sell our boards for us. What would you like to be paid?"

Wendy said, "I really don't know. I've never done anything like this before. What would you want to pay me?"

Jolene said, "What's a good salary for an adult here?"

Wendy thought and said, "I think right now about two hundred a week but that's an awful lot of money."

Jolene said, "Well that's what you'll start at then. Now how about a couple of custom boards for you to ride with your name on them?"

Wendy said, "A new board would be great. I haven't had a surfboard for the last two years."

Jolene said, "Well you'll have two now. Do you have a boyfriend who needs one?"

"No, I don't have a boyfriend. The French men don't really like young assertive women and I won't be anything else. I always wished I were like you and David. I read you two met at the beach when you were fourteen and ran off to Hawaii when you were fifteen. That's so romantic. I wish it had happened to me."

Jolene said, "It will. David and I were very lucky to find each other. Wait until the men find out you're the catalyst for the surfing scene here. You'll be fighting them off."

Wendy said, "Do you really think so?"

Jolene said, "Yes I do. You're the picture of southern California with your blond hair and you're very beautiful. You just wait until they see you surf. You'll be a celebrity overnight."

Wendy said, "Thank you Jolene. My confidence has been off since I've been here. Maybe this will fix it for me."

The two girls stood and hugged and Jolene ordered a bottle of champagne to seal the deal between us. We told Wendy of our shop in Biarritz and she thought it was wonderful. We left the staffing of it to her and she said she had friends who would like to work there which was fine with us. Jolene gave her license to do things as she wanted and told her as long as the product was moving, there would be no problem at all. Wendy worked with us there and we took her to Biarritz to show her what was going on at our other shop. Before the week was out she hired a manager for the store and decided to run the other herself. We told her to find another shop for us further north and she said it would not be a problem. We drove north to St. Nazaire where Wendy said would be a good place for another shop as the beaches were great there. We left one of her friends to run the shop in La Rochelle and the team and the three of us drove north. We got there the next day after and we did our demonstration for the people on the beach. We got their attention and they were mad for surfing in another day. We sold boards and Wendy was fantastic to have around. She was like working with family and we knew we had found just the right person to represent us in France. She was able to deal with everything and after ordering more stock for the three stores, we left them in Wendy's capable hands. We drove to Paris for the ride and caught a flight home from there. When we got back, Dale was up to his ears in orders to fill and Terry was delighted we had found someone wonderful to run things for us in France. We would deal with Spain the next summer and Jolene and I looked forward to the trip back to Europe.

We spent the rest of the summer in Huntington Beach and we were glad to be back in our own house with Maw and Mombo. They loved hearing about our adventure in France and told us they were hoping to get a chance to go there with us sometime. Dale was hoping to go there too and we told him as soon as things were caught up, we would send him there to see the operation and as a vacation for working so hard. We had made a serious amount of money in France and we invested it back into the boards which were going to be made to send there. Dale would be talking to Wendy on a regular basis to keep our products in stock and we hoped they would get along well. Dale flew off to France a month later and he loved it there. We watched things for him in Huntington and after two weeks we got a call from him saying he would be back in another week and he needed to talk with us. We were curious about what until he came home and told us he and Wendy had become lovers and asked we send him to France to make boards for us there so they could be together. His brother would do the work for us in Huntington Beach and we were delighted Wendy had found someone to be in love with. Dale was a great guy and of course Jolene said he could go and be with Wendy. This would help a great deal but we would continue to ship boards to France until Dale discovered how to find the materials there he would need to make boards. We got a call from Wendy a few days later and she said, "Jolene I want to thank you for sending me a wonderful man."

Jolene said, "You're welcome but we just sent Dale to learn the operation and meet you."

"That was enough. I haven't seen a man from the beach in so long, it was love at first sight. Dale's wonderful and thank you for letting him come and live here."

Jolene said, "Of course. I wouldn't stop you from having the man of your dreams would I? I want the two of you to be happy and to sell surfboards. You will both be celebrities there and it will be a great time in your lives. We'll be calling from time to time and you'll be calling us as well. Wendy, I want you to take good care of Dale and remember we love you. Call when you need anything."

Wendy said she would and after thanking Jolene for Dale once more, Jolene came to where I was sitting and putting her arms around my neck said, "Every day I love you more."

I said, "I love you too. How's Wendy? Is she happy about Dale?"

Jolene said, "Oh yes she's very happy. I think sending Dale to her was a great thing. Dale and Wendy needed to find each other and we needed a shaper there. I think this will work out perfectly."

I said, "Jolene did you plan this?"

Jolene grinned, "A little, but I was sure It would work out. Wendy needed a man from the beach and Dale needed a great girl. It wasn't hard to see they'd work out together."

I said, "Well good for you. Tell me what would you like to do this evening my little match maker?"

"I want to go surfing and I want to eat dinner and then I want to make love to my husband if it's all right."

I said it was more than all right and we began to close the shop and head across the street where the waves we both loved were breaking nicely. We went home afterwards and went to have dinner with Jolene's parents at their house. We ate while we watched TV and were falling asleep by the time the evening news was coming on. We excused ourselves and went home to crash until the next day. Early was when we woke up and soon we were on our way to the shop and our morning session with our favorite waves. We drove Jolene's roadster to the shop and she parked it in front as usual. Partly for advertising and partly for the purpose of keeping an eye on it during the day. Jolene ran an errand after lunch and she didn't return right away. I assumed she had gone for a drive or run a long errand until I got a telephone call at the shop at about four. It was Jolene and all she said was, "David I'm in jail. Please get me out."

I asked her what for and found that she didn't have her drivers' license with her and no registration and no proof of insurance. Those three things combined demanded the officer bring her in to the local station. I went there right away and was told because I wasn't twenty-one her parents would have to come to the station and get her out. I went immediately to her mom's house and after some explanation Laura went with me to bail Jolene out of jail. It took two hours and Jolene was in tears by the time we got her out. Laura took her home and I went to where her roadster was and picked it up. I met her at home and she said, "David it was horrible, what took you so long?"

I said, "I'm sorry love they wouldn't let me get you out because married or not, I'm not twenty one. I had to get your mother and I'm sorry I didn't think of putting the registration in the car. It's all my fault and I can't tell you how badly I feel."

Jolene said, "It's my fault too because I didn't have my license with me."

We hugged for awhile and Jolene calmed down eventually. When she was quiet we got up and went into the kitchen to get some dinner. We spent the night in and woke to go surfing the next morning. It was a typical day for us and a rather nice one as well. We went home after our evening with the waves and when we got there Mombo handed me a letter and said, "This came for you today and it looks important."

CHAPTER ELEVEN

I looked at the letter and it was from the U.S. Government. I opened it and found a demand for my presence for a complete physical to see if I was fit for being in the army. Jolene was horrified and said, "No way! No way in hell are you going into the army and fight in any stupid war!"

I said, "I agree, but what are we going to do about it. These people are pretty hard to argue with. My date for a physical is in a month and I'm afraid I have to be there or face the consequences."

Jolene said, "You are not going into the army and that's it! I'll find some way to keep you out if it's the last thing I do. I'd rather move to Europe than have you shot to death in some dumb county a half a world away for no good reason."

I said, "Well I'll go along with anything you can find as long as I won't go to jail for it. What do you think we can do?"

Jolene said, "First thing tomorrow I'm going to call one of the women's groups I spoke for and ask them what to do. They had a group opposed to the war and I'm sure they'll have some ideas."

I said, "Good, I know there are a lot of people who are getting out because of one reason or another. I'm sure it can be done and we'll just have to find a way."

Jolene said, "You're damn right we will! Even if you don't go to war, I couldn't put up with you being away from me for that long."

We were up at our usual time the next day and Jolene looked pensive all morning. She was quiet when we surfed and she was quiet when we walked to the shop. I went to work and Jolene got on the phone and started making calls to acquaintances who might be able to give decent advice on my situation. She was still on the phone and I went to the corner and got our sandwiches for lunch. I ate while she spoke on the phone and her conversation seemed very serious. I finished my sandwich and went back to work while she stayed on the phone. I worked through the day and Jolene was on the phone when I came out to help close the shop and surf or go home. Jolene chose home, as she was exhausted from all day on the phone. She waited until after dinner before speaking of the matter to me. She said, "David here's what we need to do."

I said, "What's that?"

She said, "I've been on the phone with so many people today and I think I've gotten good advice. You and I have to take a trip a few days before your physical date."

"Why's that?"

She said, "Because Los Angeles is out for draft physicals. The only way to get you out is to have you fail your physical which will be hard because you're in such great shape."

I said, "So how am I going to fail?"

Jolene said, "You're going to have high blood pressure. I spoke to a sympathetic attorney I was referred to today and he said it's pretty much a sure thing."

I said, "I still don't understand why we'll have to go out of town."

Jolene said, "We have to go out of town because of Los Angeles. They have a quota to meet here and they're taking everyone who's's breathing and warm. It's been suggested we go to Boise, Idaho for your physical."

I said, "Boise, Idaho! That's a long way away. How can I take my physical there?"

Jolene said, "There's a rule of three days before your physical date you can go in for your physical anywhere you might be. All we have to do is make up a story about our car breaking down and say there's no way you could get back to LA in time and they'll let you take your physical there."

I said, "I don't have high blood pressure, how will I get it?"

Jolene said, "I've been given the name of a sympathetic doctor here who will help us. He'll teach you how to make your blood pressure too high for the army. I've heard what you'll have to do and it's not bad."

I said, "Do tell."

Jolene said, "The key is coffee."

"Coffee?"

Jolene said, "That's right, coffee. I've been told if you drink about thirty cups of the stuff before you go in, it will raise your blood pressure through the roof and make your heart go fast. The army checks for all kinds of drugs but they don't check for caffeine."

I said, "It sounds awfully simple."

Jolene said, "Simple is good. The doctor will give you a couple of other tricks to use. You're seeing him Monday morning."

I said, "Jolene you're wonderful. Thank you so much."

Jolene said, "It's all selfish my love. I love you completely and I'm not about to let you go anywhere dangerous. Just like I don't want you under the pier. I truly wouldn't know what to do without you and I don't even want to think about you being hurt."

I said, "Jolene I love you too and I still thank you for doing all of this. You know I'm no good at this sort of thing."

Jolene said, "I know that. Now how about if we go to bed and you do what you're really good at?"

Jolene got up and took me by the hand to our room where we made love late into the night.

Monday came in a few days and the doctor was great. He gave me a few lessons in muscle control which would help to increase my blood pressure. I practiced at his office a number of times and could use the technique perfectly by the time we were to leave for Boise. Jolene and I caught an early flight the day before I would have to take my physical. We took a hotel room a few blocks from the induction station in

Boise and woke early to have breakfast before I would go alone for my physical. The only place to go and eat was the bus station and we went there two hours before the induction station opened. There were only a few people in the bus station and we sat at a table where I proceeded to drink coffee at a fast pace. I finished my thirty cups before the time was up and I was so buzzed on caffeine I was barely able to function. I walked to the station and Jolene went back to our hotel room to wait for me. I went in and told the story about my car breaking down and they bought the rap and I was allowed to have my physical there. I went through the whole thing and was astonished many of the local boys were actually trying to do their best on the physical. I kept my mouth shut and went to area after area wearing nothing but a T-shirt and my boxer shorts. When I got to where blood pressure was checked, I lay my arm limp on the table and as the cuff was put around my arm I tightened all of the muscles in my body except for the arm the doctor was holding. He took my pressure and then checked it once more and said, "Son did you know you have very high blood pressure?"

I said, "No sir, I didn't. Is high blood pressure a bad thing?"

He said, "Yes it is. I recommend that when you get home you see a physician immediately."

"If you say so. I had no idea I was sick."

The doctor said, "Well you're not sick but you should be taking medication for your condition. I'll be checking your pressure again after lunch and I hope for your sake its lower."

I said, "Yes sir thank you."

I was dismissed to the next area for a chest x-ray and after the film was done we were all told to put our clothes on and go the have lunch at the bus station where I'd been for breakfast. I took no chances and after eating lunch with my army meal ticket I proceeded to drink another twenty cups of coffee just to make sure my pressure stayed high. We all walked back to the induction station together and when we got there we were asked to strip again for another group of tests. I was called out of line for another pressure test and I went apprehensively. I did my trick twice more and was pronounced 4-F and unfit for service. I acted disappointed at the news and asked about living a normal life from the doctor. He assured me I would be able to do so provided I sought out medical help and got some medication for my condition. I left the induction station happily and walked to the hotel where Jolene was waiting. I went to our room and knocked on the door and Jolene answered immediately she said worriedly, "Well?"

I said, "It worked. It worked perfectly. I was declared 4-F and I have you to thank for it."

Jolene said with tears in her eyes, "I was so scared and now I'm so happy. Are you okay?"

I said, "Yes, I'm okay but I'm so buzzed on coffee I don't think I'll sleep for a couple of days."

Jolene said, "I don't care if you ever sleep again. I'm so happy you're out of danger. I love you so much. David I'm so happy."

We went out to dinner to celebrate and we had a decent meal in a big hotel in Boise. I was still buzzed by the time we got home and I didn't sleep at all for the whole night. Jolene kept me company for as long as she could stay awake and I spent the night watching the television in our room. I was sitting there in the chair where I was when Jolene went to sleep and when she woke up she said, "My God, you're still awake?"

I said, "Yep, I've been up all night long."

Jolene said, "Are you okay?"

I said, "I think so. I feel like hell but the coffee is beginning to wear off. Did you sleep well?"

Jolene said, "Yes I did. I'm sorry you didn't though. Do you feel up to flying home?"

I said, "Sure let's go home. I've had enough of this town. I want to get back to the beach."

We packed the few things we'd brought with us and took a cab to the airport. We bought tickets on the next flight which was in an hour and with a stop in Salt Lake City we were in Los Angeles before noon. We went and got the woody out of the parking lot and began our drive down I-5 to Huntington Beach and home. By the time we got there I was very tired and as soon as I got to our room I lay on the bed and crashed. I was completely out and slept until the next morning when Jolene kissed me awake and said, "My love, are you okay?"

I said, "Yes I'm okay. I feel all right but I'm still exhausted from everything though."

Jolene took me into her arms and said, "Thank you for being so brave. I know you did all of this for me and I dearly love you for it. Is there anything I can do for you?"

I said, "No my darling. I'd like to have some breakfast and then go to the pier and get some time on the waves."

Jolene said, "Can I make you some breakfast?"

I said, "Breakfast yes. I'd love some but I'm pretty sure I'll never drink coffee again."

Jolene laughed and hugged me very hard and we went to the kitchen after we'd dressed and then went to the beach where I felt greatly relieved I had evaded the draft and I wouldn't ever have to go and be a part of someone else's stupid war.

School would be starting soon and Jolene and I knew we would be heading back to the islands soon. We would be turning nineteen in the coming November and it felt odd to us to be getting older. As we aged we noticed our priorities were changing and luckily for us ours were changing in a similar manner. Our surfboard business was doing wonderfully and the new extension in France was doing very well. Wendy reported to us on a regular basis and we found out there were customers driving all the way from Spain to France to buy our boards. Dale was confident the two of them could expand the business to Spain and Portugal without our help and we thought we might just go there anyway the following summer for the fun of it. Our money was piling up and Terry had already been talking about retirement but he was at a loss as to what he would do with himself if he didn't have the shop to go to every day. We arrived back in Hawaii in early October and it was good to be home. Teresa had grown and I know Jolene was very happy to see her. We settled in and I got the Jeep started so we would have transportation the next morning. We woke early and went to the beach to go surfing. Most of our friends were there and it was great to see them on the waves. We surfed until nine thirty and then rode in to go to work at the shop. Terry was very happy we were back and he came with Teresa just after we opened the store. Jolene immediately took Teresa from him and settled in to cleaning the shop and making it fit for customers. Terry had two employees by this time and they were doing a great job and making life easy on Terry. As soon as Jolene finished cleaning the shop she took Teresa from her playpen and taking her surfboard she walked to the beach to play in the water. Teresa was a little over a year old by this time and I was pretty sure Jolene would want a child soon. I was prepared for this eventuality and would deal with it when my lovely wife decided she was ready. It was the week before Christmas when Jolene looked at me one night in bed with the moonlight pouring in through the open windows. She said, "David, it's just about time."

I said, "Time for what my love?"

Jolene said, "It's almost time for us to have children."

I said, "Oh, are you sure of this?"

Jolene said, "Yes I'm sure. I can feel it inside of me every time I'm around Teresa. There's something going on that's telling me this. I don't know what it is but I know I'm going to have to have a child soon."

I said, "I know you are. I've been watching the two of you and I can see it on your face and with your body language when you're around Teresa."

Jolene looked at me and said, "Will it be okay?"

I said, "Yes it's okay. You decide when you want to quit your birth control and I'll be more than happy to have a child with you. I think it's a good idea to have children at a young age so by the time we're forty they'll be on their own and we'll be able to finish our lives."

"David you were talking plural when you said children."

I said, "Yes I was. I want you to have two children like I talked about years ago. I want my child to have a brother or a sister to grow up with in addition to Teresa."

Jolene said, "Thank you. I'll do my best to have a girl and a boy for you but I want to have a girl first if that's okay. I know I don't have much control over what will happen but I can hope can't I?"

I said, "I'll be happy to hope with you. I'm very happy about this. When were you thinking about quitting your pills?"

Jolene said, "I was thinking about quitting them in January after the New Year. Will quitting then be okay? I want to be pregnant during the summer and hopefully have the baby here in Hawaii where I have you and Marcy and Terry here to be with me. I'm still a little frightened about the birthing but Marcy said that's normal."

I said, "Jolene you've thought this out wonderfully. We'll do just as you want. I'm looking forward to having a child and she can grow up with Teresa at the shop."

Jolene said thank you and the two of us rolled over and went to sleep holding each other as we did every night.

We turned nineteen with a small party and Christmas was on us before we knew it. We surfed on Christmas day and Jolene took us to where we had gotten married and we kissed again on the spot where we stood a year before. Jolene quit her birth control pills on the first of January and we waited for her to become pregnant. She was disappointed when she got her period in February but she was pleased to find she was pregnant in March. She went to our doctor when she was a few weeks late and he confirmed what she already knew. By the end of the month she was sick in the mornings and I have to hand it to my love, she never complained once and was great about sticking to what was a normal amount of food for her even though she admitted to being hungry all of the time. When she was sick she would go and do what she needed to do and then return to what she was doing before she got sick. I watched on many occasions as when we were surfing she would feel herself getting sick and paddle far outside to vomit and then she would paddle back to the line up and shake it off and catch another wave. Her courage made me immensely proud of her and I was very happy I had such a completely wonderful wife. In a couple more months her sickness was over and we flew back to Huntington Beach and our home there for the summer. We moved into Mombo's house and she was thrilled about Jolene having a baby. We had said nothing to either of our parents about the pregnancy as Jolene wanted it to be a surprise. They were very surprised when they found out and Jolene's parents were not exactly told straight away. We had been back two days and were at their house to swim and eat on Sunday afternoon when Jolene's mother looked at Jolene in her bikini and said, "Jolene are you getting fat? You're stomach used to be flat as a board. Have you been drinking too much beer?"

Jolene laughed and said, "No mom I haven't been drinking beer. I haven't had a beer since March when I found out I was pregnant."

Laura said, "Jolene you're really pregnant. Are you serious?"

Jolene said, "Yep I'm serious and it looks like David and I are going to have this baby in November."

Laura was excited and said, "Jolene this is wonderful I'm so happy for you and

David. I suppose you have everything covered such as doctors and the like?"

Jolene said, "I do in Hawaii but I'll need to get a doctor here and you could help me with if you would."

Laura said she would indeed and told Jolene she would make the call the next day and schedule an appointment in two weeks for Jolene. Stan was very happy about becoming a grandfather again and made a point of vigorously shaking my hand and telling me how proud he was. I called my father in the south and he was excited for us too. He asked if we wanted to fly down to the gulf coast during the summer and after asking Jolene we decided to fly there for ten days together. I would be able to show her where I had grown up and she was pleased get the chance to know and be able to see my background.

We left the shop in the hands of our help and got a flight two weeks later to New Orleans. We rented a car and I took Jolene to all of my favorite places I had frequented when I was young and before I moved to California. She loved seeing the old city and especially loved the food. She got to meet my old pals who lived in the neighborhood I grew up in and I was pleased to introduce her to them. Most of my old friends were still doing what they were doing when I left. I was a very different person by then and the difference between us was truly amazing. They were amazed I was married and owned a house in Hawaii and also that Jolene was pregnant with our first child. We spent two days in New Orleans and then went to Biloxi, Mississippi to see my father. Jolene liked the two-hour drive it took to get there because it was located on the coast. It was beautiful but she missed the waves that broke on the coast in California. We found my father at one of my family's hotels and it was good to see my dad. There was a yacht club a few blocks away built out over the water, and after we put our things away, we went to it for lunch. Jolene loved the old green building and the view of the coast it offered. We ate lunch and then went and opened my father's sailboat. At this time in his life he had a Swan sixty-two and it was a great boat. Jolene had never sailed before and she sat in the cockpit while I went to work with the old man rigging the boat and getting ready to spend the afternoon on the water. When we were ready I motored away from the dock and raised sail. As soon as the wind caught us I cut the diesel and let the wind move us. It was blowing nicely that afternoon and the Swan heeled over and Jolene was more than excited about being on a nice sailboat. When we had cleared the channel I gave the helm to Jolene and she turned out to be naturally good at keeping the boat on the wind and moving properly. She said it wasn't as exciting as surfing but she liked it anyway. I gave her the helm as much as she wanted and we sailed away the afternoon and cruised into the harbor as the sun was going down towards New Orleans. It was Jolene's first time sailing and she said perhaps we should look into getting a boat when we got back to Hawaii. We spent ten days sailing my dad's Swan each afternoon and eating seafood, which Jolene pronounced better than any she had eaten before. Jolene got to meet more of the friends I had grown up with and she was amazed they all seemed so young. Jolene attracted tons of attention, as there weren't many surfer girls on the Gulf Coast. Jolene with her height and beautiful face, tan skin and long straight blond hair was something which just wasn't seen in the south. I must have looked as different as she did and it was fun for us to go out and see the looks we would get in the restaurants and the clubs. It was time to go before we knew it and one morning we drove back to the airport in our rented car to get our flight back to California. We were back in our house before nightfall and we were pleased to be home. We went to bed after dinner and while we were lying there after making love Jolene said, "David, we have to make a change around here."

I said, "What's that my love?"

"We have to get our own house here. I love Maw and Mombo, but I want us to have our own place here where we can be together like we are in Hawaii."

I said, "You're right. We're too old to be living here with my parents. Do you have anything in mind?"

"As a matter of fact I do. Want to hear it?"

I said, "Sure what's your idea?"

Jolene said, "I want to go and live above the shop on the water where I can hear the waves at night. Terry has owned the building for years and I don't know why we're not living there. There's a two bedroom apartment above it and we actually own it as its part of the surfboard business."

I said, "Well let's go get the tenants to move out and move in ourselves."

Jolene said, "We can't be mean about this. We'll have to wait until their lease is up and if I remember right it'll be up in another month. Will it be all right if we move then?"

I said, "Yes that will be fine. You check the lease tomorrow and I'll plan the attack on moving in. You know this will mean we'll have to get some furniture and what do you plan on doing with the place while we're in the islands each year?"

Jolene said, "We'll rent it out when we leave. It will rent fast and we'll have no trouble finding tenants."

We went to sleep after our conversation and the next day after surfing Jolene found we could move in three weeks from that Monday. The time came and we moved out of Mombo's house and into our first California home. It was great to be living right on the beach and, except for being kept up sometimes by the crowds at the pier and on the streets, we were very happy there. We visited our parents regularly and it was always great to go and be invited to dinner. Dale and Wendy were very happy in France and were planning to be married in the fall but only after they came back to Huntington Beach so Dale's parents could meet Wendy. They would do this after the summer was done and business slowed in France and Spain where they had opened two more shops that were also quite successful. Jolene's body was getting a little bigger but she said she wasn't going to stop surfing until she could no longer lie down on her board. She was still excited about becoming a mother and I wished we could know whether or not she would have the girl she wanted. We would just have to wait and see. The summer went by faster than we could remember and the first of October Dale and Wendy arrived in Huntington Beach. Jolene and I drove to get them at the airport and gave them the woody to get around in for the time they were there. The first night they were home we took them out to dinner and found that our friends had moved in together in France and were very happy there. Wendy was thrilled to be back in California and she and Dale surfed all of their favorite spots during their stay. We surfed with them a lot and the bond between us grew. Wendy wanted to know everything about being pregnant and Jolene was happy to fill her in on all of the details.

They left to go back to their home in France and two weeks later Jolene and I flew back to Hawaii to be in our first home and back to warm water and summer. Terry and Marcy were glad to see us and we found out when we arrived that Marcy was pregnant again. Jolene was ecstatic about the news and loved that our child would have another cousin to grow up with. We moved back into our house and I started building another room onto the place so the baby would have a bedroom. Jolene put her touch on the space and it was the perfect surfer's bedroom when she was done with it. November came around and the birth of our child was going to be during that month. Jolene had to quit surfing because of her size but it didn't stop her from going to the beach with Teresa every day. She went to work every day as well and I was certain she would give birth in our shop and kidded her about it often enough for her to become bored with my jokes. She did make arrangements with the hospital in Wakiki and they promised her the delivery room was positioned where she would be able to see the ocean while she was delivering our child. The big day came early one morning in the middle of the month when Jolene had just come back from the beach with Teresa and her water broke in the middle of the shop. I walked her to the Jeep and Terry got on the phone to call all of the parents and tell them Jolene was about to deliver. I went into the delivery room with her after scrubbing up and putting on the required clothing. When I entered Jolene was having contractions which would cause her to grit her teeth and crush my hand as I held hers. She looked beautiful as she lay on her back looking out of the windows at the beach and the ocean that she could see from her bed. She said, "I think it's going to be pretty soon now."

I said, "How do you feel? Are you hurting very much?"

Jolene said, "I'm okay, it hurts but it's nothing I can't handle. I think you should go and get Dr. Wing and tell him its time for him to earn his money."

I let go of Jolene's hand and went to the nurses' station where they called Dr. Wing. He came to the delivery room a few minutes later and as he walked in Jolene was busy squashing my hand during a contraction. A few more, and with some coaching from him, Jolene delivered a beautiful little girl with snow-white hair on her head. The baby was quickly cleaned up and handed to Jolene who was sweating but radiant from the birth. She held our daughter and kissed her softly and then she raised her bed up with the remote control and handed her to me and said, "David this is your daughter Caroline. Is she as beautiful as I think she is?"

I took Caroline from her and said, "Yes she's as beautiful a baby as I've ever seen. She looks just like you and she's perfect. You've done an extraordinary job and I love holding her. She's just perfect."

Jolene lay there looking at me holding Caroline and smiling at the two of us.

After awhile Jolene asked for her daughter back and I handed the baby to her. Terry and Marcy were let into the room a few minutes later and they were in love with Caroline in minutes. They both told Jolene she was beautiful and Jolene beamed with pride as did I. They left after awhile and I went with Jolene to the room she would spend the night in. I was asked to leave when visiting hours were over and Jolene nodded. It was time for me to go and it was okay because she wanted to get some rest with Caroline. I left the hospital and drove to Terry's where he and I proceeded to get drunk and celebrate Caroline's birth. I stayed very late and then walked home to my bed and slept until it was time to go and get Jolene and Caroline Boyer Parish at the hospital. I collected my girls and asked where they wanted to go. Jolene said she wanted to go to the shop and I drove there carefully. When we got there I said, "Jolene why are we here. Don't you want to go home?"

Jolene said, "Not right now, we have to take Caroline for a swim first."

I said, "Sure, that's a good idea."

We walked down to the water and took Caroline into the small surf with us. She seemed to love the water and smiled as the salt water poured over her when the little waves broke. We passed her between us for about an hour and then Jolene carefully dried her daughter off with the towel she brought with her. We walked back to the shop and got into the Jeep with Jolene breast feeding Caroline on the way home to the village. When we got there we put Caroline into her basket that had a big handle on it for carrying her around and keeping her near us. She fell asleep and Jolene and I went about making lunch and looking at our new partner. We stayed in all day and night but woke up early for feeding Caroline and went to the shop where we put her into the playpen with Teresa who was fascinated by her cousin. The two of them stayed together except for when Caroline was being fed and Teresa kept a running commentary going to Caroline all day long. Jolene and I each took the girls to the water during the day and again Caroline loved the waves. I knew exactly what Jolene was doing with our daughter and it was fine with me that my wife train her from an early age to be a surfer. It was a great way to live and it was healthy. I knew Caroline would be as good as her mother in a few years and it pleased me that Jolene was looking to the future for our little girl.

CHAPTER TWELVE

Caroline was good for our lives and Jolene and I fell more in love in her first year than we'd ever been in love before. We surfed separately while we watched Caroline on the beach and as she got older there was a great deal of taking her out on our boards with us. When our winter in Hawaii was over we all flew to Huntington Beach where we moved into our apartment above the surf shop. Our parents loved our daughter and we took her along to all of the things we did. It was great to have Maw and Mombo and Laura as willing baby-sitters and we gave Caroline to them on more than one occasion to spend the night when we would decide we wanted to go out.

Our finances were getting bigger and Jolene made sure it would all go to Caroline one day. We had our attorney make out a will for us and we put it into our safe deposit box. Caroline loved Jolene's roadster and I suppose it was the wind in her hair and the sun on her face she liked about it. The two of them would go on long drives together and come back glowing from the sun and the wind. It was Jolene's show and I hoped I would get the same opportunity if Jolene were to have a son the next time. We surfed away the summer and before we knew it we were flying back to Hawaii and it was hard to believe Caroline would be a year old the coming November. We settled back into our lives in Wakiki and as usual it was wonderful to be home. Marcy had another girl in the winter and named her Jolene for my beautiful wife and Terry's sister. The decision was made to give her a nickname to distinguish her from Jolene and Jo was what we all decided to call her for short. Jolene was very flattered and pleased at Marcy's choice and loved having a namesake. The two little girls were to be joined by another as soon as Marcy stopped nursing and we looked forward to the three children growing up in the shop. All of us went into the water at least twice a day and we watched as our children grew. We would leave them sometimes with Terry or Marcy when the big waves would break on the north shore and we would go and get a dose of the Pipeline or one of the other killer spots we knew of. I thought that all-too soon we would be teaching Caroline to surf the big waves with us and I hoped she would love it as we did.

That November Caroline turned one and we turned twenty in the same month. We were no longer in our teens any more. We were lying in our beds with Caroline asleep in her room when Jolene said, "David, is it okay if we have another child?"

I said, "Yes I think it will be just the right time. Are you going to quit your birth control at the New Year again?"

"That's just what I planned to do if it's okay with you. I'm going to try and have a boy for you this time."

I said, "A boy would be nice but I want you to know a girl would be fine too. Caroline might like having a sister to grow up with."

True, but I loved having brothers and if she has a brother he can look after her like Terry looked after me. I love my brother and I would like her to have the same experience."

I said, "If that happens it would be excellent but I'm okay with what ever we get."

Jolene said, "Thank you David, I love you very much. You're not bored with our lives are you?"

"No of course not" I said. "I have the most beautiful wife and daughter a guy could have and I'm not ever bored."

Jolene said, "That's good. Sometimes I miss the days when we were kids on the beach and I'm having just a little trouble getting used to growing up. I love my memories and I can't help but miss the wonderful years we had when we were younger. It's been like a great story I got to live in thanks to you."

I said, "I feel the same way. It's hard not to miss our youth and I think although those years were fantastic we've gotten to do everything we've ever wanted to do. I think the best years are yet to come. The waves keep coming to the beach and as long as I get to ride on some of them with you, that's all that matters."

Jolene said, "I hope so but it's difficult to think the next six years could possibly be as good as the last. I hope Caroline will have as good a time as we had when she's fourteen."

I said, "Would you be willing to let her run off and live with her boyfriend at the same age we did?"

Jolene said, "If she finds someone like you and is as in love as I was back then yes, I'd let her do it but with our supervision."

I said, "I would too. I just hope she's as lucky as we were."

Jolene said, "Don't I know it. I hope she finds the perfect man like I did. I think she'll have the same luck. She'll be very beautiful and will be the best surfer in the world."

I said, "Of course she will and she'll have the best mother in the world to guide her there."

Jolene agreed and I kissed my beautiful wife who had made up her mind she was going to have a boy for me the next time she gave birth.

We went through Christmas and the New Year and Jolene quit her birth control pills as she had done before. It was the same scenario as with Caroline and Jolene was pregnant in March promising another birth in the coming November. We went back to the coast in June and Jolene was blissfully happy about being pregnant again. I loved the way she looked and our parents were as excited as we were.

Summer came and went and in October we left California for our home in the islands. Jolene delivered a beautiful baby boy that November and he looked just like his sister and she took him to the water with me and the other kids the day after he was born. She named him David for me and I was very proud to have a namesake. David Parish Jr. went through the same upbringing his sister was getting and I loved watching my two children and their cousins grow up on the beach. As soon as they were able to walk Jolene got them little Styrofoam belly boards and they used them in the shore break riding the small waves and having a wonderful time in the water. Jolene made sure our kids and Terry's were water safe by the time they were two and when they could swim we let them run on the beach as we had done but watched them closely when they played in the water. We had a number of friends from the village who had children the same age as we did and it was great they did the same thing as we did when it came to getting our kids used to the ocean. We found it was an old Hawaii tradition to do this and we were also amazed that our kids were rarely ill. We attributed this to the ocean they were growing up in and it felt good to have strong healthy children.

We had turned twenty-one in November and our becoming of legal age was exciting to us. At least we would be able to contribute to things which were affecting our lives by voting. Jolene was continually checking on our finances and we could have retired at any time but we thought like Terry, and really wouldn't have known what to do with ourselves without working. We had our children to bring up and as we expected the years began to roll by faster than they had before. Each year was magical and we watched as the kids got bigger and more in control of themselves. When Teresa was four Terry made her a real surfboard which was just her size and gave it to her on her birthday that year. Jolene made sure she got to surf the small baby waves in the shorebreak at Wakiki each day and she was standing up on her board in a couple of weeks. I was impressed and Jolene was ecstatic about her progress. The other children watched her and played with their belly boards along side of her. When Caroline was four I built a board her size and we were surprised she could stand up the first time she was able to catch a wave on it. This was understandable, as she had known what to do for years from being at the beach and watching us as well as the other surfers. Caroline and Teresa became surfing buddies and went every day in front of the shop under Jolene's supervision.

Soon it was the time to go to California for the summer. The girls didn't wish to be separated, so we left Caroline with Terry and Marcy who had stopped working the year before because Terry had plenty of money to live on by this time. We hated to leave Caroline but Jolene thought it would be best for her to stay in the islands.

David came with us and got to spend his third summer in Huntington Beach. We missed our little girl and decided to go back earlier in the fall than we ever had before. We flew back to Hawaii on September first and we were glad to be home. Caroline was surfing great by this time and Teresa was as well. The two of them were able to ride waves almost as big as they were and they were quite a pair out on the water. David and Jo got their first boards in November and they took to the waves as their brother and sister had done. The older kids coached the younger ones and they all began to learn together. We loved seeing them surf and Jolene was sure Caroline would become a champion by the way she watched the water and was in control of her board. Terry was always willing to watch the kids on the waves and sometimes it was hard for us to leave the kids and take our turn watching the shop. The surfing was serious with the kids and when Teresa and Caroline turned five they were enrolled at the grammar school in the village in Wakiki. The kids liked school and they were allowed to dress as they always had. They wore shorts and T-shirts and slippers on their feet. Physical education was held on the beach and surfing and swimming were what was required from them. The two girls were way ahead compared to a lot of their peers and Jolene was very proud of her girls. She volunteered to help with the classes and the teachers were always happy to have her help with the kids.

When Jolene and I turned twenty-five we decided we would stay in the islands permanently and stay with our family. We no longer needed the excitement of the pier, and other than a few visits there, we made our home in the village behind the band shell in Wakiki. That year we sold the shop in Huntington Beach to Dale's brother and he and his girlfriend moved upstairs and kept the tradition going for us there. Jolene and I were considered to be legendary at the pier and even on our visits there the locals we had surfed with for years always recognized us. It was a great feeling to be spotted and Jolene especially enjoyed it when she heard she was considered to be one of the pioneers of the sport in Southern California. We still surfed each day as we always had and spent our time between the shop and our children. Our decision to sell the shop in Huntington Beach came hard to us but we had plenty of money by this time in our lives and the trips became hard for us to deal with considering our children had to go to school and we didn't want them to go to school on the mainland. We much preferred the easygoing attitude in the islands and the kids loved their school.

Growing older wasn't hard for us and Jolene grew older in a wonderful way. She became more stunning as her face changed from age and I have to admit she became much better looking. She was continually asked to be in films or commercials in the islands and she did take a couple of jobs doing those things. On one occasion she did a television endorsement for the local Chevrolet dealer and we got a new four-wheel drive truck out of the deal. This was great for us and it was our first new car ever. I had her roadster shipped to the islands when we decided to stay there permanently and Jolene loved driving her hot rod around. The rain was a minor problem for the roadster, so unless it was a sunny day, she kept it in the garage I had built especially for it. We sold our woody to Dale's brother and I mostly drove the Jeep that seemed to be always repairable. I kept it patched together and Jolene took to driving the Chevy truck around usually with a bunch of kids and surfboards in the back.

We lived pretty much this way until the kids became old enough not to need constant supervision on the beach. We came to notice this one-day when Jolene and I were out surfing the bigger waves in Wakiki and Marcy was watching them on the beach. We were waiting for good sets on the outside when Teresa and Caroline paddled up next to us and Caroline said, "Hi mom, hi dad."

Jolene said, "Caroline what are you doing out here?"

Teresa said, "Come on Jolene, we got tired of the baby waves and came out here to ride something bigger."

Jolene said, "Okay. Do you think you can handle what's coming in?"

They both said in unison, "Of course we can!"

Jolene said, "Then let's see. Let's get you into something decent and see how you do."

The three of them paddled over to the take off spot and Jolene sat up on her board and said, "Hey you guys, this is my daughter and my niece and I want you to leave them alone and don't be dropping in on them and spoiling their rides. This is their first time on the outside so cut them some slack or you'll have to deal with me."

The gang we all knew well there whooped and yelled and applauded the kids. Jolene instructed the girls on taking off on the five-foot waves and when she was done she pushed Caroline into a good wave. I was paddling back out and saw my daughter take off on a wave which was twice her size. She handled it perfectly and dropped in and made a good bottom turn at the depth of the trough and rode up to the top and streaked down the face at a beautiful angle cutting across the face of the wave with her hand exactly as she had seen her mother do a thousand times. Caroline looked exactly like Jolene on the wave and the sight of her riding such a big wave reminded me of the first time I saw Jolene on a wave and it brought tears to my eyes. She kicked out over the wave and screamed her delight after a perfect ride. Teresa was next and did exactly as her cousin had done and worked the face of it beautifully. I was incredibly proud of her as well and couldn't wait to tell Terry what his daughter had done. I paddled out to where the girls were and as I paddled up I said, "That was great. You two are doing just great. No more baby waves for you two. You're real surfers now and I think you're wonderful."

The girls giggled and said, "Thanks. It felt really good. Can we surf some more?"

Jolene said, "Yes you can and from now on you can come out here but only when I'm here or David is out here. It can get big sometimes and you two are just a little too young yet. Now go on and see how much you two can impress me and David."

The girls paddled over to the take off spot and spent several hours impressing us and the locals who were out there with us. I turned to Jolene after they each had a few successful rides and found she had tears in her eyes. I said, "Jolene what's the matter?"

She said, "Nothing. I'm seeing my daughter grow up and I was remembering the first time Terry took me outside at the pier. I'm crying because I'm very happy and proud and look at how well they're doing. Caroline is just wonderful and so is Teresa. They're both just beautiful."

"I know, I think so too. I saw Caroline's first ride and it reminded me of you the first day I saw you ride at the pier. I think it's fantastic. Jolene you've done an incredible job teaching these girls and I do love you terribly."

Jolene said, "I guess this was inevitable. I taught them this is what they should be doing and now they are. I wonder how long it will be until Jo and David will be out here too.""

I said, "I guess it will be another year and we'll see them here too. Personally I can't wait for them to be here. I'm damn proud of those two girls and look, they're both taking off on the same wave. Let's watch."

Jolene and I sat up on our boards and watched as the two girls took off on a big wave and together raced along the front of it. They worked it up and down and both cutback at exactly the same time and went for big bottom turns when they got into the other direction. Then they raced up to the top of the wave and dropped in again working it some more and kicking out just before it closed out on them. I said to Jolene, "Now that's talent. Aren't they great? I wish I was doing that when I was their age."

Jolene said, "They're certainly wonderful. Let's go and get them. Marcy is probably worried about where they are."

We paddled out to get the girls and rode in with them, each on our own wave. When we got to the beach Marcy was up and waiting for us a bit worried about where the girls had disappeared. She said, "Where did you two go? I've been worried about you." The girls said they were sorry and then Jolene said, "They should have told you but they came to find us on the outside and they've been riding the big ones out there with us."

Marcy said, "How'd they do?"

Jolene said, "Almost too well. They were great out there and they're going to have to be out there more, but I've told them they can only go to the outside break when both or one of us are out there. They did just great and I'm afraid we have two very talented local girls on our hands. You should have seen them, they were amazing. Wait until we tell Terry, he'll be thrilled."

With that the seven of us walked up the beach to the shop to tell Terry about how great the girls were on the waves at Wakiki. We found Terry at the shop and he was excited but sad he had missed his daughter's first time on bigger waves. He announced he would take them tomorrow morning provided the waves weren't too big for them. It was a completely great afternoon and we all went home to dinner after work feeling great about our children.

Teresa was eight when they came outside and Caroline was seven and they had done what we really hadn't expected of them for a couple of years. The girls became a regular experience for us outside and we began to take them to our other spots we liked where the waves weren't too big for them. They rode magnificently and we were very proud of their abilities. A year later we took Jo and David out to the break and they repeated what their sisters had done the year before. Jolene took to waking the whole family in the mornings and we all surfed before they went to school and we went to work at the shop. Terry's kids went with us and so did Terry on most mornings, and before too long, the kids were as good as anyone on the water. We entered them in the contest at Ala Moana that year and Caroline won first place and Teresa came in second in the kids division. Jo and David were too young to enter but consoled themselves they would be competing in the contest next year.

We had our hands full with family surfing, but we loved the fact that our children were living our dream with us and loving it as we did. We taught them to be very self reliant and they were great around the house. They all could cook and we included them in making dinner each night and then cleaning up afterwords. They still liked school and were very popular with their classmates and friends around the village. Our TV got only one channel and there was little on the tube most of the time. Jolene gave them books to read and they spent most of their evenings reading or playing games when they weren't at their cousin's house. They all were expected to be at the shop in the afternoons when they weren't surfing or going to school. They became proficient at the different jobs at the shop and completely understood how to make surfboards by the time they were ten. They entered and dominated the contests around the island, and began to go surfing with their friends from school when they got old enough to do so alone. They had good reputations and we didn't worry much when the swells got big. They could handle just about anything out there and everyone on the beach knew who they were and where we were when we weren't surfing with them. Both of the girls were very beautiful and as they approached puberty I asked Jolene if she had explained to them what would be happening in a few years. I said, "Jolene what have you told the girls about puberty?"

She said, "Everything I didn't know at their age. Marcy and I decided to give them the information straight so they won't be in the dark like we were when we were young. They already know what sex is and I don't think there will be any problems."

I said, "Are they having boyfriends yet?"

Jolene said, "Not yet, but they're experimenting with kissing boys at school parties like we did. I think it's great and the boys love the way they look."

I said, "That's great. I'm happy they'll have lots of choices when it comes time for them to find boyfriends."

"I think it's great too, but they don't much like boys who don't surf. They consider the boys they surf with to be the most attractive and they like the boys that surf as well as they do."

I said, "Well that's good. It would be a shame if one of them would wind up with a boyfriend from the math club."

"David how dare you? You should hear yourself. I'm all for these kids of ours doing what they want and if they fall in love with someone from the math club then I think It would be wonderful."

I said, "I was just kidding. Do you think they will get through high school?"

Jolene said, "I think they just might. School here is so different from when and where we went plus they really seem to like it. Remember the looks we would get for coming to school wet? That's about thirty percent of the students. Most all of them go to the beach before and after school."

I said, "When do you think we'll have to start worrying about the girls?"

Jolene said, "In about another year. I can see they're beginning to develop and if Caroline is anything like me it will be almost overnight."

I said, "I don't think you've ever told me the story."

"Really? I can't believe I haven't but here it is. I was blond and cute and skinny as a rail until I was about twelve. One day my body felt different and my breasts began to grow. Within a couple of months I was out growing the first bras my mother bought for me and I got embarrassed to have the boys looking at me all of the time. I developed a waist and my ass got bigger. The next thing I knew I had a gorgeous figure and all of the boys including boys much older than me wanted to date me. I went from nobody to somebody in about six months. I could get them to do just about anything for me because they all wanted to have sex with me. I went out with a lot of them because I liked the attention and I had some pretty close calls with boys who were insistent about having sex. Luckily Terry was never too far away and he bailed me out of a jam more than once. When I turned fourteen I was just about fully developed and I looked like I did when you met me. By the time I met you I was tired of the problems with boys and then you came along and I couldn't get you off of my mind. It was love at first sight and for the first time I was glad to have the body and face I had so I could attract you."

I said, "Wow that's some story. I hope our daughter doesn't get hit on the same way."

Jolene said, "Not to worry, she's going to be much better prepared than I was. Marcy and I are already giving the girls lessons in how to put off unwanted suitors. They're going to be very beautiful you know."

"I know I can see it in them. Caroline looks just like I think you looked at her age. She's going to be a real attraction at the beach."

Jolene said, "Fortunately she's not going to be on the beach. She'll be out on the water on her board surfing better than the boys."

I said, "So what about David? Is he prepared or do I need to have a long talk about things to him?"

"David's just like you are. He has the same intelligent calmness you do and did when you were young. According to his sister, all of the girls are already in love with him and he pays attention to none of it. You see the way he is around here. He's like having another adult in the house. As you know he's always ready to work on the cars or at the shop. He takes care of business and he reminds me so much of you I'm in love with him too."

I said, "Well that's great. I just hope the kids don't have to go through the hell that some of our friends had to go through."

Jolene said, "I know that all too well. That was the reason we got off the mainland if you remember. Remember what school was doing to us? Imagine what school would have been like had we not had each other. We were together and in love and it still stunk."

"You're right about that. If I hadn't had you I don't know what I would have done. How do you think we should handle the next few years?"

Jolene said, "By just letting things happen. You're a great example to Caroline as to what a good man is about, and David has me as an example as to what a good girl is like. Remember our kids only respect the best surfers on the water. I really don't think with the combination of those things there will be much that can go wrong."

I said, "If you say so then that's what we'll do. I'm kind of excited to see what choices they'll make."

Jolene said, "Well I can tell you now that David just loves girls who are slim and trim with nice breasts like his mother. I see him looking when we get around any babes."

I said, "What about Caroline?"

She said, "Caroline doesn't care much about pretty. She seems to prefer men who surf really well out there and have a good personality. I guess a good cutback turns her on or at least that's what she tells me."

"Well it certainly sounds like you have a handle on things. I should have known you'd be on top of everything. I feel much better after finding out you've been doing your homework."

Jolene said, "Well of course silly that's part of my job. They'll talk to me much easier than talking to you. That's just kids. When I was growing up I only talked to my mother. What was I supposed to do? Go to my dad and tell him I just outgrew all of my bras and needed new ones? He would have had kittens if I had done that."

I laughed and said, "You're right about that. Ha, I can see his face now. Stan would absolutely lose it if you had done that. Imagine him standing in the lingerie department waiting for you to pick things out."

Jolene laughed and said, "That's so funny. I love it when you go off on your wild descriptions."

I got up from my chair and we went together into the kitchen and began to make some dinner. The kids came in to help and as usual it was always wonderful to have them around us. We had a nice dinner and I decided to watch things regarding my son and daughter around the shop and see what was going on with them and their love lives. It didn't take too long to see something. Two days later when Caroline was working behind the counter and I was up in the front a young man came into the shop and immediately walked to where Caroline was cleaning stock. As he walked up to Caroline, he glanced at me. I watched but kept doing what I was out front for. She too glanced at me as the boy walked up, and they talked as friends for quite awhile, smiling as they did so. Shortly Caroline walked over to where I was standing and said, "Dad this is my friend Stephen Iola. We go to school together. He's a good surfer and he wanted to meet you. He has one of our boards."

I said, "I'm pleased to meet you Stephen, are you liking your board?"

Stephen said, "Yes sir. It's great and I'd like to say it's nice to meet one of my heroes. I've been looking at pictures of you and Caroline's mother since I was a little kid."

I said, "Are you a good surfer?"

He said, "Pretty good," then added quickly, "but not as good as Caroline. She's really the queen out there. We all compare her to her mother."

Caroline was getting embarrassed by this time and said, "Stephen stop that. I'm no better than you are and lots of the other kids. Come on now, let my dad alone and come over here so we can talk."

They huddled together for half an hour and then Caroline asked, "Hey dad, can I go surfing with Stephen?"

I looked at the two of them standing together and said, "Sure, be back here to close the shop. If you see your mother out there, tell her I'm here alone and she can give me a break at any time. I want to go surfing too."

They laughed and Caroline got her board from the back and headed off with Stephen. I was pleased that she seemed to have a nice friend and decided to keep my eyes open for anyone who might be more special than someone else. Jolene came into the shop a few minutes later and I told her about Stephen and Caroline. She smiled and said he was a very nice boy from Caroline's school but they were just friends and they surfed together quite a bit. Jolene and I closed the shop early and went to ride a few waves before going home. We were paddling out to the break and saw Caroline dropping in on a big one that had just begun to break. She was doing a very late takeoff and we wondered if she would make it or not. She did about a four-foot freefall before she caught the wave with her board and began to slide down the face of it. She made the bottom turn and came back up to the crest and just as the wave began to close, she kicked out over the shoulder and began to paddle back outside. Jolene said, "One thing about Caroline, she's really got balls. That late take off was radical!"

I said, "You know it. She looks just like you on the waves. I think it's time for more contests."

Jolene said, "More contests and bigger waves. She wouldn't try that on a really big day",

I said, "I don't think so either. She got away with it because the wave was small."

We paddled out to the take off spot and saw Caroline and complimented her on her late takeoff we'd seen. We rode the waves with our daughter and pretty soon Teresa and Jo and David were out with us. We had a good family afternoon outside, and I suppose our quality time together was what people always talked about during those years. I can think of nothing better for a family to do together. We were definitely a surfing family and true to what Jolene had said, Caroline and Teresa began to develop as women when they were almost thirteen. I saw the changes in their bodies and the changes in the way grown men reacted to them in our shop and on the beach. They were both incredibly beautiful and with their age, we now were letting them do as they pleased on the waves with instructions they were not to go too far from the shop in Wakiki. They ran the beaches and there was a steady stream of young men who came to the shop to court them. They were great about putting most of them off and stayed with their friends who were able to handle the waves as well as they could. Their cousins were just as good at surfing and we would wait a year before giving them license to run around by themselves on the beach. David my son was great on the waves and loved to nose ride whenever possible. It was his passion to casually surf that way in small conditions, but when the waves got big his mother's abilities inside of him took over and he became deadly serious about what he was doing on the waves. I felt he was better than his sister and often he proved it out there.

CHAPTER THIRTEEN

Jolene and I were in our early thirties by this time and the surfing world had changed quite a bit. The boards had gotten even shorter and the things that could be done on the waves were very different from what we could do even with our breakthroughs in board construction and length. We were very comfortable financially by this time and we decided to sell the European part of our business to Dale and Wendy who had gotten married some years before. Terry left most of the shop for us to run and we let him come and go as he pleased, as the whole thing was his idea to begin with. Maw died that year from just being old and after we all flew to her funeral which was in the small California town she was born in, we invited Mombo to come and live in Hawaii. She came and took a part time job in the hospital in Wakiki and proceeded to have a lot of men in her life to keep herself occupied. We were all for this but it was tough to not have Maw around when we would go and visit. Our growing older wasn't too bad because we were both in great shape and Jolene seemed to get more beautiful every day. We were still living in our old place in the village and it still was as romantic to us as it had been the first day that we saw the place. We had kept up our routine of waking up early and heading for the beach by the shop or another surf spot we liked. More often than not all of the kids would be with us and we would hit the surf together wherever we were that morning. Jolene entered the kids in most of the contests which were available to them and the trophies piled up until we had no more room for them at the shop or at home. As puberty hit I built another room onto the house so our kids could have more privacy. I also added another bath which helped Jolene and me out as the kids were always in the shower when we needed it. The kids were still going to school and they told us it was the social fun that kept them there and not the academics. Neither of them had plans to go to college and we found they wanted to take over the shop from us when they got old enough. This was fine with us but it wouldn't happen for a few years. We loved the islands and sometimes would recall the days when we moved there when we first escaped from the mainland. We were very happy things had turned out well for us because it could have gone either way in the scheme of things. Teresa and Caroline seemed to become more beautiful each month and the stream of friends around the shop got larger as their outgoing personalities encouraged the others to come around and visit. Son David and Jo were just as attractive and their friends added to the numbers who came to the shop as well. Teresa and Caroline were beginning to get endorsements from manufactures and Jo and David were right behind them in that department. The four of them represented the shop as part of the team and they were hell on the water. That year Jolene loaded the kids onto a jet and took them to the Huntington contest in California. It was a great day for all of us and the kids dominated the event. Caroline, Teresa and Jo won the first three spots in their division and David finished second in the men's division. We loved that they were such great surfers and they liked the notoriety winning brought them. We had a great time in Huntington and there were lots of our friends we saw there who were all about finding out what we'd been doing for the years gone by when we stopped surfing on the West Coast.

When the older girls were fifteen they began to get more and more serious about their boyfriends. For the first time they began to go out alone on dates with the boys who asked and got dates with them. Jolene smiled and thought they might be finding the right boys to pair up with soon.

The two of them came to us in a few months and asked if they might get a place of their own to live. They were astonished when we said yes on the condition they take Jo and David into the house with them. Terry and Marcy were fine with the idea and we moved them into a place that had two bedrooms and was two blocks from us. We gave them the Jeep David was already an expert at repairing, and set them up there where the whole village including us and Terry and Marcy could keep a close eye on them, not to mention all of our friends at the beach. David shared a room with his sister, and Terry's children took the other room for themselves. They did as we had and furnished the place with used furniture they found at garage sales and thrift stores and worked together at restoring the old furniture. Mombo was their best friend, and there were few days when she didn't drop by or bring them some piece of furniture or some appliance she'd found for them. In a year their house was fantastic and there were plenty of their friends who hung around in the evenings. David had built a wooden half-pipe for skateboarding in the backyard and the only way we could count the number of friends visiting was to count the number of boards that were left on the outside leaning against the house. We went to a number of parties there and we were always welcome. The parties were pretty much quiet and beer was mostly what was drunk, but there was always some pot being smoked around the place. We didn't mind. When we did attend their parties, it was nice to be recognized and treated with great suspect because of our surfing abilities. Our kids liked that we were cool with their friends and Mombo loved the parties as well. Caroline told us she would sit in her chair and drink beer and all of the kids would go and talk to her at some point during the evening. She would expound on the ways of the world and give out romantic advice to those who wanted her comments. Jolene and I were pleased to be alone for the first time in fifteen years and it was fun not to have the kids to think about all of the time. They were on different schedules and we would see them continually at the local spots where we all went surfing together in the mornings or afternoons. We heard that they kept up with school and that pleased us quite a bit. We had always hoped they would want to go to college and we kept our fingers crossed It might happen.

Jolene took the kids out to more and more difficult spots during the year and they all got a taste of the Pipeline. She had a call from our friends that the Pipe was breaking big early one morning and she went over and woke them all up and together we went to the north shore with our boards to see. It was at least double overhead and Jolene and I paddled out with Teresa and Caroline leaving Jo and David to surf the sandbar nearby. The two girls listened intently to our instructions. When they were ready, they lined up on the next set that was coming into the beach and the treacherous break. Caroline was the first to take off and she made her ride perfectly. The look on her face when she got back on the outside was truly amazing and we laughed when she said, "Mom! That was the most exciting thing I've ever done! Thank you so much."

Jolene said, "Not at all. I felt the same way myself when I was just a little older than you. You might just be the youngest woman to have ever surfed the Pipe."

When Teresa took off on her wave a few minutes later and made the drop but faltered and wiped out. We were worried for a minute but she got her board and came back to try again. She made her second wave and had a beautiful ride. When she got back outside she was beaming like Caroline and we were very happy for her. David and Jo soon paddled over to where we were waiting on the outside of the Pipeline When they came up they asked if we would help them get their own waves there. We said yes and coached them about the takeoff as we had their sisters. David took off first and had one of the most perfect rides I could imagine. He was magnificent and we could hear the crowds on the beach screaming for him as he kicked over the shoulder at the end of his ride. Jo went next and had as good a ride as David did. She was incredible and she looked fantastic in the pipe as the green water broke over her head causing cheers from the crowd that were barely discernible to us from the thunder of the breaking waves. She paddled back out and when we were all on the outside the kids asked Jolene to take off and show them how it was really done. She said she would and the five of us paddled to the channel to watch her from the side of the giant wave. We watched as she scratched water in the lineup and caught the biggest wave we'd seen all morning. She reached down, and taking the right rail of her board, she set her left rail into the wave and made the drop perfectly. We watched from the rip as she screamed along the inside of the tube with the wave breaking all around her. As she became stable on the inside of the tube she stood straight up and relaxed with her blond hair blowing out in front of her from the compression that was being forced out past her body. She crouched as the wave got smaller and then stood up again as its size increased. She was blown out of the tube standing up and in complete control and the crowd on the beach was going wild for her. When she finished her ride she paddled up to us and said, "Wow that was quite a ride!"

I said, "To say the least. That was great!"

The kids smiled and told her what a great ride she had and then asked me to paddle over and take one. I obliged them and went to the takeoff spot and waited for the next set. I didn't have to wait long as another of the big sets was coming in quickly. I lined up my board and took the second wave of the set. It was huge and when I got into it I started my drop reaching for the rail as Jolene did and making the drop I worked my way into the tube where I was locked into the wave. I stood erect and was having a great ride and could see my family in the channel watching. I went as far as I could and them kicked out over the shoulder of the wave and paddled to where Jolene and the kids were. They said, "That was fantastic! We've never seen you ride that way. You're as good as anyone out here. You were great!"

I said, "As good as anyone except Jolene you mean. She's always been the best in the family. But you kids aren't far behind."

The kids said, "Can we go out and ride some more?"

Jolene said, "Well that's what we're here for, you kids go ahead."

Jolene and I took a couple of more rides apiece and then went into the beach to watch our kids surf the biggest, baddest waves on the North Shore.

When we got to the beach there were a number of reporters who came up to us as we put our boards down and began to dry off. One said to Jolene, "Are you Jolene Boyer, the first woman to ride the Pipeline?"

Jolene said, "Yep that's me except my name is Parish now. David and I have been married for years."

He said, "This is great! Do you mind telling me who the kids are you were out there with?"

Jolene shushed him with her hand to watch Caroline drop into a perfect wave and make a successful ride. Then she said, "That's my daughter who just finished her ride out there. Isn't she great?"

The reporter said, "She certainly is, how old is she?"

Jolene said, "Fifteen I think?"

The reporter said. "If she's fifteen that would make her the youngest woman to ride the Pipeline."

Jolene said, "I guess it would except for my niece who's out there. She's only fourteen."

He said, "Who are the other kids?"

Jolene said, "That's my son David taking off now. He's a year younger than his sister."

David made another stellar ride and just ripped the wave to shreds up and down the face and into the tube and back before kicking out at the end.

The reporter said, "Amazing ride! He's really talented."

Jo was next and had a great ride on the giant wave. The reported said, "Who was that?"

Jolene said, "That was my niece Jo Boyer and she's a few months younger than Caroline."

Teresa was on the next wave already and the crowd watched as she dropped in and had another fantastic ride until the wave flattened out at the end. The reporter asked, "And her?"

Jolene smiled and said, "That's my other niece Teresa Boyer. She's the oldest. Wasn't she fantastic?"

The reporter said, "These kids are amazing. Would you mind if I got an interview for Surf magazine with them when they come in? I'm particularly interested in Caroline and Jo who I'm sure are the youngest women to ever ride the Pipeline."

"Sure if you want to," and then she added, "and they want to. They're not much on interviews but you can try."

The reporter waited with some others on the beach as we watched the kids ride the giant waves together. They came in soon enough when they were tired and were soon surrounded by the reporters. We watched as they gave interviews to them on the beach. The kids talked politely to the reporters for more than an hour, and when all of the questions had been answered, we loaded the Chevy and drove back to Wakiki. The kids were very happy to have conquered the Pipeline and they were excited to have stories to tell when they got to school the next day. A few weeks later Caroline's picture was on the cover of Surf magazine and there were pictures of all of the kids on the inside in the article. I saw Jolene's face as she looked at the magazines which were dropped off to the shop that afternoon and she said, "David look at Caroline. Isn't she magnificent?"

I said, "She certainly is. I think you taught her pretty well. She looks just like you on the waves out there."

Jolene said, "She and David are better than us. Everyone does so much more with the new boards and the way they think about the waves. It makes me feel all warm inside that our kids are doing so well. I'm so proud of them."

I said, "I am too. They're great kids and I can't think of a better pair of kids next to Terry's around. I guess this was the best way for them to grow up of anything we could have chosen."

Jolene put her lovely arms around me and said, "This is like a dream come true. I've never felt like I've grown up and I still feel the same way I felt the first day I saw you in Huntington. I wished for this feeling to last forever and it really has. I'm so happy."

I said, "I am too, but you know as well as I do what a picture on the cover means for business."

Jolene said. "Oh I almost forgot about the customers and there'll be plenty of them tomorrow here at the shop. How's the stock in the back?"

I said, "We have some but we'll need more if we're going to profit by all of this exposure. You need to get the kids here to help and Caroline and Jo need to sign some boards."

I went to the back and began some new product and when school was out the kids came to the shop and started to help with what needed to be done. David and Caroline and I shaped and the others took their turns in the itch room or behind the counter. The next day we were deluged with customers and business was more than good for several days. We cranked out the boards and they flew off of the racks in the front of the shop at an alarming rate. When the next two days were done we were all tired and went to the beach early for some waves and sunshine. We surfed for awhile and noticed our kids were out with us on the water and riding as well as we could expect them too. They surfed in with us when the sun was setting and the press on the beach walked up to them and wanted to know what was up right away. The kids gave short interviews and were done in time to meet us at the shop and drive their Jeep back to the village and their home. Jolene and I ate and went to bed thinking of our kids and how much we liked them as people. They were just what we wanted and we were proud they liked hanging out with us as we liked hanging out with them.

It wasn't very long after Caroline had her picture on the cover of surf magazine that she began to see a young man about her age. His name was Louis and he had been born in Hawaii on the Island of Maui. He was quite adult and was very well mannered coming from a nice family there. Louis had come to the big island for college and he was taking classes at the university. He was a couple of years older than Caroline and they began to spend a lot of time together. He was a great surfer and already had several contest wins under his belt. We watched him surf and he was excellent on the water. They became constant companions and we could see Caroline had chosen his companionship above all others. He was with her in the mornings surfing before school and was around in the afternoons each day. We watched as they grew closer and we noticed as they began to hold hands together when they walked to and from the beach. He drove an old VW van which was tricked out for surfing and the two of them would spend weekends together surfing our favorite spots on the north shore. We could tell our daughter was falling in love and from what we could see she had chosen a very nice man to become attached to. Jolene thought he was very nice and put him to work in the shop in order to get to know him better. Louis was great and we wondered how long the romance would last with him. They became engaged the following Christmas and we were delighted for Caroline. She came to us after their engagement and said, "Mom, Dad, would it be okay if Louis and I rented the house on the other corner from ours. We're very much in love and we want to live together."

Jolene got tears in her eyes and said, "Do you really love him so much you can't bear to be away from him?"

Caroline said, "Yes Mom, I do love him that much. We want to be together like you and dad were when you came to Hawaii."

Jolene said, "Well then, you'd better rent the place and we'll help you fix it up so it will look like something."

Caroline came and hugged us both and said thank you numerous times. She and Jolene worked on the house for several weeks and before long it was beautiful and very cozy. The two of them moved into their place and we could watch their comings and goings from where we lived. They would wake at dawn and leave for the beach together and that alone reminded us so much of ourselves it could bring tears to Jolene's eyes sometimes. Teresa was next in about six months and began to go out with Richard; a friend of Louis's from school and in another six months they too were engaged and had a home in the village and all of us were happy for our off-spring. That left David and Jo who were happy to have the house to themselves and we wondered when they would be next. We waited and waited and one day Jolene came and said, "David, I think there's something you should know."

I said, "What's that my love? Is everything okay?"

Jolene said, "You tell me if everything is okay. It seems that our David is falling in love with his cousin Jo."

I said, "How do you know?"

Jolene said, "Because I've seen them walking together holding hands and I don't think that's all that's going on. They've been inseparable for quite sometime and I think they're in love. Do you think that's all right?"

I said, "I guess it is. Cousins marry all of the time in Europe. What could be wrong with it?"

Jolene said, "I don't know but I wonder if Terry and Marcy know about it and what they would think about what's going on."

I said, "Why don't we get together with them and ask?"

Jolene went immediately to the phone and called Marcy and asked them to come to our house that night and have dinner. They were there that evening and after a few drinks Jolene said, "Terry are you aware that our son and your daughter are becoming a couple?"

Terry said, "I thought so, I've been seeing them holding hands and kissing but you're right. I think so too. Does this bother you?"

Jolene said, "A little, but David says this goes on all of the time in Europe and I was wondering if it was a dangerous practice?"

Marcy said, "I don't think so but we should check. I think it's wonderful that they are. They've been together since they were babies and I think they're adorable."

I said, "It's perfectly all right with me if they fall in love. The way they've been together all of their lives I suppose it was inevitable.

Jolene said, "I'll call our doctor and see if it's okay for them to become involved with each other. It's one thing to make love but another thing entirely for them to entertain the thought of having children together."

With that we finished our meal and spent the evening talking about the business and what our girls were doing with their boyfriends. Jolene got on the phone the next day and found there was nothing wrong with the relationship as long as it was limited to one relationship of this kind every two or three generations. She was relieved when she found all was well and I have to admit I felt better as well. Our kids were really growing up and we loved watching them.

David finally came to dinner with Jo and announced to us they were a couple and would stay in the house they had been living in with their cousins. They had been afraid of telling us but were relieved that we had checked on the possibilities of their love bringing something into the world that was undesirable. They left the house that night with our blessings and we could tell they were very happy.

CHAPTER FOURTEEN

Jolene and I were still in our thirties when our children paired up and we thought it was wonderful to have lived and loved and created offspring we completely approved of. We were still young and Jolene had done nothing but get better looking since she was fifteen. We had more money in the bank than we could possibly spend in our lifetime. We would be able to leave the kids the surf shop on the beach in Wakiki and this would assure them of always being able to eat. Jolene and I decided to think about what we might do next since our children were attached to each other. So, we began to think about taking an extended vacation from everything but surfing for awhile. We lived our lives and, with a few interruptions from our kids, everything was fantastic. Louis and Richard convinced the girls to go to college and we were pleased to find they had gotten scholarships to help with their tuition. They did well at the university enjoying what they were doing as well and we were very proud of them for attending. Jo and David had no interest in going to college but were set on surfing their lives away as Jolene and I had done. They opened a surf shop on the north shore and they were successful almost over night. I was proud of them and they continued to carry the logo on their boards which were on the boards we made in Wakiki. They lived together in the village and drove the old Jeep to the other side of the island each day. They were a great team and through the other surfers I learned they had the respect of all of the surfers on the island. Jolene became more and more restless as time passed and I knew her brain was cooking up something wonderful for us to do. I came home from the shop and afternoon of surfing with the kids to find her watching to film, The Endless Summer, on TV. She was taking notes from the story and I said, "Are we going to have an endless summer Jolene?"

Jolene turned her lovely face to me and said, "That's right. I want to go everywhere in the film including some others and we can just surf until we have no place left to go. We've always wanted to do this and I think it's time we did."

I said, "Are we going to take our children with us?"

Jolene said, "Heavens no! This is for us my love. It's a gift to us for raising our children well and for giving part of our youth to them."

I said, "Well you figure out the itinerary and tell me what boards we'll want to take and I'll be ready when you are."

"Thank you David. This will take a while to arrange but I want you to know it's going to be the trip of a lifetime. Do you think we should take a photographer to document the surfing?"

I said, "I don't know. Perhaps we should. Maybe we should call Bruce Brown and see if he wants a vacation?"

Jolene nodded her head and went back to what she was doing before I walked into the room. I went to the kitchen and began to make dinner when David and Jolene came into the room. I said, "Hey there, what's up?"

They said, "Nothing, we just missed the two of you and decided to walk over. Where's mom?"

Jolene walked into the room and said, "Missed us huh? Well that sounds familiar. It's nice to see you kids. Do you two want a beer?"

They answered yes and Jolene got four from the 'fridge and put them onto the kitchen table. We each took one and as we drank David said, "Mom what do you mean our missing you sounded familiar?"

Jolene said, "Along time ago when your father and I first moved to Hawaii to be together, we were very young and in love. But, when it came down to it, we were still kids and we needed our parents and their love. You two are lucky you only live a block away and can walk over here anytime. I was almost three thousand miles from my parents and I needed them badly but I didn't know it. I realized it after they caught David and me together in Wakiki when we were just sixteen."

Young Jolene said, "I thought it was something like that. You're right. We're still kids no matter how you look at it and it's nice to see our parents. We were thinking we were supposed to be so grown up we were ignoring what we were feeling. Jolene I'm so happy you said something. You always have all the right answers."

I said, "Would you two like to have dinner here with us tonight? We're having steak and there's plenty. I was going to do them on the pit outside."

The two of them said yes and I got out two more pieces of meat and set them to thaw on the counter while we talked around the kitchen table. We talked about our plan for taking a vacation sometime in the coming months. The kids loved the idea of us following the path of the film The Endless Summer our friend Bruce had made. It was a full-length film and was by far the most successful surfing film ever made. David and Jolene stayed for awhile after dinner that night and when they left and Jolene and I were in bed I said, "So when would you like to leave on this journey?"

Jolene said, "I think in about two months. It'll take that long to organize our itinerary and we'll have to get some shots for going to Africa and India. I want to book nice hotel rooms for the whole trip so we can be comfortable."

I said, "What about maps and cars? Would you like me to do the arrangements for those things?"

Jolene said, "No, I think I can handle it all. Remember you have a surfboard shop to run and you'll need to get the kids ready to take it over while we're gone."

"You're right. I wouldn't want them to have to rely too much on Terry. He's enjoying his retirement too much to make him go back to work."

Jolene said, "That's true. He and Marcy are totally comfortable these days. Terry loves to visit the shop but I can't remember the last time he shaped a board."

I said, "That's okay he's definitely shaped his share over the years. He's easily got me beat on the numbers."

Jolene said, "Don't I know it. I'm pretty sure I personally sold about everything he ever made with the exception of some of the boards that went to France."

"Well two months will put us in the middle of January. Will it be the time of year you'd like to start our great adventure?"

Jolene said, "I think January would be fine. Do you want me to keep you posted on what we're spending on this junket?"

I smiled and said, "I'd rather not know. You know how finances bother me. You've always been the brains when it came to investing and dealing with money. I see no reason I should suddenly have to know."

Jolene said, "Well if it hadn't been for you fixing and making everything work around here, we'd never have as much money as we have. You've saved us a small fortune over the years."

We went to sleep after awhile and dreamed of our vacation until we woke the next morning at dawn and drove to the north shore for some waves. Caroline and Louis were already out on the water when we got there and it was great to see them riding the waves as the sun came over the horizon. Caroline always reminded me of her mother when I watched her surf and she was a joy to behold on the waves. We paddled out and caught a few waves with the kids and chatted with them on the outside. They said they had a class to get to and left before we were ready to go. We stayed a few more hours and then drove back to Wakiki to open the shop and go about our daily routine. Jolene spent the majority of her time on the phone for the next month making arrangements for our adventure. In two weeks we had a departure date and it was coming at an astonishing rate. Everything was set at least two weeks before we were to leave, and I was happy we both got a chance to relax before we went to the airport. Young David and Jolene took us to the airport on a Saturday morning and we flew to Los Angeles for the first leg of our journey. We then flew straight to New York and changed planes and caught an overnight flight to Dakar, Senegal. It was hot when we got there and we were tired from being so many hours on airplanes. We went straight to our hotel where we would rest for awhile and eat dinner. The next morning we would pick up a rented Jeep and in the afternoon drive to the same beach where Bruce had filmed part of his epic movie. The first place we would surf was right in front of our hotel on the beach near the harbor. The waves were good and we spent the morning riding the nearly perfect three-foot waves the ocean offered us. We drove to our afternoon spot after lunch and to our surprise there were several surfers already there. Bruce's film had quite an impact on the local culture and it was great to see fellow surfers on the waves when we pulled up in our Jeep. The spot was near a fishing village a few miles from town and Jolene was surprised our fellow surfers recognized her there. It seemed Bruce's film that had featured us had reached Africa and Jolene got to sign a few autographs as we walked to the edge of the Atlantic Ocean in the early afternoon. The locals were very nice to us and for the next week we were taken to all of their favorite spots which were easily reached by Jeep or station wagon.

Our next stop was Ghana where we found no other surfers and the waves were breaking just like they were in the film we were following. We spent the day surfing the perfect small waves and drove back to our hotel as the sun was going down. We showered and went out that night for a good dinner that filled us perfectly. We were just short of being stuffed by the time it was over and we walked the streets to see the sights until we grew tired and decided to go back and go to bed so we could get up and try another spot in the morning. We spent a few days going up and down the coast in Ghana looking for good spots. We found at least one each day and it was great to surf in places that had never been ridden before. There was little nightlife in Ghana and we tired of the place sooner than we thought. We went to the airport when we were done with the place and caught a flight to Lagos, Nigeria. Lagos was on the equator and it was very hot there. The air temperature was 100 degrees and the water temperature was about the same. It was hot enough to melt the wax from our boards but we had good surfing there. We were careful to stay on our boards as much as possible because the area was home to deadly stone fish which were poisonous enough to kill a person unlucky enough to step on one. We found great waves and stepped on none of the deadly fish. The nightlife was about the same as Ghana and we kept to our hotel room after dinner for the most part. We stayed three days and took one extra day off to go sight seeing without our boards. On the fifth day we took a flight to Cape Town, South Africa where we rented another Jeep. After settling into our hotel room we set out to find some surf to ride. We followed Bruce's movie script to a beach on the peninsula which separates the Indian Ocean from the Atlantic. We found good surf at a place named Long Beach and there were a lot of other surfers there. We spent the day there and made friends with the locals and were invited to dinner with some of them after we went back to our hotel and cleaned up for the evening. We drove up the coast to Durban a few days later and the drive was wonderful. The immense amount of animals which were strange to us were wonderful and we loved the drive. There wasn't much along the way but we slept in the Jeep and found some spots to surf where we were sure no one had surfed before. We spent a week driving to Durban because we wanted to find the beach Bruce had filmed in The Endless Summer where the rides were longer than long and the waves were perfect. We found the place after some searching and it was just as Bruce had said it would be. The place was fantastic and we rode waves which were so long we got physically tired of standing on our boars and crouching in the curl of the perfect waves. There were other surfers in Durban and they were happy to see us. They took us up and down the coast to their favorite spots and we spent two weeks riding waves in the Indian Ocean. We had to watch out for sharks there and we did as the locals did and when sharks were seen everyone just put their feet up on their boards until the beast was gone. The locals were great and quite a number of them knew of us from the magazines and the film that we'd been in.

We changed things from the path of the film and flew to Madagascar to see what we could find there. The weather and the water were warm there and we stayed in the small town of Cape St. Marie at the southern point of the country. There were no waves to speak of there but we had a good time exploring but soon left for Colombo, Sri Lanka where the surf was better. We surfed and explored there for another week before going to Jakarta on the Java Sea. There were decent waves there and we were just south of the equator. We saw no other surfers there but found several spots where the waves were good and we had a ball riding the completely uncrowded waves that the Java coast offered us.

We packed up after a week there and flew to Australia where we landed in the city of Perth. We drove to Freemantle, where we knew from the magazines there were good waves and lots of surfers. The locals were good to us and we surfed behind the shark nets which were strung offshore to keep the bathers from being attacked. The waves were good and we took plenty of time there with the locals who we would eat and drink with far into the night.

We flew to Sidney a week later and we got the same great waves and treatment from the locals who were more than happy to take us around to all of their favorite spots along the coast. We were lucky and had good surf in most of the places we were taken, and had a ball on the southern coast of the continent. We deviated from the plan there and went to Tasmania where we spent another week riding the waves the southern ocean had to offer us. From there it was off to Auckland, New Zealand where there were uncrowded beaches and good surf for the most part. We spent two weeks there and then flew to Tahiti where the waves weren't so good but the beaches and the people were so great, we spent two weeks lying around and eating in the restaurants available to us. We were beginning to run out of summer in the Southern Hemisphere so Jolene made plans for us to go and surf some spots where summer was beginning to be in season.

We flew to the Galapagos Islands where we again found good waves on the equator and we stayed in the strange place until I decided we'd had enough and we flew to Los Angeles and rented a car and drove to the south beaches where we found some of our old friends at the Huntington Pier and surfed the place where we both had fallen in love. Jolene's parents were still living there and they were pleased to see us. We spent a month there and drove to a different beach each day to ride the waves we knew would be there and reminisce about our youth.

We had missed our family a great deal while we'd been traveling and it was great to be at Jolene's where we could call and talk to the kids on the telephone more regularly. In another month we were back in Hawaii and we had been gone for nearly ten months.

Terry and Marcy picked us up at the airport and drove us to our house in the village where we put our things away and got out all of the gifts we'd brought our kids and our relations. They all came over that night and we loved seeing everybody. Caroline and Louis were planning on getting married the next summer and so were Teresa and her boyfriend. Jo and David were very much in love and they were living in the village and still driving to the north shore to make and sell surfboards each day. They were still driving our old Jeep and it was becoming too old to cross the island each day. Jolene traded the Chevy truck for the Jeep and we were back to our original transportation in the islands. We still had the roadster and the old Jeep was fun for us as we rarely went anywhere that was far. I continued to patch the old thing together and Jolene kept up the interior. Caroline and Teresa were married the following summer in the palm grove by the shop where Jolene and I were married years before. They were intent on finishing school and more and more they took over the surf shop in Wakiki for us. We kept surfing and loved not having to be tied to the shop all day. The girls kept it up perfectly and we gave them time off to deal with their classes at the university. They graduated two springs later and announced they were conspiring to have children together. That happened about a year later and within two months of each other, Teresa and Caroline gave birth to two beautiful children. Caroline had a girl she named for her mother and Teresa had a boy that she named for her father. We were all very proud and were delighted the girls each took their children to the ocean on their way home from the hospital. Jo and David were comfortable just living together and running their shop on the north shore and they did mention they would have children but wanted to wait for a year or so before having them. That was to happen quicker than we thought, as Jo became pregnant by accident and nine months later she delivered a beautiful baby girl that she named after her aunt. They nicknamed her Jojo to help keep the names straight and we were all proud of our kids. Two years later Caroline and Teresa each had another child and the both had boys. They named the boys David for me and Stan for their grandfather. Jo and David waited another year and had a beautiful daughter and named her Grace for my mother but called her Mombo as we all did my mother. Jolene was all about the grand kids and she took them to the beach each day and a lot of times with Marcy along with her. They taught the grand kids the ways of the ocean and the kids grew up at the beach as their parents had. They were swimming each day and lived in the village with all of us. Mombo was also helping with the kids and she was usually at the beach with all of them at some point during the day. They were healthy kids and we loved watching them grow up as we had raised their parents in the sun and the water. Jolene and I still surfed morning and night and Mombo would take the grand kids when we wanted to all go together. The kids developed into great surfers as one would expect and we loved giving them surfboards as they got older.

Mombo died when the kids were becoming teenagers and we all grieved her passing, she had been fantastic to all of us and was an inspiration to us when it came to our children and our grand children. She had wanted us to scatter her ashes in the Pacific across from the beach at Wakiki and we took the whole family out off

Diamond Head for the scattering. We were sad but happy she had had such a great life. We spent the day remembering her and all of the fun she had helped us have in our lives.

That was quite a few years ago now and as I'm sitting here writing down this story about our lives while Jolene, my fantastic wife, is out with the grand kids at the break at Ala Moana giving the grand kids lessons with their parents. I stayed in today to finish the story of the finest life a man could have and I still think about the first time I saw Jolene on a good wave in Huntington Beach with her blond hair trailing behind her in the sunlight and smiling as she worked her board on the wave. She still looks the same on the waves and she loves it when we both wake up before dawn and head to the beach in our old jeep. We get our boards from the shop our kids run and walk holding hands to the water that we love. Jolene is still one of the best surfers at the beach and we ride waves together and talk about the days of our youth while we sit on the outside waiting for good sets to come in. We often see our family surfing with us and it feels great to see them living the way we taught them to.

I thank the stars for the day I moved to California and for the fantastic woman who made my life complete. And when I finish typing the end of my story I'll get into the Jeep and go to the shop and get my board and see if I can find the most beautiful woman I know out on the water and ride a few waves with her. I always said that as long as the waves keep coming into the beach and I get to ride some of them with Jolene, I'd be satisfied. I'll find Jolene this afternoon and we can finish our day together. We'll go home when it gets dark and spend the evening together and go to bed where we'll make love until we fall asleep. We'll get up tomorrow and head to the beach as we've always done and spend the morning surfing and watching for some of our family doing exactly as we are. We really love what happened in our lives and we look forward to many more years on the water together. What happened by chance in Huntington Beach that gave two people the lives most people only read about, is something we think about daily and we're very happy it happened to us.

THE END

David Nash was born in New Orleans, Louisiana in the middle of the Twentieth Century. He was born of educated parents and attended private school. His family raised him modestly between New Orleans and the Gulf Coast of Mississippi until 1963 when he moved to Southern California and the small town of Huntington Beach.

He was raised on the water and was a proficient sailor throughout his youth. After moving to Huntington Beach he became a surfer / skateboarder / skier who also loved hot rods, motorcycles and rock and roll. He discovered art on the Gulf Coast eventually earning both a bachelors and masters degree in fine art in Southern California after working with extremely notable artists for more than twenty years in the entertainment industry. Still dabbling in music production Nash taught sculpture and ceramics at university level for eleven years before retiring to yacht and his home restoration business in New Orleans. He has worked in twenty-seven countries and began his writing career in the year 2000. Of all of his hobbies and interests he loves sailing the best and is active in the sport as well as cruising.

David Nash has always enjoyed life in the fast lane and has no intention of living any other way. He is unmarried with no children and still enjoys sailing, surfing, hot rods, high powered weapons and beautiful women.

He is currently organizing his effort to completely retire to his yacht, The Amnesia Castle in the islands. He plans to live out his life sailing from place to place as it pleases him until he runs out of places to visit or the authorities won't allow him to return.

It has always been his wish that his death should come from the cold kiss of the sea unless the Jamaican pirates should happen to take him first.

www.ingramcontent.com/pod-product-compliance
Lightning Source LLC
Chambersburg PA
CBHW020600250626
47154CB00004B/1299